CHRISTMAS MIRACLES AT THE LITTLE LOG CABIN

BOOK 4 IN THE NEW YORK EVER AFTER SERIES

HELEN ROLFE

Boldwood

First published in 2019. This edition first published in Great Britain in 2022 by Boldwood Books Ltd.

Cover Design by CC Book Design

Cover Photography: Shutterstock

A CIP catalogue record for this book is available from the British Library.

Paperback ISBN 978-1-80415-637-7

Large Print ISBN 978-1-80415-636-0

Hardback ISBN 978-1-80415-635-3

Ebook ISBN 978-1-80415-639-1

Kindle ISBN 978-1-80415-638-4

Audio CD ISBN 978-1-80415-630-8

MP3 CD ISBN 978-1-80415-631-5

Digital audio download ISBN 978-1-80415-633-9

Boldwood Books Ltd
23 Bowerdean Street
London SW6 3TN

For my husband and his never-ending support, without which I couldn't do this job that I love...

1

HOLLY

Holly was back in Manhattan after her trip to Seattle where she'd spent Thanksgiving with family and friends, counting their blessings, sharing in the joy of each other. But right now, with the festive season in full swing at the end of November, she wasn't sure she should have been doing either of those things. Perhaps she should've been getting the fear, panicking about her next step, because today was her last day at work. Out of choice she'd quit her fifty-hour-a-week job, kissed goodbye to a bursting-at-the-seams pay packet and turned her back on never-ending perks like invitations to exclusive events, travel, and even the odd dealings with a celebrity.

Holly had spent the best part of a decade working in the magazine industry after graduating with a degree in communications and media. She'd landed an internship straight out of college, quickly secured a full-time position with a major daily in Seattle, and then moved to *Contemporary Edge* magazine where she'd made her way up through the ranks to senior editor. She'd relocated from Seattle to New York last year and thought the geographical shift would be enough to get her out of the rut she was in, but back in the summer she'd realised it really wasn't. It had been a short-term fix. Nothing had really changed. It was still the same long days, the lacklustre enthusiasm for the daily grind she'd once thrived on. And now, here she was, about to embark on a career as a freelancer in less than twenty-four hours.

She packed up her belongings into a small box and as soon as the cleaners came round after hours, her office would be ready for the next person.

'So... last day.' Co-worker Daisy, who'd been a staff writer with the magazine for almost a decade and had gladly relocated to New York too, mostly for the night life and the shopping she'd said, hovered at the door to Holly's office in the modern high-rise on Avenue of the Americas. Most likely she'd be gunning for Holly's job but rather than feeling put out, Holly really couldn't imagine handing over the reins to anyone who deserved it more. And in a way it would help her to say goodbye.

'How do you feel?' Daisy probed.

Great! would've been her initial reaction until today, but as she pushed her auburn locks, beautifully tamed and highlighted after this morning's trip to the salon, away from her face, she realised her doubts were multiplying the closer she got to her final hours. The job security was a major factor and it scared her to think how diligent she'd have to be from now on. She'd need to remember that even if she had an epic month with lots of work, it didn't mean the month after would be the same, or the one after that. She'd have to stop shopping so frivolously in Manhattan – six months ago she'd have thought nothing of getting her hair done at the trendiest and most expensive salons, spending a couple of thousand dollars on a handbag from Coach, or a few hundred on a pair of Manolo Blahniks, another extortionate sum on a slap-up lunch at one of New

York's finest restaurants where you had to book months in advance to get the tiniest table.

'I'm not really sure,' she admitted as they went out into the area that housed umpteen small booths where staff writers, photo editors, public relations, and communications staff sat. The flashing lights of the office Christmas tree were doing their merry dance, either in celebration that Holly was leaving or in mockery that she was making a mistake so huge she'd wake up in a day, a week, a month and wonder what the hell she'd been thinking.

'You're doing the right thing.'

'Easy for you to say when you're not the one doing it.' She stepped out of the way as her boss Amelia's personal assistant, Hannah, came past in a gush of air, doing the rounds to remind everyone about tomorrow's team meeting. For once, Holly felt free to safely ignore Hannah's reminder.

'Remember, final farewell drinks at 5 p.m. today. I know your big bash was a few weeks ago, but we had to organise a little something to send you off.'

'I'll be there, don't worry.' She'd already arranged to meet Dylan, Cleo, Myles, and Darcy at a cocktail bar in Chelsea after her farewell drinks. She needed the moral support from her friends, who would remain a constant when she left her colleagues behind. Holly had met Darcy quite by chance last year in the Flower District when she'd broken down and cried over the loss of her friend Sarah a few days before Christmas. She'd only been a visitor to New York back then, deciding whether or not she wanted to relocate from the West Coast, but her emotional state has caused Darcy to take pity on her, buy her a coffee, and rescue her from possibly the worst accommodation known to man by offering her a room at the Inglenook Inn. Their friendship had lasted and soon expanded to include the others; that was the Christmas Darcy got together with Myles, who had also become a friend, and soon after, Darcy had introduced Holly to Cleo and Dylan and they'd all been good friends ever since.

'Come on,' said Daisy. 'Help me put up the rest of the decorations. It'll take your mind off everything else, and when this place resembles Santa's Grotto you'll be happy to turn your back on it.'

Glad of a reprieve from analysing her decision and with her duties and tasks already distributed amongst the team so that her last day was relatively clear, she and Daisy got to decorating the rest of the office. They strung a long line of lights along one wall, put holly and ivy on the edges of picture frames, arranged several empty wrapped boxes to represent gifts beneath the Christmas tree and then moved on to decorating work stations. Many desks were hydraulic so staff could stand or sit and save their bodies from the perils of desk work, they had kitchen supplies and refreshments on hand, and there was even a small games room down the corridor with a ping-pong table and a pool table and big squishy chairs to sink into. Holly guessed she'd have to get used to far fewer luxuries. From now on it would be a case of having her laptop perched on the bed in her studio apartment, or else finding one of the many cafés and settling herself in a quiet space to work.

She handed smaller sets of fairy lights to the people sitting in cubicles.

'Can't you decorate mine, Holl, given you're unemployed as of this afternoon?' Jason crooned from where he was standing at his monitor. In charge of communications, he thought he could lord it over every faculty of the magazine. Holly had only been working with him since mid-January but it hadn't taken her long to wish he'd get a transfer in the opposite direction.

'It's your job; everyone is doing their own work space.' She managed to plaster a big smile on her face despite her inner fury. 'And I'm not unemployed, I'll be freelance.'

'Potato, potahto.' His eyes didn't leave the screen.

Holly wondered what decoration she could lob at his head, although she didn't want to get charged for assault and battery on her last day. Maybe, instead, she'd spend more time around him this afternoon, because it would be the biggest encouragement to walk out that door with a feeling of relief and know her decision was the best one.

'Pine cones.' Daisy was next to Jason's work station and left a supply of half a dozen of the frost-coated brown pieces.

'What am I supposed to do with those?' he asked.

'I could think of a few things,' Holly muttered as they giggled their way over to the box of garlands ready to hand a few of those out.

Within an hour, the decorations had been distributed and plenty of workers had got into the spirit readily enough.

'What's happening with your apartment?' Daisy shoved the empty decoration boxes back in the storeroom.

Holly wondered whether her co-worker was after that as well as her job and for some reason it made her want to laugh out loud. 'I'm keeping my apartment.'

'It's in Greenwich Village, right?' Daisy flipped her blonde pony-tail over her shoulder and shut the door to the storeroom.

'I moved to West Chelsea. Downsized.' As a twenty-something not even nudging thirty, Daisy was still living in her parents' pala-tial residence on the Upper West Side so had no idea how crippling Manhattan rents could be. 'I'm in a studio now, but it's fine. I didn't need a two bedroom.' She'd sacrificed the gorgeous apartment on a tree-lined street but every time she mourned for her light-filled, all-mod-cons, spacious apartment in a classic brownstone, she reminded herself why she'd had to give it up.

They headed towards the kitchen area, where Daisy made them both a cup of coffee. Holly knew she had a look of dread written all over her face and Daisy was quick to pick up on the vibe.

'When you first said you were doing a photography course I could see passion in your eyes.' Daisy stirred sugar into her coffee. 'It reminded me of my Grammie, my dad's mom, dead now, but when she was alive we used to play make-believe games. My favourite was when I'd pretend to be a reporter. I'd totter around in Mom's high heels with a notepad and pen and interview Grammie. She'd make up scenarios – maybe she was a film star visiting Manhattan, or she was the President, or, once, she pretended to be a police officer who'd been embroiled in a scandal, a role she carried off really well given she was once in the force. It was Grammie who encouraged me to apply for internships. "Prove yourself, the money will come," she told me. "Get your foot in the door" was her favourite platitude, and "life's too short to follow a career you can't stand" was something she said more than once. This is your chance now, Holly. You've found something you really want to do, so think of it as your internship as you build up your contacts and get more work.'

'You talk a lot of sense.' Amazing the words of wisdom that were coming from someone much younger than Holly's thirty-two years.

'Did you meet with the boss yesterday?'

'I did.' Holly had met with Amelia who begged her to reconsider leaving the magazine, but her boss finally gave way to talks about freelance opportunities when she could see Holly's mind was made up. 'She's commissioned me to cover the new hotel opening up near Inglenook Falls. I'll go out there tomorrow and do some preliminary work.'

'Wait, are you talking about the Corbridge Hotel? The hotel your super-hot boyfriend is in charge of?'

Holly grinned. Her boyfriend Pierre had met her at the office here enough times to earn his nickname. 'That's the one. It'll be a luxury escape out in Connecticut, exactly what readers want. And I'll get to do the write-up plus the photography and add it all to my portfolio.'

'Is she paying you a good rate?' Daisy quizzed.

'I negotiated, don't worry.' This job had given her confidence, persistence, and persuasiveness. And she knew her writing skills were exemplary, knew her photography was only amateur but good enough, and, better still, Holly knew what freelancers on the magazine's books were paid and how they performed. She also promised, and knew she could deliver, work in the preferred writing style with very few editorial errors to work on.

'I've also been working on a piece for the Moonlight Loft & Terrace on Madison, where my friends got married in the summer.' Holly had ended up taking the wedding photographs when the photographer failed to show up and the owner of the venue had been so impressed with her style, she'd offered Holly work there and then for a Christmas feature. Holly had already written the article, she'd taken the photos a few days ago after landing back at JFK, put everything together and submitted it to another major Manhattan publication, who'd not only snatched the chance to have her as a freelancer but had offered her a full-time job. She'd politely declined, of course, but it had boosted her to know she was wanted. There was a high turnover in the industry and you were pretty much only as good as your last piece, so keeping a high standard was vital to Holly if she wanted to establish this career in its own right.

'Amelia also wants me to write a feature on an art gallery in Greenwich Village.'

'See,' Daisy smiled, 'plenty lined up already.'

'I'm not sure I'm the best person for it, but it'll show diversity if nothing else, which will be great for my portfolio. And it sounds as though the owner of the gallery has an interesting backstory, which is the sort of journalism I really enjoy. Plus, it's art that looks like art.'

'Not a fan of modern art?'

'It's not my thing, so this is a good commission.'

'My mom always raved about modern art until that controversial British artwork *My Bed* was all anyone was talking about. She said it reminded her of my bedroom on a good day.'

Holly laughed. She was going to miss some of the people around here. But recapping what she already had in the pipeline had made her realise she was already well on her way with her new vocation. And it felt good.

* * *

'How was the office farewell?' Darcy asked when Holly met her at the cocktail bar.

Holly had escaped after an hour, out into the big wide world, the ties to her regular job cut. 'Bearable.' She draped her scarf over her bar stool, removed her coat, and nodded a yes to the suggestion of a cosmopolitan.

'That bad?' Darcy's chestnut hair shimmered in the soft lighting of the bar.

'My big farewell bash has been and gone so I've been winding down at the office ever since. My boss made a bit of a speech, wishing me well, everyone echoed her, but by the end I really wanted to leave.'

Myles was next to join them, flanked by Cleo and Dylan. He kissed Darcy on the cheek. They'd been married less than four months, but already Holly couldn't see them any other way. Hugs were exchanged all round, drinks ordered, and finally the group were settled on bar stools to catch up.

'There are three self-employed people here who know how hard it can be but who have all made it work,' Cleo assured Holly. 'You've got plenty of support. You're going to be fine.'

'I appreciate the words of encouragement. And I'll keep everything I do in a portfolio so when I pitch to publications, I've got the backing of previous credits.'

'It's the best idea,' Dylan seconded. 'My website business grew slowly but word-of-mouth contacts are invaluable. Impress one person or one corporation, and it'll lead to more.'

'Business going well still?' Holly asked. With Cleo running her store, the Little Knitting Box, out in Inglenook Falls, not far from their house in Stamford, she and Dylan were also co-parenting four kids – Ruby and Jacob from his first marriage, toddler Tabitha, and their baby, Emily.

'Business is going very well,' Dylan confirmed.

'He's got work lined up for the next six months,' Cleo added.

'And how's the store?' Myles asked Cleo.

'She finds it hard to stay away,' Dylan put in. 'And she's got the Christmas markets out in Inglenook Falls this year to contend with.'

'Hey, I'm not so bad. Emily is a lot more settled than Tabitha ever was so sometimes I take her to the store with me when Dylan can watch the other three, or Ruby comes along and entertains the baby while I talk business. And Kaisha is the best assistant I could ever ask for, so between us we should be able to manage the Christmas market stall too. Which reminds me... Kaisha will be going back to NYU to do a fashion exhibition, and I know the *Inglenook Falls News* is always on the lookout for pieces about local residents. Could be something for you, Holly.'

Holly's spirits soared. Word of mouth certainly was great. It started off small and then gathered speed and hopefully at some point she'd be like Dylan with months of work ahead of her. 'Give her my contact details – or, better still, I can pop into the store sometime in the next couple of days when I'm in town.'

Cleo sipped her cocktail and, with a big grin that made her blue eyes dance all the more, announced, 'This is my first drink since I finished breastfeeding. I'll be legless if I have too many so watch out for me. I've got work in the morning.'

Talk turned to baby Emily, who had been so desperate to join the real world that Cleo had dramatically gone into labour on Darcy's wedding day. But the pair seemed to manage parenting well these days. Cleo had lost her way during her second pregnancy but everyone here now had pulled together, surrounded her with their friendship, and she seemed to take everything in her stride these days.

'How does it feel, being outnumbered?' Myles lifted his glass of beer when he asked Dylan the question. 'Four women and two men in your household now.'

'Don't remind me. Jacob was hoping for a boy. He's even suggesting we try again, to get it right this time.'

'No way on this earth am I ever being pregnant again.' Cleo lifted one hand and mimed a snipping action.

Myles patted Dylan on the shoulder. 'My sympathies, man, good luck with that.'

'All done, last week, day procedure.'

A debate ensued as to whether Dylan had had it anywhere near as difficult as Cleo, who'd given birth, the men of course siding with each other, and by the time Holly shivered her way home a fog had set in over Manhattan, bringing with it the feeling of winter, the hint of the holiday season.

In her apartment she turned up the heat but not so much that she'd end up with an enormous fuel bill, made a mug of hot chocolate, and settled into bed beneath the quilt, flicking on the television to see if she could find a Christmas movie to watch.

As the opening scene of *The Polar Express* came on, she sipped her hot drink and felt the stress of the last few weeks disappear. So what if she'd be living on a tenth of her income from now on? Money wasn't everything. There had to be something more to life than sitting in an office and wondering whether she wanted more.

Maybe she was about to find out.

2

HOLLY

The next morning Holly took her time over breakfast, had a leisurely shower, packed her things, and with the time ticking towards midday she slung her laptop bag diagonally across one shoulder, her purse across the other, pulled up the handle of her case and, wrapped in coat, scarf and gloves, braved the late November chill as she set off on the short walk to the car-hire place on West 34th. Planning to leave the city on a work day was liberating and Holly wondered how long it would take to get used to not answering to anyone else, to be in charge of her own time. She'd have to be incredibly self-disciplined but she was ready to give everything to make this work. Already she'd swapped the sharp suit for jeans, a luxurious ribbed sweater in the softest cream cashmere, and a pair of knee-high boots in a buttery-soft, walnut leather. She sensed she was going to enjoy dressing down rather than up – all part of her new role.

As she walked she wondered how many people were robbed of the chance to do what they loved. Sometimes it was down to financial reasons, other times it was lack of confidence or peer support, and for some people it was simply that they never found their true passion. She'd loved her work as an editor, at the top of her game, the spot of executive editor or even editor-in-chief not completely out of her grasp if she'd stuck with it. But for a long while part of her had wanted to let loose. And ever since the intensive photography course she'd taken earlier this year, as well as the never-ending tiredness from a routine she knew so well, it had been a case of no time like the present.

As a young girl she'd loved photography. She hadn't much liked posing for pictures – being on the other side of the camera was all she wanted, much to her parents' frustration as they tried to capture her key moments growing up. Her dad had bought her first camera, a cotton-candy contraption, and on her eighteenth he'd upgraded it to a sophisticated digital SLR camera with a high price tag as well as features that allowed Holly to take her photography to another level. She'd badgered her then boyfriend to travel around with her as she christened the camera. She took shots of the Space Needle, the symbol of Seattle, she photographed the waterfront with its ferry boats, delectable seafood restaurants, and views across Elliott Bay.

Since arriving in New York it had been like the unravelling of another part of her creative dream, with never-ending photographic possibilities. She'd made a study of Central Park and covered acre upon acre snapping blooms, the Strawberry Fields memorial, ice-skaters in the winter and rain slashing across the Jackie Kennedy Onassis Reservoir during one of the worst storms she'd witnessed. She'd been driven by adrenaline that night – Cleo had told her it was more stupidity than anything else – and framed in her studio apartment was one of the best shots she'd ever taken, of a lightning bolt across the water. It was next to another capturing the depths of winter in the same location, the water iced over and white, the golden glow of city buildings forming a backdrop. Some of her favourite photographs had been taken in the fall, a powerful

season with changing light casting a different screen over the city
and its surrounds. The foliage had been a delight, falling leaves
caught in multiple shots as they spun their way to the ground, the
lines upon them, the colours from red to gold, to green, to purple,
some edges curled up. Holly had seen and photographed it all.
She'd captured wide landscapes beneath the bright sunshine,
zoomed close up to intricate knots in trees, and she'd mixed people
with scenery.

Holly reached the car-hire place and turned her mind back to
the present. She signed the forms, collected the keys, programmed
the satnav, and stowed her belongings in the trunk before setting off
down West 34th to Twelfth Avenue. Hiring a car was a luxury she'd
have to exchange for public transport after today in a bid to cut
costs wherever possible, so she made the most of the heater to
escape the icy chill and savoured the scenic drive with the magnificent Hudson on her left. She passed the piers, the cruise boats she'd
taken around the island to get her bearings when she first arrived.
She set the wiper blades on as the drizzle began to get heavier and
sang along to the radio station, which saw nothing at getting into
the holiday spirit so early in the morning by playing modern
Christmas music interspersed with the odd Christmas carol. She
followed the highway wishing she could stop for a time, capture the
wintry scenes, trees on either side bare and bracing themselves for
the winter snowfall that she'd heard could be brutal to even the
hardiest of New Yorkers.

An hour and a half after leaving Manhattan, Holly cruised into
Inglenook Falls, where the rain had either been and gone or not
come at all and instead there was a layer of frost on the tips of
roofs, on the street sign and glistening on the sidewalk. She'd
booked in at a guesthouse, the Chestnut Lodge, for three nights
even though Pierre had wanted her to stay with him at the hotel.
The owners of the guesthouse, Lisa and Christopher, were good

friends of her parents and had moved out this way so they could be nearer to their daughter, Heather, who was based in Hartford. Holly had chosen to stay with them not only to have a good catch-up but so she could use the time to work on her article for the Corbridge Hotel without any distractions. Pierre had asked her a few times in the last couple of months when she was going to look for a proper job. He didn't seem to be able to get his head around anything that involved working from home or had the title Freelance.

She followed the road until a bottle-green sign with gold writing came into view to welcome her to Inglenook Falls as she joined Main Street. Holly could see why Cleo loved having her store here so much. There was a small green space across the street with a bandstand that had garlands and lights wound up its post, and a Christmas tree stood tall. Arriving in Inglenook Falls was like stepping into a different world from Manhattan, like dialling down on everything from the size of the buildings to people's demeanour. Nobody seemed in much of a rush and she thought about Pierre coming here from the hotel that sat between Inglenook Falls and the next town, asking for a 'coffee, stat!' in the local café and the owner taking all the time in the world as Pierre tapped his watch. It wasn't that he was rude. He was just a man on a mission.

The sun had hidden behind the clouds as Holly passed the post office and convenience store, and it was really the bright lights on the Christmas tree that highlighted the town today. She turned right at the end, past the green again, and drove down the street on its opposite side, past the café and eventually to the Chestnut Lodge, the guesthouse set back from Main Street but within a stone's throw of a small library and an Italian restaurant. She parked up in the compact parking lot and hauled her things from the trunk of her hire car up to the porch that stretched all the way across the front of a soft-grey, colonial home with a matching grey sign depicting its name, hanging from a white post on chunky silver chains.

'Well, hello!' Lisa was out first, a red gingham apron tied round her waist and her silvery-blonde hair swished up in a bun with a few stray wisps escaping at the sides of her face. She had on turquoise, tailored pants, a thin, cream knit over a black, roll-neck top and red beads to match her apron. 'You haven't changed a bit, my girl!' She pulled Holly into a hug and then stepped back, hands on Holly's upper arms as though to examine the latest arrival. 'The last time I saw you, you were off to college.'

Holly grinned. 'That's right. You were drinking homemade lemonade on our front porch with Mom and Dad. Mom was trying to put on a brave face.'

'That she was. Seeing her daughter go off to college wasn't easy, but she saved the tears until after you'd left.'

That was another reason to stay with Lisa and Christopher. Holly was a grown woman but her parents were already worried she'd made a mistake leaving her job and so hearing from their friends that their daughter was doing well would be far easier than her trying to tell them.

Holly followed Lisa into the guesthouse and Christopher came down the stairs and pulled her into a hug. 'It's wonderful to have you here, we think you're going to love it in Inglenook Falls. You're looking well – I shall make sure I tell your mom and dad when I talk to them.' She'd figured they both would. 'I can't believe we haven't caught up with you before now.'

'I was here for a baby shower in September but haven't been back since.'

'That's right,' said Lisa. 'For Cleo's baby, Emily. She's a cute little thing.'

'She sure is.'

'You should've popped in.'

Holly felt bad. She'd stayed a couple of hours for the shower but had headed straight back to the city afterwards so she could be ready for the office the next morning. 'Life's been crazy busy, but I'm here now. Cleo mentioned you've been to the store a few times.'

'I love it at the Little Knitting Box,' Lisa admitted. 'I'm knitting a sweater for my granddaughter so I sometimes go to the workshops, especially when I've messed up and don't know how to rescue my yarn from certain death.'

Holly looked around the entrance hall, inhaled a smell of baking, noticed small touches like a guestbook on the hallway table, ornaments lining the mantelpiece in the front lounge, framed photographs on the walls. 'You two look like you belong here. Are you loving it?' They were the perfect example of people who'd made the leap, changed their lives for the better, and it was inspiring.

Lisa smiled. 'I feel like we've been here forever, in a good way. We're less than a couple of hours by road to Heather's place, so we get to see the grandkids a lot, which is wonderful.'

'Would you look at us chatting away and forgetting our manners,' said Christopher, reaching out to take Holly's suitcase and laptop bag. 'I'll put these in your room.'

Christopher did the honours and Holly followed Lisa into the kitchen, where her host poured her a tall glass of apple juice. Despite the cold weather, her thirst needed the hit before she could warm herself up with something hotter.

'So, how's the freelance life treating you?' Lisa pressed the top of one of the golden cookies on a tray on the cooktop lightly and made a satisfied murmur at its springy surface.

'This is day one but I've got a few things lined up.'

'Well, it sounds as though you're quite the business woman. And I hope you've always done what I'm forever telling my kids to do. Ten per cent of your pay packet... goes in the bank.'

Holly smiled and nodded as she hid behind a gulp of apple juice. Despite her fat pay packet, living in Manhattan did come at a cost. She'd saved a bit but it was nowhere near ten per cent – three at best. And that was one bit of information that really didn't need to go bicoastal.

Holly and Lisa chatted about Holly's parents and their trip around the world, the places they'd visited and the ones that were still on their list and by the time Christopher came back downstairs, Holly had already been plied with two oatmeal and raisin cookies. She escaped to check out her room.

She was upstairs in the Chestnut Lodge, in a room with warm, oyster painted walls on three sides and bluebell-flowered wallpaper on the other. The bedspread had the same floral touches, along with the pillows that were lace-edged and plump. The bathroom attached to the bedroom was compact but had everything she needed.

She unpacked her suitcase – underwear went into the chest of drawers, folded jumpers slotted onto a shelf, her favourite, buttery-soft, walnut, leather boots plus her black, suede, ankle boots, runners, and shoes went on the base of the closet, and she hung up a shirt and top in case she needed to dress up during her time here. She put her cell phone on charge and took out her camera, the next step up from the model her dad had bought her more than a decade ago and one she'd never have been able to afford without a well-paid job. She'd also been able to fund the photography course where she'd enhanced her self-taught skills to encompass choosing settings, framing, exposure, focus control and motion blur. She'd been practising ever since, her hobby merging with her work, bringing ideas and techniques into her own photographs and writing.

She took out the lens cloth and gave the camera a clean, checked the battery level, and put it securely back in its case. Her eagerness to explore wasn't going to allow her to relax and so she pulled on her jacket, scarf, and gloves, looped her camera over her head, and put one arm through the strap so it sat across her body. Her official stint at the new hotel wasn't lined up until late tomorrow and as far as Pierre knew, she'd be arriving in town then. It felt sneaky to enjoy this alone time but Holly was relishing it already, and after so many years working flat out, she realised she needed it.

'Wrap up warm,' Lisa called from the kitchen when Holly ventured downstairs. 'Snowfall is predicted tonight.'

Holly called out her goodbyes as well as her thanks for the advice and stepped out onto the porch. Even the air here felt different to Manhattan. Fresher somehow. It was cold, for sure, but without the fumes of the city traffic, the honking of horns, the constant rush of people all vying to get to where they needed to go first, a sense of calm washed over her and already her fingers twitched with the need to take photographs of her new surroundings.

She reached the end of the driveway and to her right, after a line of houses set back from the street, was Marlo's café, opposite the town green. The smell from the bakery across the street drifted towards her with a note of cinnamon and cloves and she turned left to pass the library with its posters in the window advertising Meet the Author events for a children's book series. She passed the cute Italian restaurant with a ruby-red front canopy and a gold-embossed menu pinned in the window promising cannelloni with beef and truffle mushrooms, pepperoni and clam ragu, or steak with pappardelle and gorgonzola.

She crossed the street lined with ornate lamps at the top of iron poles, Christmas decorations hung up high and already illuminated, ready to stand out once the sun went down. She followed the sidewalk away from the direction of the Little Knitting Box – she'd sit and chat with Cleo for hours if she went in there, and she'd never take any photos – and beyond the school she came to the sign that had welcomed her to the town. She took her gloves off so she could feel the camera as she captured a panoramic shot of the street, the green, the stores, the decorations up high, all the way down Main Street.

She put her gloves on and stood for a moment. To give Pierre his credit, he'd found the site for the new hotel and although not far from here, it had been part of his mission to ensure it wouldn't encroach on the residents of Inglenook Falls. He thought the town deserved to keep its identity, to not be spoiled, and Holly couldn't agree more.

Beyond Main Street and past the corner where the Little Knitting Box could be found if you walked a hundred paces was the most magnificent backdrop of hills and land hugging the perimeter of this town. Holly knew from Cleo that the Inglenook Falls holiday markets were already setting up in the fields she could see in the distance and come the end of the month they would be in full swing.

Holly was used to photographing a densely populated city, with shots of people milling, crowds bobbing up and down along Fifth Avenue, a group running through Central Park with the biggest smiles on their faces, views from the High Line down onto the swarming Manhattan streets. What she wasn't used to was countryside, and so when she noticed a track past the school signposted 'Inglenook Falls Woodlands' on a dilapidated piece of wood that was none too sturdy but worth removing her gloves to take a photo of, she was anxious to explore.

Holly soon got the impression not many people ventured this way. The track would've been muddy underfoot had the ground not been so hard from the frost and the temperatures threatening snow, but she meandered her way down, knowing she shouldn't be too long as she wanted to get back to the Chestnut Lodge for a good meal. Her breakfast had been hours ago, she'd only had a couple of cookies since, and her tummy was already starting to complain at being left empty for so long.

She stopped halfway down the track when it came to a fork. She veered left and followed the track on, searching out photo opportunities, exploring. Gloves off again, she photographed the canopy of trees above her, capturing the way the light dappled the bare branches, the different shades of bark on the trunk. She'd been in Manhattan long enough to know Central Park well – with all its enclaves, its busier parts, where a jazz band often played near the lake – but this was something new, completely unfamiliar. Through a clearing in the trees more land stretched out beyond, with hills rising up and then down again. This place would be amazing come fall. A hint of pine mixed in the air as the wind picked up and she lifted her camera, capturing a glassy mist on the horizon, the sun illuminating any remaining patches of frost that it could. To her right she could see acres and acres of fir trees, emanating the smell of Christmas even from far away. Perhaps people came here for their trees every year and dragged them from the land all the way up to Main Street and home.

She hurried to put her gloves on again before her hands lost all feeling, turned to carry on, her ankle wobbling on a stone underfoot. Her heartbeat increased when she thought about the bears that likely roamed this area in the warmer months. The bear population of Connecticut had increased recently; she'd read an article about it, glad to live in a metropolis when she took in the details of how bears woke quickly if they were ever disturbed. She'd also read about how some bears came out of hibernation to forage during winter thaws, and suddenly wished there was an extra-thick layer of snow on the ground now. She looked around for evidence. Bears loved to eat berries and acorns, but there weren't any of those. She didn't have food on her person either, so they wouldn't be sniffing for that. But hadn't she also read about bears hibernating in brush piles, or rocky crevices, or piles of leaves? There were plenty of patches that looked attractive for a bear right now as she passed between trees, heart thudding at the thought of a momma bear coming out to investigate this stranger.

Stop being ridiculous, she told herself. *You're being crazy!*

She took another turn and found herself at the top of a mound looking down into a clearing. A log cabin with a modest porch out front and a tin chimney jutting out of the roof was the first sign of habitation in these woods and it took her by surprise. She crouched down, took off her gloves again and lifted her camera. She snapped away. A welcoming glow came from the window on the bottom right and when plumes of smoke left the tin chimney heading for the skies she knew that must be the living area and could imagine a cosy fire welcoming the owner or guest in from the cold. Christmas would be magical inside, she bet, snuggled up with loved ones, stockings hanging on the fireplace, waiting for Santa to come.

She shivered. Her fingers were numb from exposing her skin too frequently in the urge to photograph this gorgeous town and its surrounds, and even her legs began to feel the cold as she stood up. 'Damn.' Her scarf had unwound itself and dipped in a puddle of water that had yet to ice over. She squeezed out the excess, looped it back on and, arms out to her sides with her camera hanging against her chest from the strap around her neck, she gingerly followed the uneven path that must've been formed by footsteps going to and from the cabin.

She almost slipped down the last part, which had patches of ice formed on ground that had hardened with a combination of the frost and the sun streaking through the woodland, and as she got closer the log cabin appeared even more picturesque. She took a few photos but then wondered, was she intruding? This looked like somebody's home – there was a rocker out front on the porch, a pair of men's boots by the door, two sheds to one side that she hadn't seen from farther away, a wood store beneath tarp on the side porch with a few tell-tale log ends just visible.

She decided to give the occupiers their privacy and instead of taking any more photographs, she turned back. The sky had turned a pale shade of charcoal and had already begun to fade, and she had to get back up to Main Street. She could explore more another day.

The sound of a twig snapping somewhere nearby conjured up new visions of a bear prowling the area. She quickened her pace, climbing the path back the way she came, but she kept losing her footing on the frozen mud.

There was another sound, louder this time, and it came from behind her. And when she turned, it wasn't a bear but she still screamed.

It was a man, a big hairy man with wide eyes who looked like he'd been out in the wilderness for months. She ran on but slipped and hit her knee and when she got up and tried to run again her arms didn't save her from the fall and her head made contact with the ground. One thud and the world spun around her and the man came closer and closer, his face barely visible through all that matted hair.

And that was the last thing she remembered before the bump on her head sent her to sleep.

3

MITCH

Mitch had only come out of the cabin to chop some more wood. He hadn't expected anyone to be snooping around. And he certainly hadn't expected to have to play the knight in shining armour to a helpless woman with immaculately styled auburn hair and sharp blue eyes.

He reached down and checked she was still breathing. She'd gone down hard in her quest to get away from him and there was only a little blood, although a decent-sized bump had already formed on her forehead.

He scooped her up in his arms. She weighed less than any of the logs he'd had to haul up from the fields earlier and he carried her carefully back down the path, his all-terrain hiking boots coping expertly with the slippery surface. She stirred and groaned and muttered something incomprehensible but didn't wake up enough to realise what was going on. When he reached the cabin he pushed the door open with his foot after he'd managed to manoeuvre the handle with her in his arms, and inside he took her straight through to the sofa. She was wrapped up warm and he somehow managed to remove the camera from round her neck, the bag looped across her body, her scarf, and her coat. He draped the soft pink scarf near the log burner, weighing it down on the mantel above with a pot containing loose change. He took off her boots and she roused a little, but when she tried to speak again she sounded groggy.

He hung around a moment longer in case she woke but when she didn't, and when he was sure she didn't need to be rushed to the emergency room – she wasn't vomiting, she'd managed to open her eyes a bit and attempt to talk, although none of it had made sense – he took off his own boots and set both pairs by the log burner. Once he was happy she was comfortable, he took out a broom and swept up the debris he'd brought in. He may look a mess but his log cabin wasn't. His mum and dad had kept this place shipshape when they'd still been around and now that it was his, he wouldn't allow himself to let it go in the same way as he had in so many other facets of his life.

He leaned the broom against the cabin wall by the door and as the fire inside the log burner began to fade, he studied his guest's face. She wasn't from Inglenook Falls. Well, she could be, but she certainly hadn't lived there when he'd been a proper part of the town – something he hadn't been in a long time. She had beautiful long, wavy hair and delicate facial features with a tiny mole above the top of her lip that you only saw if you were up real close. This woman was from the city, he could tell. He saw women like her every time he had to head into Manhattan. He, on the other hand, looked more like someone who begged on a street corner than someone who had once walked tall in a suit. Back then, not only had he had a job, he'd also had people in his corner.

Her camera had survived the fall. It looked expensive. Content she was all right for now, Mitch went up the staircase made in the same cedar logs as the rustic cabin, ducking in the same place he did every time to avoid hitting his head on the curved beam above, to the landing, where he knew there was a soft cloth he'd used to clean the glass on the photo frames up here. He gave the woman's camera a once-over to rid it of dirt. He cleaned the camera bag up too and then stowed the equipment safely back inside. He looked in the little pocket at the front of the bag to see if he could get some ID for the woman. That way he might be able to return her home so she was no longer his problem. It was a long time since anyone had come to this cabin apart from him or his friend Jude, and the odd person from town who braved it to ask about Christmas trees, and that was the way he liked it.

But there was nothing in the bag. No business card, no cell phone, no clue as to who this woman who'd tumbled into his life was or where she'd come from.

Back downstairs he left her camera on the small table by the window and checked the soup simmering away on the stove in the kitchen, turned the heat down low to give him some time. The log burner in the lounge was by now crying out for more fuel – the reason he'd been outside in the first place – and he didn't want the stranger to catch a chill and make this even worse for them both. Snow was forecast tonight and he never let weather get the upper hand the way so many people in his life had managed to do.

'Miss...' He put a hand gently on her arm. 'Miss...' He patted her a little harder. She opened her eyes, looked at him briefly, but then mumbled something about photographs and cabins, trees and bears, and so, satisfied all she needed to do was sleep it off, he scooped her into his arms once more and took her upstairs where it would be warmer and he could find blankets and pillows to make her comfortable. He ducked his head out of routine when he reached the beam at the top of the staircase and in his bedroom laid her down on one side of the bed.

Lucky he'd found her and not some crazy person. Not that there were many of them around here. Locals thought he was the only one of those. He hadn't done anything, per se. In fact, he'd been the one who was wronged, the one whose heart had been snapped in two, but rather than turn to townsfolk for help he'd retreated to the safety of the log cabin, to a place he felt at home, safe from judgement, safe from more hurt.

He pulled the comforter over the top of her and found a blanket from the blanket box at the foot of the bed to add extra warmth. Again he waited for her to stir but apart from a tiny groan and movement of her head she was out for the count. He was no medic, but he knew the basics and she'd sleep some more then wake up, probably yell at him given she'd tried to run in the first place. His priority was getting her off his property but other than carrying her around town knocking on doors to ask if anyone knew her, he was stuck. He had no choice but to wait for her to wake up in her own time.

He was about to leave her and go downstairs but stopped in the doorway. What if she didn't wake up? People already thought the worst of him around here. What if they thought he'd killed her?

He went back over to her and tried to ignore all that soft hair fanned out across the pillow. Perhaps he'd check her pulse. But when he went to touch her she burrowed further beneath the warmth of the bedding, turned on her side and he could hear the steady breathing that told him he was being paranoid. Still, he got some cotton wool from the bathroom cabinet, wet it and returned to the bedroom, all the while explaining what he was doing in case she could hear him and woke up to find his hands on her and it sent her into a blind panic. He gently dabbed the cut on her head clean so it didn't get infected, and then left her to sleep.

She was going to be fine. And people round here could think what they liked.

He trudged downstairs, tugged on his boots, pulled on his coat and a hat, and ventured outside to brave the elements again. Nightfall was fast approaching and the air around him an icy snap, even down here in the sheltered area around the cabin. He manoeuvred one of the logs he'd dragged up here earlier and used a chainsaw to cut the whole thing into sections. He took the first piece, placed it end up on the bigger upturned section of log that was fit for this purpose, then took the axe and, measuring in his mind how far he was standing away, positioned his hands, swung it way overhead and brought it down. He progressed in the same way, splitting each piece of log, sometimes successful on the first swing; other times taking two or three goes. And then he took each section and made it even smaller, still using the axe, so it would fit into the basket beside the log burner inside ready to heat the cabin. This was how his dad had shown him to split wood and he loved the physical escape of the task.

As he chopped he let his mind drift to Albie. He'd be eight years old now, so the same age as Mitch was when his dad taught him how to use an axe like he had hold of now. His dad, Albert, had been an experienced logger and wood carver and both Mitch and his brother Corey had watched him for a long while before they were allowed to try this themselves. Safety had always been Albert's top priority every time his boys had been with him. In the summer months they'd worn bells around their necks to ward off approaches from bears venturing into the woodland areas, and when they were dealing with wood and anxious to use the tools it was supervision at all times.

Mitch wondered if Albie had been living in surrounds like this for the past three years, or whether he was a city kid. Hard to believe he didn't know even the most basic facts about his own son.

He chopped the last of the wood. The sky was almost black now, and he put some of the wood beneath the tarp on the porch and grabbed a couple of bundles of logs to take them to the front. A couple of feathery flakes of snow drifted down from the skies above and, head down against the cold, Mitch scooted back to the side of the house to put the axe away in one of the sheds. He wondered if the woman would be awake by now, or perhaps she was and had even made a run for it when he wasn't looking.

And for a man who liked to live most of his days as a hermit, he found himself kind of hoping that she hadn't.

4

HOLLY

Holly groaned. Her head thumped and she put out a hand to touch the skin above her left eye. 'Ouch,' she winced. 'Where am I?' She took in the deep-blue blanket laid over the top of her that was tangled with the comforter, the curves in the smooth log walls that she didn't remember from the guesthouse, and when she looked around there was no desk, no closet, no sign of her things.

And then she remembered.

She sat up straighter, gasping at the pain in her head. Was that man here? Had he brought her to his cabin, in the woods, with no way to get free?

She looked around for her cell and remembered she'd left it back at the guesthouse, charging. Stupid on her part – assuming she'd be back in no time, was perfectly safe exploring the local area of Inglenook Falls, a quaint town that could now be the last place she ever saw.

She was panicking. Her breathing quickened and she leapt out of bed at the sound of tapping coming from outside the cabin. Careful not to be seen, she tiptoed from the bed over to the window, her hand resting on the small, beautifully crafted log ledge that wasn't as cold as she expected. She saw the profile of the man who'd found her trying to get away. She saw an axe, its shiny silver blade launching high into the air before it came down on a piece of log.

The light was fading fast and if she wanted to make a getaway she'd have to do it sooner rather than later. She turned to go grab her coat, her scarf, her camera, but her head pounded and she put a hand to the bump and briefly shut her eyes. She walked over to the bed and managed a straight line, which was a good sign. She didn't feel sick either so it must've been a mild concussion that she'd mostly slept off.

She looked around the bedroom again but there was no sign of anything. Had he taken her camera? She moved back to the window. He was right out front. She had no chance of escape, and it had already started to snow.

She opened the bedroom door slowly and the waft of something cooking drifted towards her from downstairs. Certain she was alone inside the log cabin, she tiptoed towards the top of the staircase but she stopped before she went any further. In the landing area beside the bedroom, where the wooden roof finished in a point, frames and frames of photographs littered the walls. Her feet sank into the maroon rug on the floor as she took a closer look, her hand rested on the back of the single rocker placed here as though it were somewhere for quiet contemplation. The subject in most of these photographs was the same little boy, captured at different ages, and her eyes moved along the space, scanning up and down from picture to picture. There was a photograph of the boy as a toddler sitting on an upturned log with an elderly man standing beside him, laughing into the lens. It looked like the upturned log the wild man was using outside right now. Another photograph showed the same boy beside an expanse of water gingerly dipping one toe onto the surface. There were others taken in the snow, one with the boy wearing a backpack as though he was off to school that day, another of him out fishing in a little tin boat. And every single photograph was encased in a beautiful frame, each one different from the last. Some were dark timber, others light, knots of wood and markings depicted their individuality as though each one had been made especially for the shot it displayed now.

When she heard more sounds coming from the porch at the front of the cabin, Holly stopped admiring the impressive photography and tiptoed down the wooden stairs one at a time until she reached the bottom. She looked left and saw her camera on the side table. She couldn't get away with him out there on the other side of the door but she could get some photographs from the upstairs window. That way, if something happened to her and she ever got away from here, she'd be able to identify the man who'd taken her prisoner.

Trying not to panic, she headed back upstairs and, careful not to be seen, positioned herself at the window. She took photographs of him in profile, then a clearer picture of his face when the axe rose high in the air. He looked as scary as before but there was a far-off look in his eyes, even from up here, that said he had a story to tell. He was working hard out there in a way not many men Holly had ever known would be familiar with, physical labour that seemed part of his life rather than a job. And despite still being scared, Holly sensed something about this man that told her he wasn't all bad. He had straggly hair that may have been dark brown before it picked up sunlight that stained the ends and never got trimmed away, his beard was unsightly – too long – and he looked serious, at times frustrated, but mostly at ease with his surroundings like all he wanted to do was avoid the rest of the world. She took a few more photographs of him half expecting him to look up any second, but he was engrossed in his task.

With enough pictures, she headed back downstairs. Her scarf was hanging beside the log burner and she retrieved it from the clutches of a pot of change holding it in place before slinging it around her neck. There was no time to waste if she wanted to avoid the man and his axe and make it out of here in one piece. She'd wait for it to quieten on the porch and then make her escape. She found her boots by the fire, nice and dry now, and her coat was hanging on a hook in the hallway. She had to admit he didn't seem like the average kidnapper. He didn't seem like someone about to murder a woman who'd stumbled upon his cabin, but then again, what crazy person did?

She listened by the door at the front of the cabin. She could make out a noise, perhaps coming from the part of the porch that wrapped around the side. She knew she could make a dash for it so she reached out slowly for the handle, twisted it quietly and stepped outside. The chill made straight for her but she carefully pulled the door closed so it didn't fall shut and alert the man's attention.

She released the handle and gasped.

He was standing right next to her.

She wanted to scream but nothing came out. She got ready to shove past him, yell, and run for her life, but he'd already given her space and moved around her to open the door to the cabin himself. He leaned inside to retrieve a straw basket and began loading up the logs he'd dumped on the porch.

Why weren't her legs moving? Why wasn't she screaming all the way back to the guesthouse?

'Thank you,' she found herself saying.

He looked up briefly, nodded, and then carried on stowing the logs. His gloves were in shreds, they'd be useless in the cold. 'The log burner will be out soon.' It was all he said before he turned his back.

This was her chance. She stepped off the porch, took a few steps and stopped. It wasn't completely dark yet but beneath the trees in front of her it was almost impossible to make out the patch she'd slipped down, the escape route she'd tried to use earlier that day. She felt out of her depth. Like a little girl. The lump on her head throbbed, the snowflakes usually so magical in their arrival did little to quell her fear, and she thought she might burst into tears.

'It's too dark to go alone,' he called from the porch, his voice surprisingly unthreatening compared to his appearance. 'There's soup warming on the stove. You can eat and then I'll take you back up to town.'

She turned to face him, but he'd already gone back inside.

Was this was one of those moments she'd learnt about on the self-defence course Darcy had made her go to in the city last month, where she either had a flight or fight response? She had no idea. All she knew was that she didn't want to go up that track to town alone and maybe this man was the lesser of two evils if bears or, heaven help her, a madman could be on the prowl.

She went back inside the log cabin and sat on the sofa away from the man, who was in the kitchen, her creative mind doing its best not to make up all kinds of non-happy endings. He'd already stoked the log burner and it confidently crackled away. When he came closer she flinched but he only handed her an ice pack and told her to hold it over the bump on her head so it went down quicker.

The kitchen area wasn't separated with a wall so she watched the man work, stirring a pot on the stove, taking out cutlery and bowls, a plate, wiping down the sink area. He cut chunks of bread on a board, buttered them and before long, ladled out a bowl of soup.

'I'm not very hungry.' She was lying, one hundred per cent. 'I'd rather get going.'

He muttered something under his breath and then added, without looking at her, 'If you eat and keep it down, then I'll know you're fine.' He plonked a bowl onto the table followed by a side plate with bread. 'I don't want to risk you collapsing halfway up the path and having to carry you back and haul you to the hospital.'

She remained seated on the sofa a couple more minutes, but when her tummy grumbled she decided it was better to do what he wanted and get out of here as soon as she could.

'How's the head?' he asked gruffly, his back to her as he ladled out another bowl, for himself presumably.

'Hurts but not too bad. The ice pack helped.' She picked up her spoon. This man clearly wasn't used to company. He wasn't even looking at her. All she could see was his matted hair from behind, wide shoulders and a sturdy physique that must be kept in shape by all the manual labour that came with owning a place out here. When he turned and leaned against the countertop to eat his own meal, she waited for him to put some soup in his mouth first to be sure he hadn't added anything weird to it, then managed a few mouthfuls herself and half the bread. And then she told him, again, that she wanted to go.

He scooped up a few more mouthfuls before he answered her. 'Right.' He dumped his bowl in the sink and said, 'I'm sorry I scared you today. It wasn't my intention.'

She couldn't deny it. 'I thought you were a bear. I mean, not that you look like a bear, just that...' Oh, goodness, she was insulting the man and had no idea what he would do now.

She thought she heard him laugh as he headed through the lounge towards the door, where he pulled on his boots and donned a hat. She followed him and, still dressed in her coat and scarf, picked up her camera bag and watched him unhook a lantern from where it was hanging on the front porch. He lit the candle inside and walked on without another word.

Holly followed him, out into the cold, the sky a dark inky

blanket above them as he skilfully led her back to the path that had caused them to meet in the first place.

'Thanks for cleaning up my camera.' Nervous, talking was the only way she could make herself feel better as she walked closely behind him so as not to lose sight of the man or the lantern. He was so tall it was difficult for her to see much at all. 'My name's Holly, by the way.'

'Nice equipment,' he said, without offering his own name in return.

She hoped he was referring to the camera and nothing to do with her, although she'd woken fully clothed so assumed he hadn't done anything other than lay her somewhere comfortable and warm while she recovered. 'It was a gift, for my birthday. A while back now,' she rambled on, her voice an attempt to dispel her jitters as an owl hooted and the twigs cracking beneath her own feet had her jumping in fright. 'I love taking pictures. That's what I was doing, out here, at your cabin.'

He harrumphed and she sensed it was the best she was going to get. They took a fork in the paths that she remembered from before, although she might not have managed it without his help given night had fallen.

'You like photography?' she asked as the path straightened and got a little steeper. She recognised this part and was sure they'd come upon Main Street in a few minutes. 'Wow, look at all these stars.' She could take a magnificent photograph, standing right here, pointing the lens up to the inky sky.

To her surprise, his feet stopped moving. She almost bundled into the back of him, her hands touched the back of his winter jacket, his collar turned up against the cold, and she straightened herself. But he wasn't looking at her, he was looking at the sky too. 'It's a beautiful night.'

'And with snowflakes too.' Her fingers twitched on her camera even though she was standing here with this stranger who could do anything and nobody would ever know.

He lifted the lantern and carried on leading the way as though he hadn't taken pause to appreciate the world around him. Whatever he'd been thinking as he gazed up at those stars, he didn't want to think it while he was in her company.

She followed him, attempting to keep up with his pace that had increased all of a sudden as they neared Main Street. 'Who's the little boy?'

This time she did pummel into the back of him as he came to an abrupt halt. He lifted the lantern and, with his other arm, pointed ahead. 'Main Street is right there. You'll be fine now.' And without even looking at her, he turned and went back the way he came.

'Thank you!' she called after him. Thank you for helping me out when I fell, thank you for cleaning my camera and drying my boots and scarf, thank you for the food, for leading me to safety.

But she didn't get a chance to say any of that as he faded into the woods, the lantern getting dimmer the farther he got, and when she couldn't see anything of him, as though he'd never really been there at all, she turned quickly and ran the rest of the way to Main Street.

* * *

'What happened to you?' Cleo took one look at Holly when she arrived at the Little Knitting Box, taking in her muddy clothes and the purply black bruise on her forehead and leapt into mum mode.

'I'm fine, honestly.'

'No you're not, you're shaking.'

'I should probably sit down.'

'Kaisha.' Cleo got her assistant's attention. 'Would you go grab some takeout coffees from the café, strong for this one. I'll reimburse you later.'

Kaisha went off to do the honours and Cleo ushered Holly into the room out back of the store where she often hosted knitting groups, before returning to the store to take payment from Mrs Merryman for a new knitting bag she was buying for her daughter-in-law, whose husband was going to be this year's Santa Claus at the bandstand a couple of weeks before Christmas. Holly could hear the banter from where she was sitting and it was a normalcy that instilled a sense of calm.

When Cleo finally finished with her customer and came out back she asked, 'What on earth happened to you?'

'I went investigating in the woods. I wanted to take some shots, appreciate the beauty of the place.'

'Did you fall?'

'I followed a track and found a little log cabin and when the owner came out mid photoshoot I panicked and tried to run away. I slipped, hit my head, and he took me in until I came around.'

'Wait... you don't mean Mitch's cabin, do you?'

'I don't know his name. Gruff-looking man, long bushy beard, unkempt, quite antisocial when it came to conversation as it happens. He put me into bed until I came around.'

'You don't need a coffee, you need a whisky or a brandy! Did he... did he try anything?'

'What?' Taken aback, Holly suddenly realised what she meant. 'No! I was fully clothed when I woke up, he was chopping wood. Although seeing the axe wasn't too reassuring, let me tell you.'

Kaisha returned and handed out the coffees. 'I took the liberty of buying some treats from the bakery too,' she smiled cheekily. 'I've already eaten mine.'

'You're a star, you read my mind.' Cleo handed Holly one of the cinnamon scrolls from the cardboard tray before taking the other for herself. 'A caffeine hit and a sugar rush should sort you out, Holly.'

Despite the feed at the log cabin, Holly devoured the cinnamon scroll and took a generous swig of caffeine-laced liquid. Cleo must've sensed her hunger because she let her eat before she asked for more details.

'You're really lucky, Holly. People rarely venture down to the cabin in the woods. Mitch runs a Christmas tree farm from there, but doesn't sell them in town – he avoids people here. The last person to go down there was Doug, who's married to Nessa from the library, and he was brave enough to go and sort out having the big tree on the town's green.'

'It's a beautiful tree.'

'It is. Inglenook Falls always gets it from Mitch's family, but since Albert, Mitch's father, died it's been somewhat of a question as to whether we'll still be able to do business with Mitch. Like I said, he doesn't like the people of this town much.' She shook her head. 'I meant to warn you not to go wandering down that way, but you were too quick for me.'

Holly smiled. 'I couldn't wait to get out and appreciate the area. I'll be working on the write-up for the new hotel and taking those photos tomorrow, so thought I'd get in there with something for me.' She savoured another hit of caffeine and tried not to panic when she caught sight of her reflection in the mirror out back. The lump on her forehead was a decent size but with any luck it would go down soon enough and make-up would help. 'What's Mitch's story?' She'd never been able to suppress her investigative skills.

'I've never spoken with him.' Cleo poked her head out to check they were okay to talk a bit longer and when she saw Kaisha was fine, she settled down again on the stool next to Holly. 'But I've heard about him. You know how small towns are, doesn't take long for gossip to come your way. Over time, especially if he's ever walked past the store when I'm in here with a customer, I've heard little snippets about him.'

'Being the subject of constant gossip and appraisal can't be easy for anyone.' No wonder he hadn't appreciated a stranger on his property.

'Enid from the café told me most of the story one day when she was in here choosing yarn for one of our workshops. Apparently he married his college sweetheart, Shannon, but it all went sour.'

'College?' Somehow the overgrown man with the muddied cheeks and inability to string much more than a few words together didn't seem the type to be academic. 'He looked like he'd been hiding in those woods forever and wouldn't know one end of a text-book from another.'

'He used to be completely different, according to Enid.'

'So what happened to the college sweetheart?' Holly put a hand to her throat. 'She didn't go missing, did she?'

'She upped and left him, took their little boy with her, and vanished.'

'The boy in the photographs,' Holly breathed.

'Photographs?'

'He has so many photographs of a little boy, all displayed upstairs in the cabin.'

'He must miss him.'

'Why did she leave?'

'I don't know, maybe he doesn't either. But Enid told me Mitch was in charge of a large, booming retail chain in Manhattan and when they closed their doors, not only did Mitch lose the job he worked so hard at and made a success, he also felt responsible for all those employees who worked for him and lost their jobs too. Many of them had families, some of them were struggling finan-cially already, and Mitch couldn't see past the guilt he felt.'

'But it couldn't have been his fault, that sort of thing happens all the time.'

'It does, but he took it personally, as though he could've done something to avoid it. And then they lost their home, couldn't keep up with the repayments. Apparently he never picked himself up after that. The family stayed in rented accommodation for a while, coming here occasionally, but Mitch was withdrawn and barely spoke. Shannon, the wife, broke down in the café one day, talking with Enid. Maybe she didn't know how to move past it.'

'So she took their son?' Holly shook her head. 'Seems an odd way to kick a man when he's down.'

'It does, doesn't it? Albie was only five at the time. Enid said that everything seemed to pile on top of Mitch at once. I think she had a soft spot for him. She talked about what he was like as a little boy, how he'd once run out from behind an ice-cream truck and almost got knocked down in the street, and then his teen days, his time at college, his wedding and when his son was born.' Cleo broke off when Kaisha came to ask a question on behalf of one of their regulars who had curled edges in her yarn but after going to see the customer, Cleo returned to Holly and continued sharing details. 'When Shannon took Albie, Mitch apparently went mad, rampaged all over town. He went into the café, the library, the Italian restaurant, the hardware store, eyes wild, demanding answers. And then all of a sudden he went away. I never asked where, but nobody saw him for a long while. A few months later he moved into the cabin with his dad and has stayed there ever since.'

'How did his dad die?'

'He had cancer and Mitch looked after him right up until the end. Very sad. Yet another thing for him to deal with. Everyone in town could see he wasn't coping, he was falling apart – "a broken man" is how another customer described him to me when Mitch walked past here late one evening.'

Holly asked for a glass of water, her thirst perhaps a side effect from her fall, or maybe it was hearing this man's story.

Cleo watched her intently. 'You okay?'

'Honestly, I'm fine. Guilty of not drinking enough, that's all.'

'He never got over it, according to people around here,' Cleo continued when she was sure Holly was fine. 'His dad left the log cabin and the surrounding woodlands to him and his brother, but his brother never comes here, as far as I know, and now Mitch lives in that cabin like a hermit. People put their heads down when they see him – God, I know I've done that when I've had the kids in tow – or they cross the street.'

'The poor man.'

Cleo put a hand over Holly's. 'Next time I see him I'm going to thank him for taking care of my friend.'

'I should get going,' said Holly. 'I don't want Lisa and Christopher sending out a search party. I don't suppose you have any make-up with you, do you?'

Cleo pulled a face. 'I don't, but I could ask Kaisha. Do you want to cover the bump? It might be better to keep it clean; the kids are always falling down and the first thing we do is clean it up.'

'I'm going to grab something to eat at the café rather than have dinner at the guesthouse – I can't face any questions – but I want to cover the injury in case Lisa or Christopher spot it and ask what happened. I can't face it tonight, all I want is my bed.'

'I'm worried about you, if you're still concussed.'

'I'm fine now, honestly. I've got a full day tomorrow out at the hotel complex with Pierre and I need some down time. It's been a crazy day.'

'Promise me you'll text me later then. And again before you go to sleep tonight. And in the morning.'

Holly laughed and kissed her friend goodbye on the cheek. 'Yes, Mom, I will.'

Cleo asked Kaisha to loan Holly some make-up and the young girl darted to the apartment she now rented upstairs and found some foundation and concealer, and when Holly went to apply it and looked in the mirror, the bump had already lessened in size, probably thanks to the ice pack, so it didn't take long to do a half-decent cover-up job. It wasn't completely inconspicuous but it was good enough and she teased the front strands of her auburn hair so they fell across the sides of her face some more.

'Thanks for the loan of the make-up, Kaisha.'

'You're welcome.'

Kaisha had finished stacking up the basket by the door with emerald-green yarn and was about to make her way over to the fields to see what progress had been made on the Swiss chalet huts being erected for the Christmas markets, one of which the store was going to occupy this year. Even though the store was right here in the heart of town, they could still do more business at an event like that, Cleo had told Holly, where everyone is in the spirit of the season, shoppers are impulse buying and lapping up the atmosphere.

'Cleo mentioned you're doing an exhibition at NYU and that perhaps the local paper would be interested in coverage,' said Holly, trying not to keep touching the bump now she'd done such a good job concealing it. 'I'm happy to pitch to them and do the write-up plus photographs.'

'Wow, that would be amazing. Do you think the paper would be interested?'

'In somewhere like Inglenook Falls, residents always want to know more about each other; they'll lap it up.' Hearing Mitch's story from Cleo, who'd heard it from someone else, confirmed that much. 'Cleo has my details – sorry, I usually carry business cards but I'm all over the place today. Get in touch by cell phone or email and we'll talk.'

'Thanks so much,' beamed Kaisha, a colourful girl and someone you'd immediately associate with working in a place like the Little Knitting Box and being into fashion, with her cute, grey, suede ankle boots, deep-purple leggings and a floppy, multi-coloured sweater.

'Well, you'll be helping me out as much as I'm helping you, Kaisha. I'm building my portfolio and a fashion piece is something totally different for me.'

Holly left them to it and made her way to Marlo's café on Main Street, lit up in the darkness with strings of fairy lights bordering its two main front windows. And nobody looked twice at her forehead as she took a table by the window to enjoy grilled cheese, another cup of coffee, and to scroll through the photographs she'd taken of a log cabin and a man who'd been through so much he didn't seem to know his way out.

5

HOLLY

Holly woke up the next morning in the guesthouse and her hand went straight to the bump on her head. It had almost gone down completely, didn't hurt much any more, and she'd managed to hide it from her hosts last night when she came in – although they were so busy cooking dinner for other guests that they didn't have a chance to stop. She'd chatted briefly and claimed needing an early night to be ready to go out to the hotel complex today. 'It's all this fresh Inglenook Falls air,' Lisa had declared, and Holly had gone on up to bed.

She yawned and pulled open the curtains, smiling at the sight before her. It was a completely different view here from the one she had in Manhattan of another apartment building across the street with fire escapes snaking all the way up the side. A chill seeped through the glass, a tiny draft came from somewhere around the sill, and the snowy scene out over the town green was so picturesque she grabbed her camera from the desk. There were no footprints in the white powder that must've fallen softly overnight and she wanted to capture the view like this, then again later as the town woke and kids came out to play. Undeterred by the cold, she opened the window fully to get a shot of the bandstand and the lights wound up each supporting pole, the lights on the Christmas tree that would be bright against the night sky later on. She'd been so tired on her way back to the guesthouse last night that she hadn't taken the time to appreciate it in all its glory.

Now, she adjusted the zoom and took a few photos of the stores on the opposite side of the street with the backdrop of trees from the woods. Some stores had dim lighting to indicate they were getting prepared for the working day and the entire scene looked as though it could be featured in a magazine spread of America's most enchanting towns. Inglenook Falls was the perfect example of small-town America still existing even with progress.

She shivered, shut the window, and sat on the bed to flip through the photographs she'd just taken as well as those from yesterday, hooked on the pictures of the log cabin, its surrounds, the man living there. She would've expected the cabin to be decorated for Christmas yet when she'd woken up in the bedroom, made her way downstairs, and seen the kitchen and lounge room, there hadn't been any clues to the holiday season at all. No stockings hung by the fire, no tree even though the cabin was surrounded by acres of them, no garlands on the bannisters, nothing. She knew a little about the occupant now. It wasn't enough to change her way of thinking but he'd gone from being a scary, stand-offish hairy beast of a man to someone gentler who'd been hurt in a way she could never imagine.

When her cell phone bleeped she picked it up to find a message from Darcy, who was tackling the stores in Manhattan today and shopping for the rest of her Christmas gifts. Darcy had attached a photo to her message showing hordes of people crossing the street to go into Saks Fifth Avenue, and her text simply read:

Wish Me Luck.

Holly decided against mentioning the man in the woods, who she now knew was called Mitch. It was almost as though by doing so she'd be joining in with the shaming, the gossip. Instead, she sent back a laughing face emoji, because by now the Manhattan streets would be gridlocked and the sidewalks like a stampede to the front stage of a Taylor Swift concert, and Holly was glad she was out here in Inglenook Falls for a break. When she'd been on the work conveyor belt, going to the same office day in, day out, she'd blocked out the Manhattan rush, the busyness. But as a freelancer, trying to get to different places at varying times of the day, she noticed the craziness of it all.

She showered and dressed and went to face the dining room for breakfast, and with a good layer of foundation, some strategically placed wisps of hair, and a seat next to the window so that her bad side was nearest the glass, neither Lisa nor Christopher noticed anything as they chatted about her adventures yesterday. She told them she'd seen the school, the bandstand, the fields near the Little Knitting Box, and that she'd had a lengthy catch-up with Cleo. She kept quiet about the log cabin for now. She didn't want tales of being taken prisoner by the town outcast to be fed back to her parents on the West Coast.

'Two eggs, sunny side up, rye toast, and a side of mushrooms.' Christopher set a plate down in front of her. 'And a freshly squeezed orange juice coming right up.'

After breakfast it was time for Holly to get to work, and she was looking forward to seeing Pierre even though it was a little odd that it would be in a professional capacity. She gathered her things and loaded them in the car and took it easy pulling out of the parking lot in case the bump on her head yesterday caused her any problems, but she needn't have worried; she felt back to normal.

The roads were relatively clear – snowploughs must have cleared the way in the early hours – and already a group of kids had a snowball fight under way on the town green. She headed out of town, down a section of the highway, and turned off for the Corbridge Hotel, which came into view at the end of a long, sweeping driveway framed with maple trees that would look splendid with their red leaves come spring.

She pulled into the parking lot that would soon be filled with expensive cars, people on vacation, those visiting for the day to sample the lavish spa facilities. She'd seen photos of this place on and off, but now it was finished, it was all the more impressive. With its curved front spread out before her, the peaked roofs stretched all the way up to the backdrop of hills that would soon be completely covered in white once winter really settled in. The parking lot extended out on either side of the building ensuring nobody would ever need to look too far for a space to leave their vehicle, and windows at the ground level revealed a grand entrance, the bar and an expansive restaurant. The windows on the floor above were identical, depicting the three-hundred-room facility. Gold railings bordered the entrance steps and, as she pushed open the gold-handled door, the foyer was nothing less than expected with its ornate light fittings creating a soft glow above what would become the front desk when the hotel opened for business in December. She looked up at the cathedral ceilings, the vast dome of the roof extending from here into the restaurant area; she took in the light and airy corridor to her right that, Holly could see from the sign, led to the fitness suite and spa complex.

'Holly!' Pierre appeared out of nowhere, announced by the sharp clip of his shoes against the shiny floor tiles. Despite his refined appearance in his made-to-measure suit, perfectly tailored to his requirements, he thought nothing of kissing her full on the lips. 'Did you miss me?'

'Of course I did.' She met his bright smile with her own grin. He was an attractive man with dark hair, cropped short, and the sort of teeth Hollywood paid a fortune for. He was always clean-shaven and his familiar Paco Rabanne aftershave lulled Holly into a sense of familiarity when so many things had changed lately.

He pulled her closer for another hug as a workman milled around the foyer with a last-minute snag list, a cleaner polished the glass doors as though they weren't gleaming already, and a couple of women in suits bustled past with an air of importance.

Holly and Pierre had met in Manhattan in the summer when he relocated there from Chicago but it turned out they'd actually known one another a lot longer. They'd gone to high school together back in Seattle but since then Pierre had worked all over – Milan, Toronto, London, and Chicago – and he'd been open from the start that the travel bug was in him. He had no intention of getting down and dirty and travelling with a backpack, perish the thought, but international moves with work were his modus operandi. Most days Holly was waiting for him to say he was on the move again – to Dallas, Los Angeles, Paris perhaps – and she wasn't sure how to feel about it. They'd only been together a few months, after he'd been a last-minute date for Darcy's wedding, but now that she was freelance, maybe moving around was something they'd be able to do together.

He pulled back but this time he swept her hair away from her face to look at her more closely and his fingers skimmed the bruise on her forehead. 'What happened to you?'

She knew Pierre well enough to know that any mention of a gruff man in the woods – whether he was helping or not – would spark his need to thump his chest and go after him demanding explanations. 'I slipped and fell on the ice, hit my head on a tree.' Did that sound plausible? Judging by his face, it did.

'It's quite a bruise.'

'I'm fine, honestly.' She purposely turned round and looked back the way she'd come, beyond the glass doors at the front of the hotel. The blue skies gave a fabulous outlook from inside the hotel and a backdrop guests would be sure to fall in love with. 'It's an impressive scene.' Across the parking lot were dense fields, covered with frost-tipped trees. Maybe those fields led all the way to the little log cabin she'd stumbled upon yesterday.

He moved next to her. 'It's what people will come for.'

'You must be pleased with it all.'

'No time to relax yet.' His green eyes fizzed with excitement. His job sounded complex and his time was in demand, and he thrived on it. Holly had been exactly the same for the last ten years. 'It took a while to find this site, but I think it's surpassed expectations.'

'You mean the view?'

'More than that. The spa complex, which you'll love, the rooms, which are to die for, and the other part of my plan.'

'Are you allowed to share?' He was one of those men who even when he stood still looked like he'd have to move at any second. His mind was switched on 24/7.

'I want to extend the site, buy some extra land, add on a golf course.'

'What do locals think to that?'

'I suspect there may be some opposition at losing some of the woodland, but it'll be good for them too. Hotel guests will use the course but it'll be available to anyone in the two towns the hotel sits between: Inglenook Falls and Bampton. It could be a real boost to the local economy when it brings in tourists, it would create new jobs too. Are you taking notes?' He grinned and kissed her spontaneously, taking her back to the long, lazy days of summer spent in Central Park on a weekend, soaking up the sun with not a care in the world. They'd talked about work, discussed Manhattan's high and low points, raved about the latest restaurants or trends to hit the city, flipped back to school days, and laughed at how they'd been back then.

He put a hand on the small of her back and led her into the restaurant. 'Come on, let's get some coffee and we can talk some more.'

She sat on the sofa at the side of the room presumably ready to seat guests waiting for a table when this place was buzzing.

When Pierre asked if she'd like something to eat she replied, 'Lisa and Christopher do wonderful food at the Chestnut Lodge so I've overindulged. I don't think I'll need to eat for a while yet.'

'You know you could've stayed here. I have a suite while I'm needed at the hotel and you'd be spoiled for choice when it came to a menu.' He located the coffee pot at the side of the room and took a cup from the stack beneath.

'I appreciate the offer, but it was lovely to catch up with them both. I think Mom will worry less if she can hear from someone else that I'm doing fine.' She thanked him for the coffee with cream added in the top. 'Are you ready for the grand opening?'

'Almost. I can't believe it's only a week away. We're a little behind schedule but I'm looking forward to getting the place dressed for Christmas, it'll be spectacular.'

'You must be really proud.'

'I am and thank you for saying so.'

After one more sip of coffee for now, Holly took out her notepad and made a few preliminary notes ready for her write-up.

'You look so serious,' said Pierre.

'Hey, don't mock, this is my job so it's professional for at least the next fifteen minutes.'

'I guess I can do that.' He put a hand on her knee, which suggested otherwise, but soon removed it when she shot him a look.

When Pierre was called away by the workman seeing to the snag list, Holly took the opportunity to make a few preliminary notes. The final write-up would reflect the hotel in action but coming here now gave her a chance to get a feel for the place, write the shell of the article, and take photographs. Some shots would work better without people filling the space – the immense foyer, the windows that stretched from floor tiles almost to the sky it seemed, the trees sparkling with frost in the distance on a clear day, which she wouldn't necessarily be guaranteed again. She jotted down some of her first impressions, mainly about the views, the no-expense-spared feeling she got the second she arrived here. She imagined the hotel would look even more magnificent once those maple trees lining the driveway changed colour with the seasons.

'Sorry about that.' Pierre returned and sat next to her again, close enough for people to realise they weren't business associates but rather bed partners, but she let it slide this time. 'Now, what would you like to know?'

She took out her voice recorder. 'Do you mind? Saves me making so many notes and lets me focus on the finer details.' She'd reviewed hotels before; she'd hit the mark with an article on Christmas at the Inglenook Inn that had pleased her boss, readers of *Contemporary Edge*, and had driven business to Darcy, who co-ran the inn. But it felt different when she knew this was a piece for her freelance portfolio, so she wanted to ensure apprehension didn't cause her to miss any details.

'Of course I don't mind, whatever you need.'

'Perhaps some background first. What led the Hatherleigh Group to this area, why build a big hotel here, what your thoughts on tourism in the area might be.'

He shared some history of the company and talked about his search for a site. 'Out here between Inglenook Falls and Bampton is close enough to the city that it's doable for a day or two,' he explained, 'yet far enough that people coming here from Manhattan, Brooklyn, New Jersey and the surrounds will feel like they're away. So as well as catering for the guests who want a long, leisurely break, perhaps with the family, we'll also be grabbing the section of the market who want weekend escapes, spa retreats, golf when it's up and running. We have a top chef working for us and we'll offer some of the finest cuisine around. The restaurant will be another huge draw for guests but also for people living in the area, so it's an additional section of the market we'll be able to tap into.'

'What do you think the hotel complex will mean to the local economy and the residents of Inglenook Falls and Bampton?' When she asked the question she thought of Mitch living a hermit-like existence, only venturing out to sell Christmas trees. Maybe he'd miss out on hearing about the development altogether.

They moved on to talk about the merits of Bampton and Inglenook Falls, how the towns themselves were also an attraction for tourists, and they discussed locals' reactions, most of them positive so far.

'This site was ripe for development,' Pierre continued. 'If we hadn't stepped in to build this hotel it would've ended up being developed for housing, I suspect. But this way, we've kept the beauty of the place, I think it looks like the hotel is part of the landscape. I knew this development could happen without encroaching on either town when it came to physical proximity. Locals can come here to enjoy the facilities or they can ignore us.'

Pierre went into more detail about the chef they'd hired, where he'd worked before. They talked about the spa's facilities and he made a note to send Holly the menu of treatments so she could include at least an extract in her article – a guaranteed hit for their target audience, no matter which part of the country they resided in.

'Come on,' he urged when she set her empty coffee mug on the table. 'Let me show you around the place some more.'

She took her camera from her bag and looped the strap around her neck as she followed him through the foyer, pausing to snap a

couple of shots of him talking business to the contractor with the
trademark pencil tucked behind his ear and a hard hat even though
Holly doubted he'd need one inside. They went upstairs to see a
typical hotel room, its sparkling bathroom, minibar and accessories, and Holly met the housekeeping manager, to whom she
chatted about all the little things that made guests welcome, from
high-thread-count linen, down comforters, and plump pillows to
super-soft towels, fresh flowers in the room, and a plate of welcome
cookies.

Pierre left Holly with Miranda, who was in charge of the spa-
complex operations, so she could get some photographs of the pool,
the jacuzzi, steam room, and sauna, the plush-carpeted corridors
leading off to separate rooms for treatments, the opulent facilities
that sparkled with newness. Positioned out back of the hotel, this
area couldn't be seen from the front but, now, Holly could appreciate its magnificence. The glass allowed one-way views of the
alpine region behind where guests would be able to follow hiking
trails or venture over to the nearest ski fields. Miranda hoped
people who skied would be enticed to come here to wind down
afterwards and relieve overworked muscles. And Holly knew this
part of the article would be popular with the magazine's readers,
because the complex was stunning. They seemed to have thought
of everything, from the finishing touches of fresh, white roses and
lilies tied at the stalks with natural silk bows and set onto small
tables dotted around, to the couches and armchairs in the welcome
area where Miranda told Holly guests would be offered herbal teas,
champagne, or where menus of treatments would entice and they'd
begin their pampering experience the moment they stepped
through the glass doors. Holly saw three of the eight treatment
rooms where paraffin wraps, pedicures, mom-and-daughter mani-
cures, anti-aging facials, and massages would happen. And she
heard about how a mixologist could personalise a blend of essential

oil and herbs to have used as a scrub, how people could enjoy the infinity pool or the hot and cold plunge pools.

'It's out of this world,' Holly told Pierre when she met him in the foyer, where he was giving instructions to someone fixing the finish to a floor tile, its imperfection impossible to see unless you were standing right on it.

'I thought you might be impressed. And there'll be substantial discounts if you want to come here. Bring your friends, make a weekend of it.'

'You know, I might do that. Cleo would love it, she's a busy working mom, and Darcy, well, she works far too hard as it is.'

'Then tell them to come along soon.' He kissed her cheek and touched her face lightly with his fingers, longing in his eyes. 'You know, if we were being watched, someone may tell us to get a room.'

She couldn't help but smile. 'You already have one.'

'I certainly do.'

'I have to work.'

He tilted her chin upwards and planted a kiss on her lips. 'I thought you might say that, and so do I. You'll keep. Dinner tonight?'

'If I get a good session of writing done this afternoon, you're on.'

'Come on, Holly, you're your own boss now. It can't be all work and no play.'

'I need to closely guard my writing time.'

'I've heard they do a mean osso bucco, your favourite.'

'If I do my write-up.'

'And tiramisu.' He kissed her again.

By now she'd totally relented. 'I'll see you tonight.'

6

HOLLY

Holly had written up some notes as soon as she got back to the guesthouse, using the pictures on her camera to jog her memory. She transcribed her interview with Pierre word for word in a notebook. Doing so, without the help of software, helped her to work through the information in her mind and absorb it all the more. She wrote out her interview with Miranda too, including some great quotes for her article.

And now, Holly felt she'd earned some time to relax before going out to dinner. She steamed up the ensuite bathroom by taking a long shower with her favourite Crabtree & Evelyn products and slathered herself in her favourite body lotion afterwards. She wound her naturally wavy hair into large rollers to give it extra bounce and as they took, she read through what she'd been working on today. She felt confident this article would be exactly what *Contemporary Edge* was after and, most of all, she congratulated herself on a successful day freelancing. If this was the buzz you got from being your own boss, she didn't ever want someone else to be in charge of her again.

She picked out a ripple-stitch knit dress in smoky grey with long sleeves. She peeked out of the window and, sure enough, the biting air she'd felt the second she left the hotel and again when she left the confines of the car to come into the guesthouse had given way to snowfall, light for now but enough to ditch the heels she'd been planning to wear and opt for the ankle boots instead. She put on a light layer of make-up, concealing the remnants of her bruise, and added a touch of pale-pink lip gloss. She took out the rollers from her hair before running her hand through the strands to loosen up the waves.

Downstairs she gave Lisa a twirl. 'Will I do?'

'You look beautiful. Are you eating at the hotel?'

'No, we're staying in Inglenook Falls and going to the Italian.' The restaurant was so close she could probably have managed in her heels, but she was already beginning to feel more at home in comfier footwear. 'I've heard good things about it from Cleo, although she still sends Dylan into Manhattan for her favourite puttanesca pasta occasionally.'

'I won't tell Giuseppe,' Lisa winked.

'Maybe you should.' Christopher had been picking up stray pine needles from the floor in the lounge where a tree stood proud, and he threw the debris onto the roaring fire in the front room where guests could freely congregate. Holly wondered whether this tree had come from Mitch or whether her hosts had been too afraid to venture down to the woods. 'Maybe they could adjust their recipe and win Cleo over,' he suggested.

'We women like what we like,' said Lisa.

'Don't I know it.' Christopher planted a kiss on Lisa's forehead before he went to get the door, and it reminded Holly very much of her childhood when her own dad would come home from work and make the same homely gesture to her mom. It wasn't an ignition of passion, but a symbol of a love that ran much deeper, sustained by a mutual understanding of each other.

Holly smiled at Pierre, who'd shaken Christopher's hand upon his arrival to pick her up, and she didn't miss Lisa giving him the once-over too. 'I feel like I'm leaving my parents' house and I have a curfew,' Holly whispered as they shut the door behind them and stepped out onto the porch. She buttoned up her coat, her hair loose and bouncy around her shoulders.

'I did feel like I was being judged,' he joked.

'You'd better behave then.'

'I suppose I should.'

She hooked an arm through his as they made their way down the path and the crisp night air wrapped around them. To their right the lights on the Christmas tree on the town's green looked spectacular with snow settled on some of its branches and now the sky had darkened. Holly could already imagine the Santa Claus coming into town, him sitting in the middle of the bandstand, the line of kids that would snake down the steps onto the lawn covered in snow.

They made their way past homes all decorated for the holidays, most with outside lights around porches, on the roof, decorations in front yards that kids walking to school would marvel at. They passed the library, which had shut for the evening, and the waft of rich Italian food grabbed them and pulled them towards the restaurant, where they were seated at the table by the window. Separated only by candlelight, the coloured wax etched on the side of the bottle it was standing in, they perused a menu each. Pierre ordered a bottle of red wine and Holly turned to look across the street. She could make out the top of the track she'd come up from the log cabin, and she found herself contemplating what Mitch did in the evenings. Did he hunker down in that cabin as soon as it was dark? Go to bed the second the sun went down? Or was he nocturnal, braving the town late at night rather than in the day? Did he ever come here to grab a bite to eat, or were restaurants a thing of the past for him?

'Have you already chosen?' Pierre must've noticed her focus change.

'Osso bucco, of course,' she smiled. She'd been planning on trying something different but she'd already seen it at the top of the menu items and hadn't looked at much else before her mind had wandered.

Once the waiter delivered the bruschetta they'd share, they fell into an easy conversation about today and the photos and narrative she'd captured for her article.

'When you get the golf course up and running we could pitch to a number of publications.' Holly took a piece of bread, topped it with the tomato and onion mixture. 'There are plenty to choose from, print or online.'

'You know the industry well.' Pierre lifted his glass to make a toast.

She finished chewing and lifted her glass to meet his. 'I do.' And that's why freelancing was going to work out.

'You'll get another job in no time.'

'I have a job, and I'm my own boss.'

'Hang on, hear me out. Another job, but I didn't say it had to be what you were doing before. You could branch out to other areas: public relations, communications.'

'I think I'll stick with what I'm doing for a while. So, tell me more about this golf course – what's the next stage?' One sure-fire way to avoid talking about herself was to get Pierre talking business.

The waiter brought their main courses – the osso bucco for her, chicken and mushroom risotto for Pierre – and Pierre topped up her wine glass. 'I'm driving so you'll be having most of this.'

'Are you trying to get me drunk?'

'I wouldn't dream of it.' He grinned across the table at her. 'But think about what I said.'

'About what?'

'Working in a different area to editorial and journalism. The company I work for employ a lot of communications and public-relations staff and you'd excel at it.'

She popped another piece of meat into her mouth, wondering how many times she had to market herself as a freelancer.

'You do look happy,' he said then, a forkful of risotto poised and ready to go. 'So do it for a month, two months, or three even. But I know you, Holly. You thrive on being busy, you love the pace of New York City. Any city.'

She gulped back a generous swig of wine and nodded as though agreeing with him. When she'd first met Pierre she'd been swept along at a pace they both enjoyed. But Holly's photography had given her a different viewpoint on life and the more she enjoyed it, the more she began to think about what else was out there for her besides long days at the office.

The low hum of music and chatter filling the restaurant allowed Holly's voice to blend in after she set her cutlery down. 'This is a fresh start for me, Pierre, and I'm giving it my all.'

He dabbed his mouth with the thick white napkin provided. 'I'm being an ass, aren't I?'

Somehow his summation made her happy. 'Better for you to point it out than me.'

'I apologise. And I'll stop being so opinionated. Can I interest you in some tiramisu as a peace offering?'

'Sounds good to me.'

With dessert in front of them, Pierre told her more about the plans for the grand opening. 'We'll have the fireplace in the reception area beyond the foyer going on opening day, the whole place will be decorated. The staff are ready to go, we've worked with an interior-design specialist whose Christmas displays are out of this world, and by the time you come back, you won't recognise the place.'

'I assume a breath-taking Christmas tree will be part of the proceedings.'

'We've had some trouble with that,' he admitted.

'And yet you look unflappable.'

'Can't fall apart.'

'What happened?'

'There were heavy floods up at the farm that was supplying it, the truck with the tree got into difficulty and the tree is... well, it's no more. Thankfully nobody was hurt in the incident, that's the main thing, but it does leave us in search of something suitable, and the party is next week. I'm on it, believe me, but my guy Lionel is fussy, it's the reason he's on my staff. He wants nothing less than perfection. Anyway, he says he's found an alternative supplier, has transportation for Friday, so we're almost there.'

'Thank goodness for that. I'd hate to have to Photoshop a tree into the pictures.' The article wouldn't run until New Year, but it would be sure to raise the hotel's profile and lead to bookings for next season.

He topped up her wine some more. 'When are you thinking of having the spa weekend?'

'Maybe in the New Year. I might organise a girls' weekend with Cleo, if she can get some time out from the kids, and Darcy, if she can get away from the inn.'

'Your friends are very busy people.'

'They are, but we'll make it work. It's funny, I've not known them long but I couldn't imagine life without them now. I love that we're all close enough to meet up at least every month, even if it's me popping into Cleo's store, or Darcy making time for a quick lunch in the city. I hope Darcy and Myles stay around for a while longer.'

'He's a high flyer. I doubt he'll want to stick around if there's opportunity elsewhere.'

'I don't know, I think he loves Darcy too much to do that to her. They had a whole discussion about it before they got married.' She hadn't told Pierre the finer details but Myles's flourishing career had almost led to the wedding being called off at one point and Darcy had wavered at the terrifying thought of losing her independence and sense of purpose when she'd seen the same happen to others who'd married and given up their careers. But they'd pushed through and were settled in the city, at least for now.

'And what about you? Would you spread your wings again and go elsewhere?'

'I hadn't actually thought about it.' She picked up another piece of coffee-and-brandy-soaked sponge on her fork, the elegant, rich layers almost too much. She had thought about travel, perhaps with Pierre, but it felt too early in their relationship for that conversation.

After dessert they left the restaurant chatting about the menu the hotel would serve – the very best cuisine with the freshest of ingredients.

'I could pitch to some of the culinary publications if you like,' Holly suggested. 'There's a real art to food photography so I'm not sure about that aspect, although I'm a fast learner.'

'Indeed you are,' he said proudly as they strolled slowly along Main Street, their breath in puffs against the cold. But then he spoiled it by adding, 'and that's exactly why you'd be a good fit for the Hatherleigh Group, Holly. You'd be an asset to the business, not because you're my girlfriend and you're insanely hot, but because you've got a business approach that comes naturally. Tell me you'll think about it, that's all I ask.'

'Of course I will.' She would, but not with a view to doing it, more with a view to how she was going to make him realise it wasn't what she wanted. Not any more. The only way, it seemed, to prove her determination to him, would be to expand her portfolio and make this succeed, and all his doubts did were make her all the more adamant.

They'd almost reached the entrance to the Chestnut Lodge and she planted a kiss on his lips. 'I'll be fine from here. I'd better get some sleep, I'm driving back to Manhattan in the morning.'

He went to kiss her again but she turned at something appearing in her peripheral vision. A pickup had pulled up at the side of the street, a figure climbed out, dropped something into the mail box, and the man turned to look at them both standing by the streetlamp past the library.

She wouldn't mistake the man anywhere. It was Mitch, from the little log cabin in the woods.

Pierre put his arm around her protectively and pulled her close as they walked on. 'I'll walk you right to the door. I don't much like the look of him.'

She almost said it was okay, she knew him, he'd helped her. She looked over to smile at the virtual stranger, but it was too late. Collar upturned, he was already climbing back into his dark grey pickup.

And then he was gone.

7

MITCH

There was a time when Mitch had been a part of this rat race in Manhattan but now, with buildings surrounding him, he felt out of his depth.

He caught the train today – the thought of Manhattan traffic too much – and he disembarked at Penn Station before making his way along 34th Street. He needed to get to the Lower East Side and embraced the walk, turning his collar up against the cold. He came into the city as little as possible, disliked crowds, but then again, somehow here he blended in more than he did in Inglenook Falls. There, people crossed the street when they saw him. He hadn't missed the way mothers cuddled children closer, discreetly took them in another direction, how locals surreptitiously glanced his way before going about their business. At least here he was one of so very many.

He wondered how long it had taken for the gossip mill to turn and spurt out his history to that woman, Holly, after she escaped from him and went up to the town that day. She was obviously here for a while, because he'd seen her last night with a man. Maybe she'd moved here, maybe they both had. Despite her Manhattan style and groomed appearance, Holly's eyes had reflected surprise but not unkindness when she glanced his way, because he'd earned at least a smidgen of her trust after their unplanned encounter. But the man had looked at him in the same way everyone else did: circumspect, with an unwillingness to give him a chance to prove he wasn't all that bad.

Mitch crossed over Fifth Avenue, trying to avoid thousands of shoppers out to get their holiday gifts. The waft of expensive perfume, coffee, the steam coming from a nearby grate all enveloped him and reminded him of the place and season. Lights flashed up high from stores on every corner and street performers yelled about the holidays and pushed leaflets at him about upcoming events. Sometimes it was easier to take the things and sling them into the nearest trash can than to insist you weren't interested.

Since he'd met Holly and she'd come right out with it and asked him who the boy in the photographs was, Mitch had been thinking about Albie all the more. Not that he'd ever stopped. Albie was in his psyche, his every waking thought, but when Holly had mentioned him he'd got angry. He'd stormed back to the cabin, slammed the door so hard behind him the logs quaked in fear. He'd stood in the kitchen in an attempt to calm himself down, hands on the sink, eyes closed, head hanging towards the floor. Albie would be eight now, he might look very different. He might possibly have forgotten Mitch even existed or that they'd often gone down to the log cabin together to roam amongst the trees, play hide-and-seek in the woods until Albie's laughter gave him away every time. And what Mitch had accepted as his fate and the result of him being such a cosmic failure, he'd all of a sudden refused to accept any longer.

That day Holly had mentioned the photographs of his son, Mitch had wanted to tell her proudly who the boy was. Albie, who was three and a half feet tall when he last saw him, with the same blue eyes as Mitch, hair that curled at the slightest chance and a small birthmark on his left shoulder blade they'd joked was his first tattoo. Albie, who had a huge toy car collection and liked to race them up and down the hall and who laughed at his dad when he stood on a car and uttered a naughty word only meant for adult ears. That day he'd wanted to tell Holly how he'd cradled his newborn son tentatively at first as though he might break, how he'd sat up with him at night when he had croup, and in the darkest of days when he felt like a failure, as though he couldn't claw his way back to existence, seeing his son or hearing his voice, the sound of his laughter, had a power to soothe like nothing else.

The day after Holly had mentioned those photographs, Mitch had tugged a piece of paper from the printer and written a letter. He'd felt like he was at school, sitting an exam, concentrating on making his writing legible to impress whoever would be first to cast eyes on it. He wrote to Shannon's parents, found an envelope and a stamp, and when evening came and fewer people were milling about, he'd gone into town to post it. He'd felt hopeful – he shouldn't have been. He'd done this a number of times already and heard nothing from them or Shannon in return, but he had to show all of them that he wasn't going to give up.

It was while he was posting the letter that he'd seen Holly again, this time with that man. And as he recalled her mention of the pictures he held so dear, Mitch had resolved to take further action. He'd driven back to the cabin and searched online for a private detective.

And that was what he was doing here in the city now. He crossed over Park Avenue, then Lexington, and finally turned in to Second Avenue, which led him all the way down to the Lower East Side and to the PI's offices, where he waited in a bright, airy office with a fish tank gurgling away in the corner as though it were a therapist's arena rather than that of a supersleuth. And instead of a cigarette-wielding man with a paunch who narrowed his eyes as smoke took over the room, the PI, Travis, was conversational, well-spoken, and took notes as Mitch talked.

'As time goes on,' Travis advised after Mitch had shared his story, 'it becomes harder and harder to find someone. People move on, change jobs, change names through remarriage, kids change school – the reasons are infinite in that regard. And it can be hard to find someone who isn't trying to hide, doubly hard if they're doing their best to stop you getting to them. Did she leave with your consent?'

Mitch shook his head. 'I wasn't in a good place back then.'

'Doesn't matter.' He scribbled down more notes. 'I'm assuming once she's found, if I can indeed manage that, you'll be looking to go for custody.'

'I hadn't thought that far ahead.' Dollar signs of attorney fees churned over in his head when Mitch thought about how far this could go. He had visions of the courts dragging up his whole sorry story, how he'd once walked tall and proud and had retreated into this shell of a man, how he'd left town for a time to stay in a place he was ashamed to talk about.

'The fact she made the decision to take your son, unilaterally, works in your favour,' Travis assured him. 'Family law takes a dim view of it.' He must've sensed Mitch's despair. 'But let's take one step at a time. I'd suggest you take a look at my contract, have a think, and if you go ahead you'll need to complete the paperwork and send a photograph of your son.'

He had plenty of those. 'How much will all this cost?' He'd been responsible for losing their family home and now he survived in a log cabin on land his father had left to him and his brother. Corey had no interest in the income Mitch currently made from it because it was down to his own hard work. But he did want the land to be

sold somewhere down the line or for Mitch to buy him out. Mitch
totally got it. Corey had moved on from Inglenook Falls, he had
four kids, wanted to put each of them through college, and hanging
on to a woodland he had no interest in was not in his ten-year plan.
He was also older than Mitch and had had a rough time with their
mom, whom he'd nursed through her dementia, taking on the
main share of her care – even taking a year off work to do so – to
enable their father to run the Christmas tree farm. After she died
Corey had gone back to work, glad to escape, but then Shannon
had left Mitch and Corey had watched another member of his
family spiral towards the unknown. Now, he looked after himself,
his family, and probably didn't see why Mitch couldn't do the same.
He and Mitch had got on when Mitch had been part of the
Manhattan rat race but they'd since drifted apart, and if Mitch
refused to buy his brother out eventually, it'd only make the rift
worse, and he knew his father would never have wanted that. Mitch
rarely saw Corey now, and the kids and his wife never came near,
but Mitch didn't want to sever the ties for good. God knows he'd
messed up enough in this life. No, he couldn't shoulder another
huge financial burden. And Shannon had been gone for three
years, she could be on the other side of the country, in another one
entirely even, or simply hiding and refusing to be found.

'It's almost impossible to say.' Travis broke into his thoughts.
'Charges vary depending how long it all takes, what work has to be
done. But I work on an hourly rate of sixty dollars, and then there'll
be extras like background checks.' He elaborated with a few cases
to illustrate how hard it was to specify a figure and cases ranged
from costing a few hundred dollars to in the thousands. 'Here's a
copy of the contract, and my business card.' Travis pushed both
across the desk. 'Take a look at them, think about our talk.'

Mitch thanked Travis for his time and stepped out onto the
sidewalk, darker for the rain that pummelled the city now. The city

of bright lights, possibilities, yet hiding corners of drudgery, hope-lessness, utter despair. Shelling out money on any extras at the moment wasn't good sense, yet he wanted to do this, he wanted to find his son. But then, if he ran out of money doing it, what would Albie be coming back to? Certainly not a father he could be proud of. He'd find a man who had lost it all, again.

Deflated, he made his way back towards Penn Station. His jacket didn't even have a hood and so his hair was soaked through, water snaked inside his collar, chilling his neck. The dollar signs kept churning around in his mind, costs mounting as Shannon and Albie disappeared farther from his grasp. They might even realise he had someone looking for them and go to greater lengths not to be found.

When he reached 34th Street he was shunted along the block past Park Avenue, on to Madison, voices echoing around him, not with festive joy but taunting him. He'd thought he might brave the Christmas windows on Fifth today or at Macy's, remembering the last Christmas he'd spent with Albie, when he'd dressed as Santa Claus in case he was seen putting the presents out. That was the year Albie had got a sledge for Christmas, a proper wooden one made by Mitch's father. He wondered if he still had it, whether it reminded him of the little log cabin. Did Albie even believe any more? What age did the magic stop?

He'd made no progress at all coming here today. He'd thought it would set the ball rolling in his search but instead it had instilled the fear that the hunt would cripple him financially or, worse, drive Albie and his mum further into hiding.

At least when he knew nothing of their whereabouts, he could live in hope of a miracle.

* * *

Main Street glowed with the promise of Christmas on Mitch's arrival back at the station in Inglenook Falls, but down in the log cabin in the woods there was no promise of anything as Mitch went straight to his computer. He set himself up with social media accounts, used his real name, no photo. That way, if Albie had bypassed the rules of having to reach a certain age – was it thirteen? – to have half these accounts, he could find his father if he chose. Mitch spent a while longer in each social media tool searching on Albie's name, then Shannon's as well as Shannon-Marie, her full name. He used her maiden name and his own surname but came back with nothing. He did the same on Facebook, Instagram, even Twitter and ended up scrolling through pointless posts, pictures of food – people sure liked to share what they were having for breakfast! He went into his email to see if there was anything from Leslie Carmichael, Shannon's mother, or Frank, Shannon's father, but of course there was nothing. He'd added his own email address to every letter he'd ever sent as well as his cell phone number, plus the location of the log cabin, which of course they already knew.

From the social-media accounts he'd set up, he moved on to deleting unnecessary spam from his email. He ignored an advertising newsletter for liquor from the store in the next town where he'd signed up once to get discounts on beer when he was at his lowest ebb, and then he noticed another email from someone he didn't recognise. It was from Lionel who worked for the Hatherleigh Group, according to the footer of his email. He was part of the team opening the Corbridge Hotel, which Mitch remembered seeing something about on a flyer that had been tucked beneath his wiper blades one morning when he parked up on Main Street. He read on to find they were asking for him to supply them with a Christmas tree. Strictly speaking he didn't liaise with anyone in town, although local Doug had braved coming to the cabin to ask for the tree on the green and so between them they'd sorted manpower and a vehicle and had the tree erected in time for Thanksgiving. They'd done it in the early hours one morning so Mitch saw as little of the residents in Inglenook Falls as possible, exactly the way he liked it. Doug had tried to persuade Mitch to go to the tree-lighting ceremony but he hadn't bothered; nobody wanted the town outcast to dampen proceedings.

Mitch whistled through his teeth. The Hatherleigh Group had sure done their research. A truck would be able to pull up from the highway adjacent to the very end of his land. They were suggesting they fell and lift the tree out of the field with their own equipment at their own cost, and they wanted a twenty-footer, well-shaped blue spruce, by Friday.

Mitch thought of his father planting each and every one of the blue spruces that stood so tall now. With the exception of the one for the town green, Mitch rarely cut down the larger trees. He didn't tend to sell anything taller than nine feet in the towns he went to, so it was hard to think he'd be losing another one of those beauties. Then again, he knew what his dad would say. He'd tell him it was business, it was why they'd been planted in the first place. And Mitch couldn't deny the financial offering was very satisfying indeed.

Before he could change his mind, Mitch typed out a reply. He told them to meet him Friday morning, early, as soon as the sun was up, to select their tree.

Maybe he was one step closer to having something good come his way. Because this money could be very handy indeed.

8

HOLLY

The snow was really coming down as she turned from West 11th onto Bleecker Street and crossed over to the Magnolia Bakery, and Holly was glad to be out enjoying the prettiness of flakes falling from above, making the most of Manhattan at Christmas time rather than being imprisoned in an office.

Last year Holly had been too devastated over her friend Sarah's death to really appreciate the festive season, she'd had more than her fair share of champagne to dull the pain, but this year she wanted to take it all in. Yesterday she'd been on a long walk through Central Park, the crisp winter air giving a new perspective to the manicured lawns, the surrounding trees, the main attractions. She watched the ice-skating on the Wollman Rink as she sipped a hot chocolate topped with whipped cream, she saw horses and carriages load in guests bundled up against the cold on the south side of the park, she marvelled at The Plaza with its lit-up miniature Christmas trees out front and garlands strung above the entrance. And last night she'd gone with her ex-colleague Daisy over the Brooklyn Bridge to see the lights of Dyker Heights with every inch of some homes covered in so many lights they were unrecognisable.

Holly joined the line at the Magnolia Bakery ready to be served and when she saw the confetti speciality cupcakes, she sent her love up to heaven at the thought of Sarah's smile every time she'd grabbed one of these treats. The coloured sprinkles were her friend's favourite, the friend she missed so much. She'd passed away just before last Christmas and Holly still expected to see her on a street corner, waving across to greet her, to introduce her to this city she'd been living in so long she'd become a real part of it. That had been another reason for Holly's relocation here. Sarah had always wanted Holly to work away from Seattle, if only for a time; she'd said it was liberating and would help her find herself, even if she went back to her home town eventually. So being here now felt as though in some way she was honouring her last wish in their friendship.

'Next!' The voice roused her from her daydreams. Holly came back to the present and selected three s'mores cupcakes from the store, and with them safely tucked inside the cardboard box for transportation, she went back out into the snow and made her way to the Inglenook Inn. Sarah would berate her for any sadness right now, tell her to put a smile on her face and live life to the full while she could. So that's exactly what she was going to do.

The Inglenook Inn was ready for the holiday season. She followed the steps up towards the door. A glow from the fireplace illuminated the bay window, small pine trees stood proudly at the top on either side of the stoop, a garland on the door was tied with purple-and-white-checked ribbon, and the lush foliage set off frosted purple berries, pine cones, and tiny bunches of cinnamon sticks. It was a welcome haven in the middle of the fast-paced city, and Holly knew she was in the right place. This was where she'd spent last Christmas and where she'd made firm, everlasting friendships at a time she'd really needed them.

'Holly, hey!' A voice came from behind her.

'Cleo, you're on time!' Her friend was trotting up the steps behind her with a tray of takeout coffees in hand.

'Oh quiet, I'm not that bad. I told you I was getting the five o'clock train.'

'I also know you're a busy working mom with four kids to look after.'

'Well, Dylan is doing the looking after tonight – I wasn't about to miss seeing my girls.' She leaned in and kissed her friend on the cheek and they did their best to hug despite the beverages and treats they needed to protect.

'I thought I heard voices.' Darcy had pulled open the door to the Inglenook Inn. 'Come in out of the cold.'

'I almost want to linger outside.' Cleo wasn't budging from the stoop. 'I want to go see the Christmas windows on Madison, Fifth Avenue, go see the tree at the Rockefeller Center.'

'Drag her in here,' Holly advised, 'or she'll never stop going on about it.'

The girls took off coats, scarves, and gloves, hung them up in the hall, then settled themselves on the sofa in front of the fire as Darcy busied herself finishing off behind the desk. Darcy made a phone call, dashed into the kitchen to see Rupert, the chef, and was back in no time at all with three plates for the cupcakes.

'All my guests are happy tonight, so I can have a little relax,' she said. 'We've got the Rogers family, who have gone to see a show at Radio City Hall, Mr and Mrs Ortega, who've taken their three children ice-skating in Central Park, the five twenty-something girls staying on the top floor came back to dump their shopping bags before hitting the town, and Mr and Mrs Sanchez have sat down to dinner.'

'You sound exhausted,' Holly smiled.

'It's Christmas, it's a crazy time, but I love it.'

Holly took out the box of cupcakes from the safety of the paper bag and distributed them on the plates as Cleo handed out the coffees. 'Then let's make the most of our time before anyone else tries to grab you.'

'What sort are they?' Cleo peered at the cupcakes.

'S'mores cupcakes,' Holly grinned. She savoured her first sip of caramel latte.

'Now we're talking.' Darcy had her caramel macchiato but set it down to take a bite of some of the best cupcakes in town.

'Have you had your guests making s'mores yet?' Holly asked. Last Christmas Darcy had been the glittering hostess, teaching a couple of young boys over from Ireland with their parents how to make the American delicacy by first toasting marshmallows over the open fire and then making them into a chocolatey Graham cracker sandwich.

'We had some yesterday.' Darcy peeled back a section of her cupcake case. 'They're always a hit with guests, I think it reminds them of fun times. Which is what a holiday is all about.'

'It sure is,' Cleo agreed.

Holly bit into the honey graham cake with chocolate filling and meringue icing, the topping and insides of the cake oozing in richness.

'How's work going, Holly?' Darcy wanted to know.

Holly was pleased her friend called it work and had actually asked about it. Dylan had told her that when he first went freelance people either asked if he'd had time to do any websites lately or didn't bother to enquire at all. 'It's as though I've retired', he told her once. 'Or I'm playing make-believe jobs at home rather than anything actually bringing in money.' His ex-wife Prue had messed him around with childcare days on occasion too, always assuming he was free to take the kids because he was at home. 'Put your foot down and guard your writing time,' he'd advised Holly from the beginning.

'It's going really well. I'm pretty much finished with the write-up for the hotel, and once I can add in the pictures for the opening night I'll send it all off to my editor. The piece won't be out in time for Christmas but everyone loves a new vacation venue. I expect there'll be a few bookings for next year on the strength of the coverage too. I also wrote the article for the Moonlight Loft & Terrace, and I've been looking into supplying shots to stock imaging libraries.'

'Wow, it sounds like you're getting off to a flying start,' said Cleo.

'Dylan did a wonderful job with my website, which helps, and I'll add to it as my portfolio gets bigger and more diverse. The piece with Kaisha and a fashion exhibition will be great to add something a little different. I want to show editors that I can turn my hand to anything.'

Darcy held up her coffee cup and the others followed suit and made a toast to Holly's roaring success. 'And long may it last.'

'Hear, hear!' Cleo agreed.

'It won't matter that the article is after Christmas either,' Darcy encouraged. 'I had a client requesting a function here for Thanksgiving last year after he saw your feature go out well after New Year's, but we were fully booked. Anyway, he came to look at the place, loved it and booked for this year instead.'

'That's great to hear,' Holly smiled. 'Thanks for the encouragement, Darcy, I appreciate it. I also have an appointment this evening with an art gallery owner to gather some preliminary information before covering an exhibition for her later this month,' she went on to reveal.

'Where's the gallery?'

'Nikita Moreno's in Greenwich Village.'

'I know it,' Darcy registered, 'cute little place. And none of that modern art I know you don't like.'

'I'm sure it has its merits,' said Holly. 'But no, I like art that looks like art. Pierre has some weird piece in his apartment that according to him is an "abstract acrylic", but no matter how many times he tries to tell me about it, I still don't appreciate it as it looks like something I could've done in second grade.'

Cleo laughed. 'I hope you didn't tell him so.'

'Of course not. We'd not been dating long and I wanted to appear sophisticated, worldly.'

'And now?'

'I still haven't admitted I hate that piece!'

With the cakes gone, Darcy added another log to the fire and settled back into the armchair next to the sofa. From here they could all look out the window, at the snowflakes settling around the window pane, the very tops of hats on people who bobbed by.

'How's the head?' Cleo asked Holly.

'It's much better, thank you.' She'd almost forgotten about her little accident, the slight discolouration lingering on her forehead the only reminder first thing in the morning before she covered it with make-up. The bruise had gone through a myriad of shades – from blackish purple to a deep red, and now it had traces of orangey yellow that she thought blended in much better with her auburn hair.

'What have I missed?' Darcy wanted to know.

'I had a fall.'

'There's a bit more to the story than that.' Cleo set her own empty plate down on top of the other two and sipped her coffee. 'She met the most feared man in Inglenook Falls.'

'Don't say that,' Holly admonished, 'he wasn't that bad. Okay, he *looks* that bad, but he isn't really. If he was, he would've left me there to get hypothermia.'

'He probably wanted you off his land,' Cleo suggested.

'I need details,' Darcy probed as though they'd both forgotten she was sitting there.

Holly shared the whole story in front of the crackling fire, how she'd gone from the guesthouse to explore the local area and found some amazing photo locations when she took the track down into the woods. She told Darcy all about running away from a man with a bushy beard, long, ratty hair, mud on his face, and how she'd woken up in his bed.

'You must've been terrified.' Darcy sat forwards to hear more but just then, Mr and Mrs Sanchez came through to express their gratitude for the delicious meal, and the beautiful room they were staying in. Darcy talked with them for a while and when she returned to the girls, said, 'And I always thought Inglenook Falls was such a sleepy town. You wait until I tell Myles's mom, Martha. She thinks it's all so quaint. I'll have to tell her there's a lot more to the place.'

'You make it sound so sinister,' said Holly, 'which is probably this man's problem in the first place.'

'What do you mean?'

'People have been talking about Mitch for a long time, apparently. It sounds like he was in a bad place when his wife upped and left, but I reckon all the talk surrounding what did and didn't happen has made him retreat all the more and, now, the more he hides away, the more people are wary of him.'

'Did he talk to you when you were at the cabin?' Darcy picked up her takeout caramel macchiato. 'I mean, you don't scoop someone up, put them in your bed, and expect not to have to talk to them.'

'He was a man of few words,' said Holly. 'He made me eat something, then led me out of the woods so I didn't get lost. I tried to talk to him, told him my name, but when I mentioned the photographs of the little boy on the landing upstairs – his son – he shut down and went back to the cabin.'

'What happened to his son?' Darcy asked.

Cleo filled her in. 'I can't imagine how lonely he must be. I feel terrible that every time I've seen him, I've crossed the street to avoid a confrontation. Jacob asked who he was once, and why his hair was so messed up, why he was all dirty. I didn't say much, I said I thought he worked on a farm. The kids at school apparently refer to him as the man in the woods, and none of them will ever dare go in there. He's like this monster in their minds. Doesn't seem fair, does it?'

'No,' said Holly. 'It doesn't.' And his eyes weren't that of a monster, they spoke of pain, of suffering, and he'd cared for her that day and kept her safe. 'The thing that's weird is that given how bad he looks, his log cabin is immaculate.'

'Really?' Darcy couldn't hide her surprise.

'He took his boots off at the door. What kind of hermit bothers to do that? His kitchen was clean, he can cook, his bedroom was like a suite in a guesthouse.' Not that she'd hung around for longer than she had to. But she remembered the little wooden squirrel beside the bed, the beautiful picture frames arranged on the cosy landing with a carved rocker to sit in, the hand-carved pieces in the kitchen.

'I can't believe you've seen his bedroom,' Cleo laughed. 'It really doesn't fit with the image of the man I see in the street. You know what? I'm going to make a real effort to talk to him from now on. I'm going to say hello and *not* cross the street.'

'That sounds like a start,' said Holly.

'What does he do out there in the woods?' Darcy asked. 'How does he earn a living?'

Cleo explained the Christmas trees. 'He supplied one for the town's bandstand as his father did every year before Mitch took over the running of the place, and according to Enid in the café, he sells trees in surrounding towns and makes and sells wooden frames.'

Holly realised those beautiful frames on the landing must be his work and she felt an even stronger empathy for this man, because the delicate ability to craft something so special was at odds with the ogre people assumed he was.

'You know, Myles's office is minus a Christmas tree at the moment.' Darcy put down her cup.

'Didn't he use Pierre's recommended supplier?' Holly knew what had happened to that.

'He did, and the place can't deliver because the truck is out of use. Myles was complaining last night that their office must be the only one in the whole of Manhattan bereft of holiday cheer without the tree to greet them every morning. His boss keeps saying he'll organise something, the admin staff have pretty much all gone down with the flu and so nobody has sorted it. Why don't we ask Mitch to find a tree?'

'It's a nice idea,' Holly agreed, 'but there are plenty of places closer by for Myles to use.'

'Of course there are, but come on, Cleo said she wants to help this guy by being at least a bit nice to him. Maybe we could do the same. We could get him to deliver a tree here, to the city, make it worth his while financially. Myles's boss will sign off any cost – he's probably fed up with hearing about it. This could boost Mitch's business and give him a little push outside of his comfort zone. You never know, it might be the start of something more.'

'I admire your optimism,' said Holly.

Darcy retrieved her iPad from the desk drawer and together they used searched engines to find details of Mitch's Christmas tree farm. There wasn't much, a substandard website that most people would click away from unless they were desperate.

'Look, there's an email address.' Cleo pointed at the screen.

Darcy sighed. 'This guy seriously needs to update his website. It's shocking. There's a dull photo of trees at the top but nothing that screams Christmas, no festive cheer, just black writing and white or grey borders. Dylan would love to get his hands on this. I bet he could work wonders.'

'Let's not go overboard,' Holly suggested. 'This guy barely talks, let alone confers with a website designer about his business. I mean, you're totally right, the website is awful. But I think with this man, we may have to take baby steps.'

Darcy got hold of Myles on the phone and after a brief explanation, told him to email Mitch, say that Mitch had come recommended by a local, and tell him they'd be willing to pay a hefty price tag plus transportation costs if he could get the tree to them by the day after tomorrow. And Myles, being so in love with his new wife, composed and sent the email there and then while Darcy was still on the line.

'Come on, girls, all this talk of festive spirit makes me want to get out and about and enjoy Manhattan. Let me go check with Rupert, see if he'll be in charge for a while.'

Within minutes they were wrapped up in coats, scarves and gloves, and explored the city. They checked out the two windows of Macy's that took up an entire corner block and were four or five persons deep as shoppers and children vied to see what was happening. They took the subway all the way up to Central Park and made their way to the Barneys Christmas window. From there they went to Bloomingdale's, Lord & Taylor and eventually Saks Fifth Avenue. They saw snowy scenes and villages, film characters, different countries depicted behind glass, more Santa Claus figures than ever before. They drank hot mulled cider bought from a street cart and the cloves, cinnamon, nutmeg, and spices carried them across the street to see Saks's light show projected onto the side of the tall building. At regular intervals New Yorkers were treated to twinkling colours, the depiction of a fairy-tale castle, the magical city that came alive in darkness for the holidays.

Holly was right where she wanted to be, in a city that she loved, and she wished Sarah could've met Darcy and Cleo, been a part of the solid friendship they'd formed. Holly's gran had always said that Christmas was more about the people than the gifts, it was about giving rather than receiving, and the older Holly got, the more she understood. Last year she'd been upset and had fallen apart in front of a stranger – Darcy – who'd given her a room at the inn and let her stay over Christmas as a guest. Without Darcy's kindness Holly would've been eating a lonely meal for one in a shabby apartment with rats keeping her company. When Holly was little she and her gran would always wrap up a few little gifts to leave beneath the wishing tree at one of the big department stores in Seattle, they'd invite Mr Sampson from number sixteen to Thanksgiving every year after his wife died, and her gran had always taught Holly to give a charitable donation every month out of her paycheck. It didn't matter if it was only a few dollars, as long as it was a little something. Even now, Holly couldn't walk past anyone standing on the street collecting money for a good cause without popping a few coins into the box.

Maybe this year, between them, they could do something to help someone else in need at Christmas. Mitch, at the little log cabin in the woods, deserved a chance at happiness as much as anyone.

* * *

Holly introduced herself to Nikita Moreno, the petite owner of the art gallery in Greenwich Village with the same name. After her time out with the girls she'd hurried back to her apartment, grabbed her camera, notebook, and voice recorder and was ready to go.

Nikita held out a hand. 'I'm delighted to meet you, Holly. And a big thank you to Amelia at *Contemporary Edge* for accepting my pitch to the magazine. I wasn't at all sure whether I'd get anywhere.'

'Well, you must've done something right or she wouldn't have said yes,' Holly put the woman at ease. From the background information Amelia had already given her, Holly knew this woman had worked her way up from the bottom and her humility was humbling.

Holly set her camera down beside Nikita's desk and at Nikita's suggestion draped her winter coat across a wide-backed mustard seat. 'It's a wonderful space you have here.'

'Thank you, I love it. Let me show you around. And don't worry, art is my passion but I won't get too technical for the magazine, I'll give you an overview for your readers.'

'That sounds perfect. We usually try to keep our art write-ups generalised and readers who are more interested will be sure to follow up with the social-media links or via your website, or even coming in in person. Would you mind if I use this?' She took her voice recorder from her bag. She always felt she should ask in case people found it intrusive. 'It'll help us have a normal conversation without me keeping my eyes on a notepad.'

Nikita swished her hand through the air. 'Not a problem at all. Follow me, let's get started.'

The gallery was up three concrete steps from the street in Greenwich Village and inside, the large windows and soft white walls created a mecca for art lovers. Soft pine counters and shelving were laid out haphazardly, somehow fitting in with the feel of the whole place. Shiny floors the colour of roasted chestnuts gave the space a luxurious finish and Holly's boots tapped their way along as she trod lightly as though not to disturb the paintings. White accessories – a vase, a heart-shaped plate propped up, a large bowl – adorned the shelves and at one side a glass-fronted cabinet showed off the edges of frames waiting for customers to make their selection.

Nikita led them over to the first section of paintings wrapped in seamless, white-edged frames. 'These are by the artist who first exhibited when I opened the gallery.' She gave some of the artist's history, where she'd exhibited before, where she was exhibiting aside from here. 'She's a master of acrylics, although she won't accept the accolade.'

'This one is beautiful.' Holly looked more closely at the scene of a lake in the fall. 'Is it nearby?'

'It's out in Litchfield County, where the artist is from. Then the painting next to it is of Chapman Falls.' They stood in front of another acrylic piece, this time of water cascading down rocks, so powerful Holly could almost hear it and feel the droplets of water carried in the air.

'Amelia told me some of your history.' Holly turned from the painting.

Nikita smiled. 'I tried the sympathy vote. I told her my past because people are always intrigued when someone makes something out of nothing.'

'You're spot on there. The human-interest angle is powerful. It'll give readers something extra.'

'That's what I'm hoping,' Nikita admitted as they paused by a large piece on the wall, this time painted by Nikita herself.

'You're very talented.' Holly admired the oil painting of Lovers Leap State Park, as the label beneath informed. The view from the top of a rock showed trees parting to reveal a scenic river and a sky so blue you had no doubt as to what season you were in.

'I have a passion and make an okay living from my own work, but I always wanted to have a gallery. I get a thrill discovering new artists, especially those who are new and have never exhibited before.'

'Has business steadily grown?' Holly felt an affinity with anyone who'd chosen to go out on their own. Maybe it was why she'd gelled so well with Darcy, Cleo, and Dylan, who were doing the same.

'We're doing well, but I always want to do better. I'm competitive.' She winked. 'You need to be in this business. I always have a list of artists whom I'd love to feature and publications I'd like to appear in, so I make a point of following up leads whenever I can. Sometimes they come to something, other times, nothing. But you must always try.'

Holly was learning exactly that with freelance journalism. She had a few commissions but there were also plenty of feelers she'd put out that had come up with precisely nothing. 'Could you tell me a bit of your history, for the record?'

'Sure.' They stayed in the same place as Nikita gave Holly an overview of how she'd fallen in love with the art scene, how she'd lived in a friend's garage to make ends meet, how she'd got lucky and found work in a Walmart and then even luckier when an art collector walked by where she was sitting on the sidewalk – after she'd been moved on by the police several times from other positions – and offered to put her paintings in his gallery in New Jersey.

'I think he felt sorry for me,' Nikita explained. 'But it was a turning point.'

'The paintings sold?'

'The first very quickly, but, more than that, he offered me a part-time job. I moved out to New Jersey and worked my ass off, learning everything I could about the business. I told him I wanted my own gallery one day and he became my mentor along the way. Lovely man. He died last year and it broke my heart. He gave me so much in that small act of kindness.'

Holly saw an oil collection of boating scenes, many from the Hamptons, a couple from around Manhattan itself down by the Hudson, and she gathered a plethora of information about Nikita and how she'd come to eventually secure these wonderful premises in Greenwich Village and turn her life around.

They moved on to another artist. 'This is the artist I'll be featuring in a couple of weeks.' The exhibition Holly would be covering. 'Campbell Baldwin is new and very talented, I'm sure you'll agree.'

'He certainly is.' Holly looked at the paintings. There were eight framed pictures in total, the first three captivating winter scenes featuring frost-laden hills, a building on a street corner with icicles hanging perilously down, a scene capturing a deserted park beneath the moonlight, its benches, railing and trees weighed down with snow.

With the preliminary interview done Holly took shots of the gallery while it was empty. She'd get more in a couple of weeks when it was packed with people. She liked the juxtaposition of the shots that told a story themselves. And by the time she left the gallery, Holly was buzzing at how tonight had gone. Another piece to add to her portfolio. Although she still knew she'd never be able to summon enough enthusiasm to appreciate the modern art in Pierre's apartment.

9

MITCH

Mitch sat in the rocker on the galleried landing of his log cabin to enjoy his morning coffee. It was the way he liked to start his day, sitting beneath the timber roof, the scent of wood surrounding him, a view of the top of the staircase his father had put in with wood not afraid to show its true colours, both dark and light spots revealing its connection to nature on the bannisters and the treads that climbed their way up to this floor. And he felt close to Albie sitting here. Sometimes he even talked to him, which he knew was supposed to be the first sign of madness – but what did he care what anyone else thought? It was what kept him sane. Although if he was going to get Albie back someday, he couldn't be like he was now or his son would probably be so scared he'd pack his own bags and leave.

Mitch had to meet the businessman this morning – Pierre something-or-other – and fell one of the most beautiful trees on his land. But it was business. He was almost disappointed he wouldn't get to see the tree all decorated up at the hotel; he bet it'd look magnificent. And so it should. It had been on the land for decades and was worthy of a good send-off. Seeing it lit up and magical would almost take away the disappointment at seeing it go.

He thought about Holly again and how she'd tumbled into his life briefly but with an impact. He still remembered the fresh, intoxicating smell of her hair as he'd lifted her up and carried her inside, the softness of her skin when he'd checked the bump and dabbed the small cut to ensure she was going to be fine. And when he began to wonder what Albie would think of her it gave him such an odd feeling that he necked the rest of his coffee and went downstairs.

In the kitchen he eyed the business card for the PI. Pinned beneath a magnet against the fridge, it taunted him to get things moving; but not yet, he needed to wait, be sure he could manage it financially first and then make sure he was ready emotionally for what it might unearth.

He grabbed his fleece jacket from the hook near the door, added another coat on top of that, a hat, a scarf wrapped tight, and found out his gloves that had seen better days. He tugged on his boots over thermal socks, pulled on the gloves, and prepared to meet the icy blast. It had snowed some more overnight, a good few inches, and it would be bitter out in the fields so early this morning.

Mitch met Pierre and his assistant out on the fringe of his land, adjacent to the highway, where some of the tallest trees stood, and when he introduced himself he could tell Pierre recognised him as the man in the street earlier this week when he'd come out of the restaurant with Holly. But neither of them mentioned anything and it left Mitch wondering whether Holly had shared details of their own rendezvous in the woods. He suspected she hadn't or this man, kitted out in a long woollen coat with a split up the back, would have something to say about it – perhaps shake his hand for coming to the rescue, or maybe warn him off touching her ever again.

Mitch wasn't going to enjoy this, so the quicker they got it over and done with the better. But it didn't stop him having his fun as he led the two men through some of the muddiest patches in the fields to reach the trees that would suit their requirements. Pierre continued to spout their exact specifications as though Mitch was too stupid to have remembered them, or maybe he was worried about what Mitch was going to do with the enormous bundle of red rope he carried over one shoulder. And as they walked on Pierre continued to talk about the Christmas tree business, as if he knew a single thing about it. He kept saying how it must be nice to work Thanksgiving until December and then have a long vacation. There was a hell of a lot more to it than that, Mitch wanted to tell him.

'These trees are outstanding.' This from Lionel, Pierre's lackey but the more bearable of the pair.

'Have we already met?' Something about him was familiar to Mitch.

Lionel didn't seem to want to answer. 'You may have seen me on your land before.'

He remembered. 'Ah yes, trespassing.'

'Sorry about that, I was hunting for trees.'

Mitch had chased him off, yelling and threatening all kinds of things he'd never have done, out of anger at finding him there unexpectedly.

'How long have they been growing?' Lionel seemed to want to move on so Mitch forced himself to think of the financial incentive to this meeting.

'A long time. They grow roughly a foot a year.'

Lionel whistled through his teeth. 'How do they grow so straight?'

'They don't,' Mitch grunted. He kept a permanent watch on his crop year-round to protect trees from pests and Mother Nature, and he used a sophisticated irrigation system. Pruning happened mostly between March and August, when he'd ensure the trees were growing in the traditional shapes people favoured. These trees didn't grow into perfectly formed specimens on their own – some downright resisted with their bare spots and unruly branches, and all of them had to be regularly sheared to maintain their shape. These trees had been nurtured for years with the help of a ladder and a long power hedge trimmer and now behaved themselves well enough with minimal supervision, like the adult version of the unrulier kids in the other fields that he had to pay a lot of attention to. It was a huge job – he had thousands of trees – so to assume he only worked a couple of months a year and put his feet up for the other seasons was naive.

'I'll tag the tree with this red rope.' Mitch gave a wry smile for his own benefit rather than theirs and walked on. 'When you find it.' Jeez they were hard to please. They still hadn't settled on anything and they'd covered a lot of area but at least there was snow on the ground rather than a downpour of rain. Now that would be interesting, watching the men slip and slide – especially Pierre, in those fancy shoes that were slowly losing their shine.

'Is the track that runs the other side big enough for a truck?' Lionel puffed moments later as they progressed along the stretch of trees. Mitch stopped when he realised the two men had paused in front of one that caught their eye. Either that or they'd both had enough of doing this.

'How big a truck are we talking?' Mitch asked. When they told him he replied, 'Not a problem, you'll get that in fine. I'll tag the tree, go back, and get the equipment I need to chop it down.'

Lionel got straight on the phone to give instructions to the manpower he'd told Mitch he'd arrange and Mitch felt sentimentality rear its head, but he couldn't let it. This was business. He dropped the rope, unwound it, and tied it around the tree, then looped it over the fence behind. 'You'll be able to see the rope when the truck drives down. I'll wait for the workforce before I fell the tree.'

'We'll be good to go in an hour,' said Lionel.

'I'll have the money go straight into your account,' Pierre added.

'Appreciate the business,' Mitch told them. He'd already forwarded his bank details yesterday.

'How many acres have you got here?' Pierre asked before Mitch could make a speedy getaway.

'Eighty.'

'All filled with Christmas trees?'

'Twenty acres are... thirty thousand trees.' And counting. Some of the land was empty, but if he got his butt into gear he could expand and see profits increase.

Pierre nodded his approval. 'You should open this place up, you'd do a roaring trade.'

Didn't he think Mitch had already thought of that? If he wasn't such an antisocial bugger he could open the farm to people from far and wide to come select their own tree, but he wasn't ready, at least not yet. He'd shifted near to a thousand this year so far by loading up and driving out to the surrounding towns, but he couldn't deny it was time-consuming and he'd do better sitting down and working out a proper business plan.

If Mitch thought the man was looking around the land admiring it for what it was, an area of outstanding beauty, he'd make the effort to talk to him about it. But he wasn't. He was sizing it up, dollar signs in his eyes. And so Mitch set off, back to his truck parked on the track that ran alongside his land, carved out from years of his father and others doing the same. 'Look out for icy patches,' he called back over his shoulder, 'there are a few around.' And he didn't want to have to rescue either one of them.

* * *

Mitch met Pierre and Lionel an hour later and they felled the tree with the help of the workforce and machinery they'd arranged, had it loaded on the truck, and he sent them on their way. He filled the next couple of hours chopping more wood for the log burner at the cabin, which ate the stuff up in the long winters. He had enough in the basket inside for now so he stashed the logs he'd chopped beneath the tarp on the side porch, and inside, out of the plummeting temperatures, he made up a batch of beef and barley soup, ate some with a hunk of bread, and then it was time to get all his layers on once again and get back outside to fell trees ready to sell in Bampton and the little town adjacent to it.

He braced himself against the freezing temperatures and retrieved a chainsaw from the shed. Sometimes he liked to fell trees with a saw and an axe – he liked the physical labour of the task, the way it took him back to basics, the sound of the tools against the wood as he broke through the trunk. But when he had so many to chop down, power tools were the only way to go. As he drove the truck he thought about the cash he could rake in from these trees. He didn't care if it took him six months, a year or more to raise the money to find Albie. This was what he wanted. It gave him purpose, drive, and heaven help anyone who stood in his way.

The many acres Mitch now owned had been organised well with wide tracks running adjacent to many, smaller tracks leading to others, and it was manageable with his truck. He'd park up as close as he could, fell the trees, load them up, drag those he couldn't get so close to. Today he'd parked up in one of the most central fields where many of this year's ready-to-harvest trees were. They were a good height for selling to townsfolk, not so tall they wouldn't fit on top of their car or in their living room, but big enough they'd impress. Shannon had never accepted the idea of one day running the Christmas tree farm. She liked the Mitch of the suit and tie brigade, the one bringing in a steady and reliable salary. And back then, he'd thought the same. It'd only been when his life fell apart that he saw a different way forward for himself. And even if Shannon hadn't left, he suspected they never would've lasted as a couple with him changing in ways they hadn't predicted. He liked to think he would've eventually wanted this outdoor life for his son too.

In the farthest acre, with Mitch's footprints the only marks on the ground of pure white snow that had dusted its surface, Mitch got to work. By his estimations, if he started selling in Bampton by late-morning he could get rid of most if not all of the trees by the time the sun came down. He felled sixty trees in all, each measuring between six and eight feet. When he'd worked in an office he'd slowly noticed a little extra layer creeping on around his middle, but it was the opposite out here. When he got in the shower at the end of a long day, the physical labour was a sign he wore proudly on his body. He was mid-thirties with the physique he'd had in his college days. He may have straggly hair and an unkempt beard, but he couldn't mess up the taut abs, the defined chest and arms, and the muscles in his legs seemed to be keeping up too. Mitch smiled to himself. Was it any wonder his dad had been in such good shape right up until he got sick? He'd never hunched over with old age, he'd never bemoaned going outside and around the land or groaned when he got up from the floor like so many others his age did. If cancer hadn't got him, he'd have been by Mitch's side doing this right now. And with Albie too, they would've made a handsome trio.

Mitch batted away the emotion. That wasn't going to put food on the table or pay his bills. He took the tree-netting machine from beneath the cover of his pickup where he'd stashed the tools. He set up the fold-down table he'd brought with him, placed the netting machine on top and with net hooked over one end, he pushed each tree from its trunk, all the way through. The tree ended up skinnier and easier to transport this way and each time he netted one he loaded it onto the pickup. He'd batch the trees into groups of twenty, most in the tray on the back, some on the roof tied with rope, and then he'd take them all to Bampton, where the selling would start. Depending on how many were left over after Bampton, they'd move on to the next town, then the next, and so on until all the trees were gone.

He rubbed his hands together and blew into his gloves to try to get some feeling back in them. His body was warm but his fingers felt about ready to drop off. When they felt better he took out his cell phone and called Jude, who lived in Bampton, to give him the heads up that he would soon be on the move. He'd enlisted Jude's help last year when they'd struck up an unlikely friendship. Mitch had felt sorry for the boy when he'd tried to buy a Christmas tree outside the local deli. Mitch had just sold his last one and the boy looked heartbroken when he'd heard and had slumped into the store a few doors down. As Mitch was clearing away and getting ready to leave, he'd heard two women talking about Jude and how he lived with his grandmother who, despite being in good health, was growing old and now needed help with shopping, cooking, and keeping the house clean. Jude shouldered most of the burden of her care as well as school and being a teenager, and Mitch had been so overcome by the unfairness of it, perhaps because Albie had been dealt a bum deal too, that when he saw Jude emerge from the store he'd driven him out to the farm and let the boy choose a tree himself that he felled there and then, teaching Jude how to wield an axe. Mitch had taken the tree to Jude's home and after realising how tough this boy had it, Mitch had asked him to help on a regular basis if he'd like to earn some extra cash. Jude had been coming regularly to the Christmas tree farm since then to prune trees, weed, prepare the soil, and help plant new saplings. And Mitch had enjoyed the company, the light relief to the cloud of remorse and sadness he carried around with him. Their friendship had grown stronger although each of them respected one another's boundaries and never asked too many questions.

'Mitch, hey.' Jude was already there waiting for him outside Bampton's candy store, where the owners had agreed they could line trees up along the side wall with more out front. In this season, their busiest of all, the boy was a great salesman, happy to talk to anyone. Sometimes it was as though Mitch was his sidekick, not the other way around.

'Hey.' Mitch climbed out of his pickup and, knowing Jude had taken his gran to the doctor's, asked, 'How's your gran?'

'It's only a cold, nothing serious. And she ate breakfast this morning so the doc is happy.'

'That's great, buddy.' They began unloading the trees between them.

Jude, a gangly teen still growing into his body, had a hat pulled over his blond curls, a few of which had sprung out on one side. 'These smell good.' His breath made white puffs in the icy air as he set down another tree he'd hoisted up onto his shoulder.

'They sure do.' Mitch leaned the trees up against the wall as the snowfall stopped and all they were left with were patchy sidewalks, a glistening frost on the top of the fence on the street opposite. 'Did your gran like the tree you picked last week?'

'She says it's the best she's ever seen.'

Mitch handed Jude a Stanley knife. 'Want to do the honours while I unload some more?'

'Of course.'

Last year they'd left the netting on, thinking it would be easier for whoever bought them to transfer them, but so many customers didn't want to buy unless they'd seen what the specimen would look like all opened up. So this year, they were unwrapping every last one.

'I'm thinking I might expand the business next year,' Mitch told Jude as the boy sliced the netting from another tree.

'Planting more trees?' Jude moved to the next. He paused to look over to Mitch's slightly battered pickup waiting to go back for load number two. 'You might need a bigger truck.'

'Very funny. But I wasn't thinking of transporting them all.' He lifted another tree from the pickup and walked it over to Jude. 'I was thinking of planting in another couple of acres, perhaps even opening the farm up to the public.' He wasn't completely comfortable with it but since dealing with Doug to sort the tree for the green in Inglenook Falls, Pierre and Lionel to arrange the tree for the grand hotel opening, and what with that woman Holly to totally unexpectedly fall into his life, not to mention his talk with Travis, the PI, he'd come to realise he needed to take action. He couldn't go on like this.

Jude's face was as expected. 'But you hate the public.'

It hadn't always been that way. 'I suppose I do.' The smell of Christmas was in the air three hundred and sixty-five days a year for him as the trees grew, but still the power of the sharp, sweet scent washed over Mitch. He put the tree down. 'And that's where you come in.'

'I'm listening.' Jude sliced the netting from another tree.

'Dealing with the public is something I thought you could do. It'll help with your resume when it's time to leave high school, go to college. I'd put you in charge – you'd be the face of the business.'

'Nothing wrong with *your* face,' said Jude. 'Nothing that a good shave wouldn't fix anyway.'

'Are you trying to lose this job before it's even yours?'

'As if?' Jude batted back in good humour. 'Nobody else would do it for you.' He cut the bottom piece of netting completely away and opened up the branches of the tree, arranging them just so, for customers to see its true beauty. 'People are scared of you, you know.'

'I think maybe you're right.' The memory of Holly trying to run from him came into his mind. She'd looked terrified. Less so when he led her back to the safety of town, and her eyes had only shown surprise, not fear, the night he'd seen her in the street.

Jude tackled the next tree. 'I heard someone call you a yeti last time we were here.'

Mitch's laughter rang out across the street making the woman coming out of the candy store jump. She crossed the road pretty quick.

'You've got a real way with women,' Jude joked.

'Don't I know it.' It had been a long time since he'd cared what anyone thought, let alone a woman. He wondered for a moment whether Holly was still hanging around Inglenook Falls or whether she'd already gone back to the city. 'So, are you interested?'

'You open to the public and I'm your man. I'd need to work around Gran, but other than that, I'm happy to put in the hours.'

Mitch took the last tree from the pickup and leaned it against the wall for Jude to prepare for display. 'Your gran is lucky to have you.'

'I'm lucky to have her.' Jude put the Stanley knife to the netting, sliced it, and exposed the branches. 'She's done everything for me, right from when I was little. I chose to be with her.'

Mitch wanted to know more. He took some loose change from his pocket. 'Here, go and buy two coffees from the café on the corner. Mine's black, no sugar.'

Jude came back with a coffee for Mitch and a can of Coke for

himself. 'I don't drink coffee,' he said by way of explanation when
he flipped the ring pull.

'It's cold, don't you need to warm up?'

He took a few long gulps. 'Nah. Thirsty work this, you know.'

'What did you mean when you said you chose your gran?'
Mitch knew Jude could avoid a subject if he really wanted, they
were the same that way.

The can went to Jude's lips again and after he swallowed, he
looked at Mitch the way he usually did, amused and a little bit
guarded. 'I thought you weren't big on talking.'

'I'm not, but I thought we were buddies.'

'We are.' Another swig from his can.

'So, what's the deal?' The coffee was red-hot and Mitch had only
managed a couple of sips but it at least kept his hands warm.

'My parents argued, like all the time.'

'Most married couples do.'

'Not like this. They fought, they yelled, they used me to piss
each other off.'

'How?' It didn't seem a good time to reprimand him for his
language.

'I dunno... Mom would drag me to ice hockey games at the last
minute if Dad had something planned, whether I wanted to go or not.
She only did it to get to him. And once, he whisked me away when
Mom had promised to take me sledding. I thought I'd do the sledding
with him but all the stuff was in her car so all we did was went to a diner,
ate sausages and bacon and fatty hash browns, and he took me home.
The snow was too dangerous the next day and we couldn't go out, so I
sat at home in front of the TV, turning the volume up as they yelled.'

'That doesn't sound much fun.'

'It wasn't. Mom walked out when I was six. I still remember it. I
remember her suitcase in the hall, her crying, her yelling at Dad.

He yelled back and threw her case out front, told her to go. And she did.'

They didn't say anything for a while.

'Mom never moved back in but a few nights later I was woken up when someone came into my room in the middle of the night. She ushered me out of bed; I was too sleepy to ask what was going on. Dad had been drinking and was out of it on the couch and she took me to the car and drove away. I didn't see Dad for months until he found me, wherever we were – I don't even know – and he did the same, took me back.'

'Jeez.' What shit had this kid gone through?

'I remember a court date, a judge, and a lot of talking. I begged to go live with Gran, she begged them to let me, and I don't know the official reasons, I never much cared, but that was what happened. I went to live with her, my mom and dad stopped by to see me every few days but they didn't seem to want me as much when I wasn't their bargaining chip.' He shrugged as though it was fact, no emotion involved.

'I'm sorry, buddy. It must've been hell for you.'

'I owe everything to Gran.'

He was caring for his gran the same way Mitch had cared for his dad, the way Corey had cared for their mom. It's what families did. But Jude had missed out on the generation who should've been there for him before it was his turn to be in charge. He wondered what Albie would've done had he and Shannon stayed together and fought like Jude's parents had.

'Do you have any help at home?' Mitch asked.

'It's not so bad, don't go feeling sorry for me.'

'I don't.' Mitch liked their banter, it always went this way, even with the serious undercurrent. 'But do you?'

'Our neighbour, Mrs Matthews, helps us out when she can. She and Gran have been friends since they were small. Believe me,' he grinned, 'they tell me stories, *all* the time.'

Mitch smiled as Jude tossed his empty Coke can towards the trash can at the edge of the sidewalk.

It deftly clattered inside and the boy held up both hands. 'Score!'

Ever since he'd met with Travis in the city Mitch had been motivated to get his finances in shape, get things moving, and find Albie. But he couldn't stand the thought of hurting his son even more. And maybe Albie was really happy now, content, going in the right direction. Maybe he didn't need Mitch coming in and throwing everything into disarray. He was a mess, at least physically. His head was getting in the right space but he still wasn't a part of the town he'd once loved and he didn't blame people for shying away from him. He regularly let it be known he wasn't up for company.

'How about we make a deal?' Mitch suggested. In the light of not knowing what the hell to do in his own life, this was a way forward at least.

'Yeah?'

'You work for me but I'll keep it really flexible, even if it means I have to face the public myself.'

'Hey, maybe I could leave school, work on the Christmas tree farm full time.' His eyes lit up.

Tickled by the boy's enthusiasm, he played the parent role. 'You finish school, get good grades, then maybe we can talk.' The teen would probably have other ideas once he could spread his wings and experience the big wide world out there.

'You're on. And for what it's worth, I think it's about time. I wondered how long you'd haul trees like this when a lot of people would jump at the chance to come out and choose one. And you'll really talk to people?'

'Of course. I'm talking now, aren't I?' Mitch closed the back of the truck ready to go and get the next load.

'Not the same thing!' Jude called after him before turning back to make sure the trees were presented in the best way.

And as Mitch drove away up the grey street covered in the slush that came after vehicle dirt mixed with beautiful white snowfall, he felt as though he was finally heading in the right direction.

10

HOLLY

Manhattan was in the icy grasp of winter as Holly took the train to Inglenook Falls on Saturday for the grand opening of the Corbridge Hotel. Yesterday, Pierre had sent her a photo of the foyer as it was decorated for Christmas and Holly couldn't wait to see it again. Somehow Pierre had found the biggest and most impressive tree she'd ever seen and staff were on ladders reaching its highest boughs to string lights and hang ornaments. Holly's fingers were already twitching at the thought of taking more photographs of it tonight to cover the event.

As the train pulled into the station, Holly changed out of her comfy footwear into heels suitable for the party, and with darkness already fallen over the town, snowflakes whirled their way from the sky to the ground and settled on her coat shoulders as she stepped off the train and made her way to the front entrance.

Pierre had sent a car to collect her and bring her to the party but she hadn't expected him to come himself. 'I thought you'd be too busy getting ready for the opening,' she said after he'd engulfed her in a hug and planted a kiss on her lips.

He stowed her camera bag and extra bag containing shoes in

the trunk before they climbed into the back of the car. 'I took time out to come get you, thought it'd be a nice surprise.'

Her parents would approve of this man with his instant charm, his air of success, his confidence, the way he treated Holly. Back in tenth grade, Holly had dated Boyd Carson, a jock from the football team, every ounce the popular guy, and after they'd been dating for a month she took him home to meet her parents. They'd asked her to do so. No more meeting at the Dairy Queen that sat almost equidistant from their houses. They wanted to know who their daughter was seeing and he'd been understandably uneasy beneath their scrutiny, although Holly had put it down to him being young and unpractised in these situations. But seven months later, after Boyd found he couldn't focus on anything other than football and Holly started dating Jesse, it was a totally different story. Jesse, more into academia than sports, had met her parents and shaken their hands, and before he'd even taken off his jacket and her mum had hung it in the closet with the others, he'd had them eating out of his hands.

It would've been the same with Pierre. This was the type of man her parents saw her with – and, to be fair, the type of man she'd always seen herself with one day. But since she'd handed in her notice and her lifestyle had altered – for the better, she knew – she'd found his business acumen and his drive so very different to what she was looking for.

'Earth to Holly,' Pierre laughed as the car cruised through town, slowly in case of ice, and then wound its way through the darkened streets leading to the hotel.

'Sorry, I was daydreaming.'

'There was I thinking you'd be relaxed now you've cut back on your hours.'

'Don't worry, I am.'

'But you didn't hear what I said.'

'I'm sorry.'

He took her hands in his as they sat in the back of the car next to each other. 'I told you you look beautiful tonight.' He leaned across and kissed her again.

'You can't even see what I'm wearing under my coat.'

He grinned. 'The heels tell me enough.'

Holly hadn't needed to treat herself to anything new for tonight. She had plenty of outfits to choose from. One of her concerns with moving into a studio apartment had been whether she had room for her entire wardrobe because her handsome salary had meant far too many frivolous shopping trips in a city renowned for its designer stores. Tonight, she'd selected a favourite little black dress she'd picked up at Nordstrom last winter. Partially sheer at the bodice, waist and hem, it finished a few inches above her knee, and she'd teamed it with a pair of high, satin sandals with ruffle detail across the toes. Completely unsuitable for snow but perfect for a glamorous party. She'd worn her Converse to Penn Station, her dress hidden beneath a black coat in a blend of Italian wool with cashmere, a wide draped collar keeping her warm and comfortable.

When they pulled up outside the Corbridge Hotel, Holly let out a gasp. 'Oh, Pierre, it looks amazing.' The outside had so many lights it was like a slice of Christmas paradise.

'I'm glad you like it.' He thanked the driver, who had already opened his door to come round and help Holly out and across the slippery surface

'Thank you, Paul.' Holly smiled at him. They seemed to be on a first name basis since he'd driven her places with Pierre quite a few times before. 'Between you and me, I'd be a lot more comfortable in my Converse.'

'You and me both,' Paul whispered back after he'd taken Holly's bags from the boot. They both focused on his shiny chauffeur shoes. 'Don't tell the boss.' He tipped his hat and left them to it.

'What are you two whispering about?' Pierre put an arm around her waist.

'Nothing much. Do you mind if I get a few shots before we go inside?'

'Sure.' He looked on as she opened one of her bags. 'What are you doing?'

She took out her Converse. 'I hadn't thought about this part. I want to get some shots for my article, and the lighting out here is spectacular right now. It's clear, the stars are bright, the moon is out – it's perfect. If I wear my heels I'm bound to slip.'

He moved closer, his body pressed against hers. 'But inside there's champagne, canapes, people to meet and greet, even the big boss and the head of the media department.'

'And I'll meet them soon. This is work.' She steadied herself against Pierre's arm as she wiggled off one heel and slipped a sneaker onto that foot. She repeated the dance with the other shoe and then pushed her heels into her bag, took out her camera, and looped it around her neck, and put the bag behind the small planted Douglas fir out front to one side of the door. 'That way it won't be in my photos,' she laughed. 'Go on. You go inside and meet people, socialise.'

'Don't be too long,' he smiled.

'Promise.'

She walked to the side of the parking lot. There was a drop-off area, where Paul had set them down moments ago before driving on and out of the other entrance, and the space behind her was starting to fill, but from her position now, she had a great view of the hotel and its surrounds all dusted in white. There were a couple of icicles hanging from the sign on approach – she'd seen them as they'd driven in – so she trudged back there and snapped a few shots, the hotel background making a striking photograph with its alpine backdrop. The scenery was enchanting with stars twinkling above, the moonlight casting a shimmer across everything. Golden lights dotted the windows of the building at all levels, like little jewels, and each section of the covered walkway running along the entire front of the hotel had lights hanging to illuminate the way.

Small Christmas trees were spaced at regular intervals out front of the hotel and the finishing touches were spot on. Holly waited for one of the staff to tie a burgundy taffeta ribbon around what looked like a fancy tree-bark-effect bucket on the tree at the far right, switch on its lights to match the other five trees and disappear inside, before she took more photos. She snapped away, capturing guests' arrivals, the smiles on their faces, ready for the most wonderful time of the year. She took pictures through the downstairs windows – of people gathering in the restaurant, the soft glow from the subtle lights reflecting on their faces; another few looking into a reception room where an elderly couple were ensconced on a couch, chatting away, with a small plate of canapes between them.

When she had enough photographs she went back over to the undercover walkway, pulled out her bag, and changed her shoes. Once her heels were on, she took out a rose-gold, box clutch that matched her diamond solitaire earrings, ruffled the edges of her hair, picked up her bags, and went inside to see a tree that looked even more impressive than it had in the pictures Pierre had sent. Standing at about four times her height, it was adorned with glass bauble ornaments, angels, and cherubs, red velvet ribbons tied to the ends of branches, thousands of lights woven in and out between greenery that left Christmas on the air. Little red-boxed gifts hung strategically from branches, from the bottom layer of the tree all the way to the top, and gold-wrapped boxes with generous matching gold bows were placed at the foot of the tree. The garlands hanging on the side wall of the foyer matched the green of the tree and their white lights gently flickered, making the entire place look like it was already in a magazine.

'What do you think?' Pierre, dressed in a crisp, dark-navy suit, a white shirt, cuffs measured precisely, came to her side and stood so close she could feel his warmth.

'It's wonderful.' She looked towards the back of the foyer at the reception area where, as Pierre had promised, the fire was burning away with a cosy effect that tied everything together for the season.

'I'm thinking next year, I'll add in an ice rink for this place.'

She stood back and turned to him. 'Wow, that's seriously impressive. I thought it was a golf course you were going for.'

'I can have both.' He stood back a little, ever professional, always appraising his surroundings. 'There isn't another outdoor rink in or near Inglenook Falls; locals will be all over it.'

'They certainly will,' Holly approved. Was there anything this man couldn't do? 'And where did you find this tree, it's gorgeous?'

'The local tree farm.'

Her head whipped around but then she remembered she'd never told Pierre about her encounter with Mitch. 'I've not seen it.'

'It's well hidden. In those woods tucked behind Main Street. Lionel spent some time scouting around for another tree and found it by chance. It's exactly what we wanted. Not too sure about the owner though. We saw him once before, down on Main Street, you might remember.' Holly shrugged. 'I thought he was a down and out, but he's got a bit of savvy about him. Just not enough to really make that business a roaring success.'

'What do you think he should be doing differently?'

'A shower and a shave wouldn't go amiss, and maybe learning some communication skills.'

'I guess if he works on the land—'

'Doesn't matter. You still need to face customers. I wouldn't let any employee, front office or back office, look like that.'

No, she didn't suppose he would. 'Did you invite him tonight?' Her heart beat faster at the prospect.

'As a matter of fact, I did. But only because we invited every single Inglenook Falls resident. It's good for reputation, good to befriend locals and it helps us and them. He never replied.

Their discussion faded when her friends arrived. 'Darcy, how wonderful to see you.' Pierre kissed her on the cheek and did the same with Cleo. 'Welcome to the Corbridge Hotel.'

Holly hugged Cleo and then Darcy. 'I'm so glad you came!'

'Myles sends his apologies,' said Darcy, 'but he's stuck at work so couldn't make it.'

'And Dylan is on babysitting duties so he sends his apologies too, Pierre,' said Cleo. 'The whole place looks wonderful though.'

'Thank you for saying so, Cleo. And talking of babysitting, don't forget we'll be providing that here too.'

'Really? Then I'm sold already.'

'I think it'll be a big draw for parents to have some alone time in the spa or share a few drinks over dinner. We're dedicating a couple of rooms at the rear of the hotel for a kids' club, with fully trained staff, and it'll be suitable for all ages.'

'Well, it sounds amazing,' added Darcy. 'And you're right near the ski fields, aren't you?'

'We sure are.' He pointed towards the rear of the building. 'There are ski fields, toboggan runs, and plenty of space for snow play.'

'My kids would love that,' said Cleo, 'but I've got my eye on the spa the second it opens.'

'You can check it out tonight, you're most welcome.'

'Really?' Cleo was first to follow Holly's boyfriend towards the direction of the spa and the others were close behind.

When Pierre left them to it, Darcy told Holly that Myles had been in touch with Mitch from the Christmas tree farm.

'And did he order a tree?' Holly wanted to know.

'Eventually. Mitch wasn't too happy about going all the way to the city but Myles told him he'd cover all the added expense and given the short notice he'd make it well worth his while. I get the impression Mitch needs the money, although what he could possibly spend it on out there I'll never know.'

'Remember... we don't know the man, not properly,' Cleo reminded them both. 'We shouldn't add to the gossip.'

'Yes, Mom,' Darcy teased.

Holly wondered how Mitch would get on taking a tree into the big city, liaising with Myles, who was chatty, a clean, crisp business-man. But he'd obviously managed with Pierre, so perhaps this would get him talking again and sooner or later he may find himself integrating back into the community. Or was she dreaming? Maybe Pierre was right, maybe freelancing didn't keep her busy enough because here she was trying to poke her nose in where it definitely wasn't wanted.

Miranda gave them a tour of the spa and following talk of setting up a girls' weekend here, they mingled with the crowds. As well as lots of business folk they didn't know, there were plenty of people from Inglenook Falls coming to investigate what this place was all about. Nessa from the library was here along with her husband, and Cleo introduced Holly, and then Holly met Enid from the café and they got to talking about running your own business. Lisa and Christopher had come along tonight and were delighted to see Holly again; she met a few of their friends and they said that they weren't in the least bit worried about the hotel taking their business.

'We're different to this place,' Lisa declared. 'Our clients aren't looking for all the extras. They want boutique, quaint, near Main Street with the bandstand and the green, people they can get to know during their stay, the cutesy Italian restaurant that doesn't charge extortionate prices.'

'Keep your voice down,' Christopher urged. 'People will think we're against it.'

'Christopher is very much looking forward to the golf course being added.'

'Sooner the better,' he confirmed. 'I need the escape.'

'I met someone called Meredith from New Jersey,' Cleo giggled when she joined them again. She was holding another glass of champagne, intent on letting her hair down tonight now she'd stopped breastfeeding. 'I've already talked her into trying out the knitting workshops.'

'You little networker,' Darcy approved.

'I also heard talk of an ice rink,' Cleo went on. 'Is it true, Holly?'

'Who knows, Pierre is always surprising me with how far he can push things.' She grabbed a cucumber and whipped-feta canape from the silver platter that floated past balancing on the arm of a waiter.

'I'm happy with a roaring fire at the Inglenook Inn,' Darcy concluded, taking a canape for herself. 'Pierre's pulling out the big guns.'

'Between you and me...' Holly lowered her voice, 'I fell in love with the Inglenook Inn last year and even a place as impressive as this wouldn't sway me.' She'd snapped a few shots of the fireplace earlier, and it certainly had the wow factor, but this hotel was staggeringly huge and what it had in grandeur took away from the cosiness the Inglenook Inn could offer, and the Chestnut Lodge too.

'You're a good friend.' Darcy hugged her. 'I'm glad I found you.'

'The feeling's mutual. Now, you'll have to excuse me.' Holly lifted a glass of champagne from the passing tray for herself. 'I need to get some photos while everyone is mingling.'

'We have food, we have champagne, we'll be fine,' Cleo assured her.

Holly went to retrieve her camera from Pierre's office but the man himself commandeered her attention on her way back. 'I'm going to do a quick speech, can you hang on?'

'Perfect, I'll get some shots of you in action.'

Another woman was hovering beside him. 'Holly, let me introduce you to Lucy Hall. She's head of media and communications at the Hatherleigh Group.'

'It's lovely to meet you.' Holly could see exactly where this was going.

'I've been telling Lucy all about your work with *Contemporary Edge*,' said Pierre.

'I hear you're quite the editor and I've been buying that magazine for years, just my thing, especially on a long flight.'

'Well, that's lovely to hear. I don't work there any more though, I'm freelance.'

'And how are the commissions going?'

'I've made a good start to my portfolio.'

'She's doing a piece on this launch tonight, for *Contemporary Edge*,' Pierre informed the woman.

'Great, the more coverage the better. We'll be doing our own on the website and in a major daily but reaching more of an audience is key.'

'She's also got plenty of other pieces lined up,' Pierre added, 'including an art exhibition, something in the fashion realm.'

Lucy pulled a business card from her purse and handed it to Holly. 'If you're ever in the market for a permanent role then I'd be *very* interested. And we offer an extensive salary package, which Pierre can tell you all about. I recruit all around the country too.' She smiled as though she and Pierre were already in cahoots. 'You two would make quite the travelling pair.' Her chiselled, mousy bob didn't move an inch even when she laughed. 'A match made in heaven.' She touched a hand to Holly's arm. 'Call me.'

'See,' said Pierre when Lucy floated off and he prepared to take front and centre of the crowd congregating in the foyer. 'What did I tell you? You're in demand already.'

'You must've talked me up before tonight.' She wasn't sure whether to be thankful or a little put out.

'I may have mentioned you once or twice.' He winked, stood on the fifth step of the staircase leading up to a mezzanine area, and when he tapped a pen against the side of his glass the hum gradually faded and he was able to say a few words about the hotel, the history of the search for a perfect site, a bit about the towns on either side and how locals had been accommodating and welcoming, the effect on the local area and its economy, a series of discounts he'd be offering to residents. He certainly pulled out all the stops in making whatever he set his mind on successful.

Holly waited for the speech to finish and then it was time to get back to work. She took pictures of the foyer filled with dressed-up partygoers, captured the shiny trays and the details of delicious canapes; she photographed guests laughing beside the Christmas tree with champagne in hand. The Christmas tree Mitch would've grown, cultivated, and chopped down, and knowing Pierre and how desperate he was for tonight to be a success, Mitch would've got a tidy sum for it too. She went into the kitchens and chatted with waitstaff, the chef, and the sous-chef, careful not to get in anyone's way. Mostly she absorbed the atmosphere. She took photographs of the gleaming kitchen kitted out with all mod cons, the steam rising from the commercial gas range as one of the kitchen hands took out a tray of roasted cinnamon pears. She took close-ups of a line cook using his knife skills to finely chop garnish to go onto the awaiting plate of oysters. She captured shots of drinks being poured, even the teenage girl who had her first job ever, washing up at the hotel and passionately extolling the virtues of this hotel coming so close to Inglenook Falls. She told Holly how she'd tried to get a job at the café but they had reams of applications from locals, so as soon as this place advertised, she jumped on in there.

'Is she bugging you?' Pierre poked his head around the doorway to the kitchen to address the chef.

But the man bellowed with laughter as he busied himself around the kitchen. 'I'm used to talking while I work, don't mind at all.'

Holly tucked her camera away. 'I'm done now, I've got plenty. Thanks so much.' And she let the chef get back to issuing his orders.

Holly intended to write up some notes as soon as she finished here tonight and so she'd turned down Pierre's offer to stay over, choosing to get the last train home with Darcy to the city. It meant she could stay up late, scribble as much down as she could, then tomorrow she'd write the rest of the piece.

After Pierre made a quick call to his driver and Holly had rounded up the girls, he waved them off, and as the car drove away Holly looked back through the rear window, at the hotel so magical beneath the moonlight.

This was the kind of place where dreams came true. The kind of place that would've wowed her once. But now, Holly was beginning to wonder whether life had a few surprises in store for her.

11

MITCH

Why he'd agreed to this he'd never know. It was six thirty on a Thursday morning and here he was on his way from Inglenook Falls, tucked away in Connecticut, to New York City to deliver a Christmas tree. He'd been up since 4 a.m., he'd felled the tree that he'd tagged the day before – no way was he going to select it in the dark – and on his own he'd managed to get the tree netted and haul it up onto the tray of his pickup. Luckily this company didn't want a twenty-footer but a modest ten feet of festive beauty, which protruded from the tray but fit well enough. Mitch had tied reflective ribbons to it so some jackass didn't drive up his behind on the highway or in the city.

It had been a busy but weird week. The day of the grand hotel's opening, he'd been selling trees with Jude in a town a few kilometres from Inglenook Falls when he'd got a call from Pierre again, requesting another eight trees. All of them needed to be pretty much the same height at roughly three feet, no more than four. Pierre wanted them all in pots, placed at intervals where windows of the hotel were separated by concrete wall, and he'd pay through the nose to get them that afternoon. So who was Mitch to say no?

Mitch had taken Jude back to Inglenook Falls and told him to run in and ask the owner of Marlo's café whether he could sell trees outside today. They still had seventeen trees left and now they'd been felled Mitch wanted each of them to go to a good home. He'd helped Jude line the trees up, shaking his head at Enid's offer of a coffee on the house – although Jude accepted the Coke, telling Mitch you *never* say no to anything free! – and then he'd gone back to the farm and to three fields over where he knew there was a cluster of trees that had reached around three feet but not yet four. He felled eight and put each into its own individual bucket. He didn't have fancy pots, he'd explained to Pierre, who said one of his staff would sort something – of course they would, this man snapped his fingers and got the things he wanted – and he'd set them all in the tray of his pickup and driven them over to the hotel by the time darkness descended. He'd pulled up at the side of the new building where his truck was out of sight, knowing tonight was about glitz and glamour and nobody would want him to lower the tone with his grubby vehicle, no matter how beautiful these trees were. Of course, he'd been invited – the entire town was, he assumed – but when Mitch had received the invite along with his mail, he'd tossed it into the nearest trash can. Part of him had wondered what Pierre would've done had he turned up tonight, but any antics he toyed with were quickly quashed when he realised his facial hair and grubby clothes didn't quite go with the requested dress code of smart.

Mitch had called Pierre's number when he arrived outside the hotel and the man had sent out a very nice lady named Sue who had a gold shiny badge with her name and job title, although Mitch hadn't taken much notice of the latter. She'd told him where to place the trees and he'd done so, sneaking a look at his enormous Christmas tree in the foyer. It looked mighty fine decorated with ornaments and hundreds of lights, and a sense of pride washed over him before he mumbled some instructions to Sue about caring for the potted trees. But she seemed more intent on getting the buckets decorated. She had a roll of wrapping paper that looked remarkably like tree bark tucked under one arm and a roll of burgundy taffeta ribbon with a wired gold edge looped on her wrist. And while they were standing there she'd waved to Pierre, who, for some reason, had jumped into a sleek black Mercedes and left.

Sue requested Mitch wait after they'd positioned all the pots so she could stand back and check all the trees were in exactly the right place, and after a bit more dragging and wiggling with the farthest one away, she was happy. She'd also been joined by four other staff, all holding rolls of taffeta ribbon and the same wrapping paper, and a fifth staff member came out with a box full of sets of lights. They were like little elves, ready to add a little sprinkling of Christmas magic.

Mitch left them to it and walked back across the front of the hotel, eager to disappear out of sight as more people began to arrive in a cloud of expensive perfume, in their perfectly shiny cars. His cell pinged with a text as he escaped round the side of the hotel to his truck, and it was Jude telling him he had one lonely tree left. Mitch sat in his truck a while longer. He could see in his rear-view mirror that more and more guests had descended. He'd have to time his escape to go unnoticed. While he waited he brought up the website of Travis the PI on his cell and thought again about what it would be like to bring Albie back into his life, and whether he could do it to his son after what Jude had told him about how his parents had used him as a pawn in their game.

Eventually Mitch put the keys in the ignition. Pierre really had cut tonight down to the wire by leaving the finishing touches so late and for some reason it amused Mitch that someone so perfect had shown even he could be disorganised. Because even with fairy lights along that walkway, the front of the hotel had been missing something before they added the potted trees. If the hotel staff cared for them properly they could last a long while, but maybe some things were just for Christmas.

He was about to put the pickup in reverse when he saw the sleek Mercedes pull up again. He'd wait for Pierre to disappear inside. The money for the trees had been transferred to his account so he didn't need to talk to the man again. 'Oh, come on, get on with it.' Mitch was getting impatient and wanted to get going but Pierre was chatting with someone Mitch couldn't see. All he could make out was the other person bending down near one of the potted trees, perhaps smelling the scent. People often did that. Hell, even he did that and he was surrounded by them every day.

When Pierre moved and went inside the hotel, Mitch saw beautiful long auburn hair with loose curls licking across the shoulders of a dark coat, and he only knew one woman with hair like that. He could remember how it smelled too – fresh and expensive, like a garment in a designer store that you were forbidden to touch. He could remember the feel of her body in his arms as he'd taken her into his cabin, up the stairs to his bed.

He watched her some more, his fingers on the ignition key. She must've come for the party, but what did she have on her feet? Were they Converse? He had a pair of those for the warmer months, but what was she doing in them at a party? And then he saw the camera looped around her neck. She'd be here taking photos, the same as she'd been doing that day at his cabin. He watched as she retreated to the back of the parking lot, behind all the expensive cars. She gazed up at the sky at one point, looking at the stars, her hair blowing away from her face. Her earrings shone in the moonlight, she was smiling even though she was alone, and she looked happy. Not throwaway happiness when you shared a joke with someone like he did with Jude, but genuine happiness, where you had everything you could possibly wish for in your life. No regrets. She snapped away with her camera, moving left and right, capturing guests as they arrived, waving to the odd person who passed by. And then when she was done she went over to one of the trees, tugged the end of her laces, slipped off the Converse and deftly put on a pair of heels. With her back to him Mitch could see long, slender legs going all the way up in black stockings to whatever she was wearing beneath that coat, and his imagination said it was something sexy.

Mitch had waited until she'd disappeared inside the building before reversing out from the side of the hotel and pulling out of the parking lot, on his way to meet Jude who had texted 'Sold!' after parting with their last tree.

Since that night he'd dreamt of Holly, of her being at the log cabin, of him taking her to places that made her smile the way she was smiling outside the hotel. They were worlds apart, yet here he was again, in her kind of world, the throbbing city he'd once left behind. He crossed the bridge connecting him to Manhattan and wound round and down the freeway on the east side of the city into a world full of skyscrapers, businesses demanding the highest service from their staff, people who knew where they were going. There was a lack of patience here compared to Inglenook Falls. And he'd already met with traffic. There was no quiet time for this city and he could feel his irritation rising. He may as well have shown up at lunchtime given how many trucks were around, people running across the street against the pedestrian lights and risking arrest or, worse, their lives. He stopped at intersections, kept his eyes on lights and his attention focused. Driving in the city wasn't for the faint-hearted. There was no forgiveness if you missed your turning, slowed to find your way.

Eventually he pulled up outside the office address given to him by a Myles Cunningham, who had organised the delivery, and called him on his cell phone to announce his arrival as they'd arranged. Mitch had only said yes to doing this because, like Pierre, this man had offered a great deal of money. Maybe this guy had more cash than common sense when any fool would know he could easily pick up a tree from somewhere a hell of a lot closer than Inglenook Falls.

Minutes later a knuckle rapped on his window and when Mitch wound it down a hand protruded through the open space. 'You must be Mitch. Delighted to meet you, I'm Myles Cunningham.'

'Good to meet you.' It was more than Mitch usually managed. Maybe he was getting used to a bit of civilisation, and this man was less standoffish than most. 'Is there anywhere better to park?'

'Here's fine. If you get a ticket I'll cover it, but we won't take long. I've got some help.' He pointed to a guy lurking in his wake, another suit, who looked like he'd rather be enjoying the office warmth and a strong cup of coffee right now.

Mitch got out of the pickup and pulled down the hatch at the back as the other man, called Rufus, joined Myles to help out. With the cheque from Myles now in his rear pocket, Mitch took the saw from the back of his pickup and reiterated his tips for looking after the tree.

'Whoa!' Rufus stood back, a look of horror on his face.

Myles chuckled. 'You might need to put the saw down, Mitch. You'll get arrested here in Manhattan.'

City slickers. Mitch got going with what he needed to do and made a fresh cut on the end of the tree. 'It'll help it take up more water, make it last from now until Christmas.'

'Appreciate it,' said Myles. 'Right now it looks like the Grinch stole Christmas up there in the office, it's miserable.'

'You know, you could've got one from much closer to the city.'

Myles rubbed his hands together. It was freezing out here and the guy had come out in a shirt and tie. 'You came recommended.'

'By whom?' He was curious and Jude's voice was ringing in his ears, telling him to be customer focused.

But then he had his answer because along came a woman Mitch definitely recognised, and it was clear she knew Myles too by the way they nodded at one another.

'I'll see you around.' Myles was quick to scarper and manoeuvre the tree through the revolving office door with Rufus.

Mitch shut the back of his pickup and went round to the driver's door.

'Don't run off.' Holly's soft voice reminded him of that day at the cabin. And when he felt her hand on his arm, he stopped. But he didn't turn around.

'You did this on purpose,' he said.

'Kinda.'

Her nonchalance almost made him smile except he hated being set up. 'I appreciate the business, miss.'

'It's Holly. You know that, Mitch.'

His name on her lips stopped him. 'What do you want from me?'

'Nothing.'

'Why are you here now?'

'I live in Manhattan.'

'But not in the Financial District you don't.' Was this what it felt like to be investigated? If it did, he couldn't do that to Albie. Because it felt intrusive, he felt threatened.

'Okay, you've got me there. I'm writing a feature on a new retail outlet that opened in the fall.'

'They want to see you this early in the day?'

'I'm a little early.' She pursed her lips together. 'A couple of hours early.'

'Ah, I thought so.' He leaned against his truck. Why was she trying to be so nice? People had tried before, but he'd batted them away – and they'd known him of old. Here was someone who'd barely shared a conversation with him, so why the interest?

'I'm not up to no good, Mitch, I promise.' Her shoulders slumped a little as though she was giving up. 'I wanted you to know people appreciate you. The town's tree is beautiful, the whole of Inglenook Falls says so.'

'We supply it every year.'

'That's nice.' She was bundled up in a gold sparkly scarf that set off her hair, her eyes left his to look down at matching gloves. 'The tree at the hotel is amazing too. Did you see it all decorated?'

He grunted. He was out of conversation and he wanted to leave. He'd caught a glimpse of his tree in the hotel foyer when he'd dropped off the others, but hadn't hung around long enough to appreciate its magnificence. Then again, he already knew its beauty, he'd seen it grow over the years and helped nurture it into what it was today.

Holly was just saying something about showing him photos on her cell when he saw his escape. A parking inspector gunning right for him. 'Gotta go.' And he jumped into his pickup and pulled away from the kerb.

He only looked in his rear-view mirror once to see Holly, head down against the cold, crossing the street.

Pushing thoughts of Holly from his mind, Mitch had two stops to make on the way back from the city, to stores he supplied with handmade picture frames. He made standard sizes for them so they'd be easy enough to fit for customers and it not only brought in a bit of extra money, but it kept him practising the skill. His father had passed down the Christmas tree farm, but also his talent in making things out of wood, although Mitch had a long way to go before he'd ever declare himself half as good. His father had long had a love affair with all things wood. He'd built the log cabin along with a couple of friends, he'd made the rocker that sat on Mitch's

landing, and he'd made other items around the cabin, including the
fruit bowl in the kitchen as well as the pallet kitchen clock with
three different types of wood to give it its striped effect, the squirrel
on his nightstand with the curve of its tail and its claws clasping a
nut. Mitch's mum had loved the squirrels and his father had made
her two. Mitch now had one, Corey the other, the biggest reminder
of their mum and how she'd loved it down here at the cabin, getting
back to nature.

Mitch finished up with the last store and then with the timing
exactly right he stopped off at the post office in town. He knew that
on a Thursday a teenage girl worked at the counter and so he
wouldn't have to face the locals or be asked many questions. He
picked up his mail, bought some stamps, and went on his way,
following the street, past the houses and all the way back to the top
of the dirt track beyond the sign into town that led his vehicle all
the way into the woods and alongside the sheds outside the little
log cabin. His foray into the big wide world was done for now, until
next time.

It was icy underfoot when he climbed out of his truck. The
snowfall had eased off but what was on the ground often lingered
longer here and was harder packed with the shelter afforded by the
trees. Hopefully the biggest dumps wouldn't come until after
Christmas. He wanted to sell as many trees as they could before
then, rake in the funds, then he could be snowed in for a few weeks
for all he cared. At least it would give him a break from having to
see people. He'd seen and spoken to more people in the last week
than he had in the whole year.

Inside the cabin was relatively warm compared to the outside.
Mitch opened the log burner and added more logs, lit the kindling
and let it take hold. When his cell phone rang again he cursed. All
he wanted was to crack open a beer, take a long, hot shower and
slouch in front of the burning logs, alone, but at least it was only

Jude. His face and voice softened. 'My star seller. What can I do for you, Jude? You're not after a bonus are you?'

'Course not, that would be rude.' Jude knew how to keep him laughing at least. In fact, he wasn't sure what he would've done without the boy during this last year when he'd felt hopeless and unable to dig himself out of his misery. 'Word on the street is that they're looking for a tree for the library. My mate Cal told me. His mom works there.'

'How big?' He stiffened at the thought of doing business with a local again, but beggars couldn't be choosers. He'd braved Manhattan, he'd braved the hotel. He could brave the local library on Main Street.

'An eight-footer, they said.'

Mitch raised his eyebrows and wondered whether this was another part of Holly's strange game, trying to integrate him back into society like some kind of mental patient. Which actually wasn't far wrong. 'Why don't they have one already? It's well after Thanksgiving.' All these people who left it late when they were running a business. It wasn't exactly community friendly, and they had the gall to criticise him.

'Barbara, that's Cal's mom, had new shelves put in, they were in a mess, so they agreed to have a fake tree.'

Mitch harrumphed. 'Not the same.'

'They realise that now. It's silver. It's not even green.'

'Sounds horrific. And did she specifically ask for a tree from my farm?'

'Well...'

'Didn't think so.'

'Cal heard her saying she'd have to get one from somewhere but hadn't had time. She's sorting it tomorrow, so you need to be quick.'

'I don't beg, buddy.'

'I'm not asking you to. But you're the closest supplier, your trees are the best. Now are we going to do business or what?'

'You talk to them, negotiate the sale, arrange for them to choose it, and you tag it in the fields, I'll cut it down.'

'And how will I get it to them? I've only got a bicycle.'

Mitch grinned. 'I'll put it on the roof of the pickup, but you can help unload it. In fact, get your mate, Cal, too.' That way they could both drag it in there and he wouldn't have to.

'So I can tell them it's a yes?'

'Tell them yes, but let me know when they're going to be snooping around the fields.'

'Would you rather they came after dark?'

'I don't appreciate the sarcasm, Jude.'

'You love the sarcasm. I bet you're smiling.' He had a point. 'I'll see you tomorrow.'

After he'd hung up, Mitch checked the log burner and with a bottle of beer in one hand headed into the kitchen to grab a snack. As he turned to put his bottle on the counter, he caught sight of himself reflected in the glass oven door.

How had he become this person? He looked at his hair, the unsightly beard, the dirt on his face that rarely bothered him. How had he turned into this sad near-recluse, alone, miserable, with no end in sight, the only people in his life a kid who had more confidence than he did and a woman who seemed determined to drag him back into civilisation?

12

MITCH

The snow had come down again and by morning a few inches covered the ground. Mitch had heard on the radio that main roads were fine, but some of the smaller towns were dicey and snow-ploughs would have their work cut out today. But he could no longer deny he needed to go to the store. He was low on everything; the small food cupboard had nothing but some stale Graham crackers and a packet of dried pasta, with the fridge coming a close second in the pathetic stakes with a piece of mouldy cheese he threw away, a tub of butter, and some well-past-it milk.

He jumped into his pickup to get the task over with. Some days he could drive the stretch of Main Street without being too bothered, other times he felt like the whole world was looking at him, laughing at the mess he'd made of his life. Today was thankfully the former, and an hour later he was back with enough supplies to keep him going for a while. He was no chef but he could put together decent meals and usually cooked things in batches that he could unfreeze as required. He'd make a big batch of chilli con carne, or a stew that would last for ages, and other than that he was perfectly capable of chopping up potatoes and vegetables and slinging a piece of steak into a pan. Holly had even eaten a portion of his homemade soup the other day. She'd waited until he had some first though, probably wondering whether he'd sprinkled arsenic or that funny tranquilising drug Rohypnol into it.

A knock at the door interrupted his unpacking of groceries and Mitch peeped from behind the curtain at the lounge window. It was only Jude.

'The people from the library want to select a tree,' the boy told him the second he opened the door. 'You said you needed to know when.' Mitch suspected he was out of puff from tramping down the track at full speed.

'I appreciate the warning.' Mitch grabbed the keys to the tool shed. 'You'll need something to tag the tree with.' He pulled on his coat, stepped out, and shut the front door behind him to keep the warmth inside the cabin. 'I've got some coloured rope. It's heavy, mind. Can you manage?'

'Cal will help me.'

'Good.' Mitch unlocked the shed and took out a length of red rope. 'Make sure you leave some of it in a higher branch so I can spot it.'

'Will do.' Jude took the rope but Mitch could tell he'd soon be asking his mate to help. It was pretty heavy. 'Are you ever going to tell me what's in the other shed?' Jude asked, eyeing the structure beside this one. When Mitch didn't answer he persisted. 'You hiding a dead body?'

Mitch laughed. Jude had asked him before but inside the shed was a part of Mitch he didn't need to reveal to the folk around here. It was part of what kept him sane. He trusted Jude; maybe he'd tell him one day, but not yet. 'That's some imagination you've got, kid. There's nothing but a load of old junk in there,' he lied.

Jude gave up on his line of questioning. 'Don't you have anything else?' He tried to heave the rope up onto his shoulder. 'Like ribbon, that'd be lighter.'

'I'm not a haberdashery.'

'A haber-what-ery?'

'Never mind.' As Mitch trudged back onto the porch he called over his shoulder, 'No letting them snoop around the cabin.'

Jude left the rope out front to collect when he'd fetched the others and scarpered back up the way he'd come. Mitch disappeared back inside, where he finished unloading groceries and stocked the fridge, all the while staying well away from the windows.

It was over an hour later when Jude came and knocked on the door of the cabin again. The kid's cheeks were pink from the cold. 'All done. I've tied the rope around one in the end row, fourth field over past the track with the old shed at the edge. I tied the rope around the base of the tree and then strung it against the fence so we'll spot it from a distance. Didn't fancy taking until nightfall to find it again.'

'I know where you mean, don't worry.' Mitch beckoned him inside in the warm. 'Where's your hat?'

'Forgot to bring it, didn't I?' His ears were even showing the cold. 'I'd better not stay too much longer,' he added with a glance at his watch. 'Gran will want dinner.'

And she'd more than likely worry. 'Don't worry, we'll sort the tree and then I'll take you home. What's on tonight's menu?' Mitch ushered Jude over to the log burner to warm himself up.

'Fish pie with carrots on the side.'

'Fancy.'

'Our neighbour made it. She cooks a lot of meals for us.'

He was glad they were eating right. If not, he was going to send

Jude back with something whether he liked it or not. 'You can borrow a hat from me,' Mitch decided. 'I don't want you freezing while we're out in the fields.'

Jude pulled a face. 'You could be housing field mice in that hair of yours for all I know.'

Mitch's laughter rumbled around the cabin. 'That's enough cheek from you. I've got a clean hat upstairs. How about I make you a hot chocolate and then we'll go chop down that tree?'

'Got any Coke?'

Mitch shook his head. 'Hot chocolate or nothing. I think I have some left.' He hadn't used it in a long while.

'Go on then.'

'Is your mate Cal on standby?'

'Yup. He's expecting my call.' He waved his cell phone in the air.

'You're way too young for your own one of those.'

'It keeps me in contact with those that care.'

Mitch wondered how many times he'd practised that line with his gran before she'd bought him one. He wondered how he'd feel if Albie were here now asking to have the latest technology, how he'd police his son's use of it.

He made the hot chocolate using the last of the powder and then found Jude a clean hat. They trekked down to the field and felled the tree and between the two of them carried it back to the truck and loaded it in. Jude summoned Cal, who arrived to meet them outside the library at the same time as Mitch's pickup pulled up outside.

'We'll do all the talking,' Jude instructed Cal. When Cal gave him a look he gestured to Mitch and said, 'He doesn't like people.'

Cal gave Mitch the strangest look but Mitch carried on with his business, amused at Jude looking out for him. He undid the back of the pickup and between them they eased the tree out so the boys could march it into the library. But Mitch couldn't let them try to erect it themselves so he reluctantly followed behind. He hadn't thought about this part but he'd be quick, sort the tree, and get out of there.

The stand the library had was thankfully a good one and with a bit of manoeuvring and only cursing in his head, Mitch, with the boys' guidance, had the tree standing tall and proud, and, more importantly, straight, in no time.

'It looks cool!' Cal told the woman who had to be his mom. She was new to the library since Mitch had last been in here. But Nessa, chief librarian and former friend of Shannon's, knew him well and when she appeared from a room out the back she smiled at Mitch, hand against her chest. He regretted stomping into her house once, demanding Nessa tell him where Shannon had gone, where she'd taken his son. He'd frightened her that day and for that he was sorry. She was at least thirty years his senior and he should have had respect for such a pillar of the community, not scared her witless. But he'd been desperate. And since that day he hadn't spoken to her again.

When Nessa looked at him a second time it was his cue to leave. He pulled some notes from his pocket and paid the boys, giving them both a little extra to stay and help sweep up the dirt they'd brought in with them, and then turned and made his getaway.

'It's good to see you, Mitch.' Nessa caught up with him the second he stepped from the library out onto Main Street.

He raised a hand but didn't turn. But she followed him to his pickup. Ordinarily he would jump in, shut the door and speed off, but this woman meant well and he owed her after he'd scared the hell out of her that day. He remembered jabbing a finger at her, yelling that she knew something, and then he'd thumped the wall and she'd burst into tears.

'How are you, Mitch?' she asked.

He managed to look her in the eye but said nothing.

'I never knew she'd do a runner, you know. Shannon,' she added, as though it could be anyone else she was talking about.

He stared straight ahead. The way her voice wobbled with nerves made him feel so much worse. 'Have you heard from her?'

'Nobody has.'

'Would you tell me if you had?'

'I would.'

He nodded in acceptance, climbed into the pickup and took off.

Back at the cabin he busied himself chopping ingredients to make a batch of beef and barley soup and as he did so he thought back to the last woman to share soup at this table. Curiosity soon got the better of him and with the soup simmering away he switched on his laptop and opened up a search engine. He looked for the Corbridge Hotel to find coverage of the opening night, which had already appeared on a blogpost, and bingo, there was Holly's name and photograph. He searched on her name and brought up a link to a staff profile at a magazine called *Contemporary Edge*, which he was pretty sure he'd heard of. But according to the write-up she'd left there and a bit more investigation told him she'd gone out on her own. The camera all made sense now. But hang on, why was she being so nosy around the cabin, taking an interest in his life? He had an unsettling feeling that she was doing more than trying to be nice. God help her if she dared to make him part of some elaborate story. He hadn't gone to the press when Shannon upped and left, although he'd been tempted. He hoped his instincts had been right about Holly and that he could trust her. Lord knows he didn't need anyone else causing a mess in his life.

He switched the soup down low. It could simmer a while longer before it was ready, and it was time to restore some of his sanity. He unhooked a key from its resting place near the front door, tugged on his coat and boots, and went out to the shed that had had Jude so inquisitive earlier.

This was his sanctuary. Had been for a long time now. It had got him through some very dark days, and now he needed what was in here all the more.

13

HOLLY

Holly spent her morning in a café tucked away in Greenwich Village. It was one of her favourite places, close to the Inglenook Inn, and since discovering it last year she'd been a regular. She always tried to sit at her favourite table by the window and now sat with her laptop in front of her as she finished up a tuna bagel on pumpernickel. She'd been poring over some art gallery write-ups in an attempt to get into the right headspace for the article on the upcoming exhibition at Nikita Moreno's. It would be important to strike a balance between the technicalities and the human-interest side for the article to appeal to their readers and so she'd been familiarising herself with formal elements of art such as texture, colour, and the type of paint used as well as the canvas material. She'd need to be able to talk to the artist who painted these particular pieces and discuss the reasoning behind them. She wanted to find out what the painting represented, whether any specific parts were significant or perhaps distorted, maybe exaggerated.

She finished her latte and shut down her laptop. Enough art for now. She felt ready to tackle the exhibition, but first it was time to change the pace. She headed back to her apartment to work on a short story, a fiction piece, a complete step outside of the box. It felt frivolous working on something that she'd not done before, but she was going with her creativity this time round and her portfolio would be even more diverse if she managed to get this piece published. She'd also scored extra work last week, supplying photographs to a stock imaging library. She'd only been able to give them repeatables, which were photographs that anyone else could go and capture should they choose to. They didn't command a huge price, but it was another income stream and while Holly was still very much in the amateur photography stages, it was a great start.

Settled in her apartment away from the hail that had begun to batter the window pane, she sat on the bed against the wall, laptop on a cushion on her lap, and began bashing away. She'd not written fiction for years and it was harder than she remembered, and after an hour of going round in circles, realising she needed to plot even a two-thousand-word story, she took out a pad and started planning. But she couldn't concentrate. Her mind kept flitting to Mitch and seeing him in the city that day. He'd known she'd planned the entire thing and she cursed herself for not having given Myles the heads-up to pretend they didn't know one another. Then again, Mitch hadn't yelled at her and he hadn't run a mile, so perhaps it hadn't been such a terrible thing for him after all.

The hail outside stopped and she flicked to the photographs on her laptop, uploaded on a regular basis from her camera, and she went through the shots of the little log cabin in the woods. Quaint in its appearance, it showed no hint of the man who lived there or what he'd been through. She wondered how much laughter there was inside those walls, how much contentment there'd once been. She scrolled through the shots of Mitch taken from the upstairs window when she'd thought she'd need them for evidence, and now she knew his story she could read the pain on his face even though it was hidden by hair and dirt; she could see a slump in his shoulders despite the working on the land that obviously gave him his sanity. She scrolled to another picture of him, this time bending to pick up a collection of logs, but a knock at the door to the apartment disturbed her.

She went over to look through the peephole but there was nobody. It was most likely a delivery guy with access to the building dumping a parcel on the mat for her to find, or for someone to steal. Her last delivery had been a new strap for her camera – okay, not hugely expensive, but she still would've been pissed if it had gone missing.

She opened the door to find a bunch of flowers appear at waist height and Pierre step out from behind them.

She grinned. 'You shouldn't have.' After a hug she leaned in to smell the silky rose petals.

'Of course I should.'

'What are you doing here, I thought you were out in Inglenook Falls all week?' She led the way through to the kitchen.

'I had a meeting, so thought I'd stop by and take my girl out for a coffee.'

'It's great to see you.' She filled the vase with water. 'And these are beautiful.' She arranged the flowers inside and set the vase on the countertop.

'Only the best for my girl.'

'Give me a minute, I'll freshen up and grab my coat.' She put the vase in the centre of the low coffee table opposite the television and it was only when she went to the bathroom that she realised the photographs of Mitch were displaying on her laptop. She hoped the screensaver had kicked in or that Pierre was hovering by the door.

When she came out he was waiting near the door, so to avoid any attention being focused on her laptop and the photographs that may or may not be still showing, she pulled on her boots and her coat over jeans and a flecked navy batwing sweater, and shut the door behind them.

* * *

After their coffee and once Pierre had gone on his way, Holly decided she didn't have a hope of concentrating on her writing so instead turned her mind to photography and made the most of the respite from the awful winter weather. It was pretty when snowflakes fell, but hail was another thing altogether.

Holly was slowly getting to know Manhattan but there was always more to discover. In the summer she'd gone to the more well-known places: the Empire State Building, the Rockefeller Center, the High Line, Central Park. A couple of months ago she'd visited the iconic silhouette of the Guggenheim Museum on the Upper East Side and soon discovered through people watching and listening to snippets of conversation that visitors didn't only go there for the art, they also went for the architecture and profound beauty of the place with its internal concrete ramps climbing up the walls towards the glass roof that felt closer from down below than it did when standing at the top. She'd sold a single shot of the view from the bottom to a stock library, then she'd gone on to take the Roosevelt aerial tram that passed over the East River and she'd sold a shot from that outing too, depicting the sun setting and the tangerine sky as it enveloped Manhattan's skyline. Last week Holly had discovered Greenacre Park on the Upper East Side with its dramatic, twenty-five-foot-high waterfall, an oasis in the city. She'd captured some amazing shots there too, hoping she could sell them to a stock library, or if not then maybe she'd find inspiration for one of her stories.

Today she was heading for a waterfall tunnel on 48th between Sixth and Seventh and made her way to the 14th Street Station to head uptown. Apparently every New York office worker knew about this tunnel. She didn't! Freelancing was turning out to be so much more than a job change. It was an adventure and had altered so many things. She was more aware of money and making it last now she was earning less, she had a new respect for public transport and the way it connected city hubs, and she felt better for all the walking as she traipsed the Manhattan streets to explore or meet with new clients.

She got off at 50th Street and made her way towards 48th and Sixth. How had she not known about this before? She felt like a kid in a candy store, discovering the latest treat to hit the market. She always felt a lift when it came to photography. Even if you were taking pictures of something you'd photographed previously, there was always a new way to capture it, whether it was the mix of people at the same scene, a different light across a building, or a transformation in any changing season.

After the waterfall, Holly headed to Bryant Park, where every year they held the Winter Village. Last year she'd snatched some last-minute gifts from there, plus a couple of things for herself, but she hadn't had time to wander and fully appreciate it then because she'd had to get back to the office. Today, she could take her time.

She took in the scene of shoppers bustling about, some looking for gifts, others with ice-skates dangling over their shoulders ready to meet friends at the ice rink she could see from where she was standing. She made her way through the crowds, gloves off and hands braving the elements, camera looped around her neck. She captured the set-up and different vendors, pausing to take close-ups if space allowed and the image felt powerful enough to want to capture. She saw artisan-crafted earrings, moreish treats made out of chocolate, jewellers showcasing their finest wares, shoppers checking items off their Christmas lists as bags dangled from arms and overzealous kids hyped up on candy from one of the kiosks begging to go home. She grabbed a hot chocolate and, sipping the velvety liquid, moved closer towards the rink, where bright splodges of colour from hats and scarves whipped by, faces laughing, others flecked with fear at falling as arms jutted out to the sides in an attempt to keep balance. She watched for a while and after she'd thrown her empty cup in the trash, she captured the scene spread out before her, the colours of the lit-up Christmas tree behind the rink.

She weaved in and out of the crowds making her way back between vendors. She chatted with a woman selling fancy soaps, another selling cute socks. She admired photographs and paintings at an artwork vendor and reached out to touch a frame in the shiniest of oak wood with curved edges. She had a very special photograph she still wanted to frame but up until now hadn't found what she wanted. Maybe one of these would go with her favourite shot of her friend Sarah. She'd taken the photograph when Sarah visited Seattle in the fall before she got really sick. The leaves you could see in the background had turned to red, russet and gold and overhung the nearby boating lake, water shimmering around rowing boats as they glided across its surface. But the best part of all was the smile on Sarah's face as she cradled a bright orange pumpkin in her arms, the leaves crunched beneath her feet and a light breeze lifted her hair away from her face. She'd insisted they carve the pumpkin when they got to Holly's place and she'd been prattling on about costumes and how they had to dress up 'for the kids'. Neither of them had any and Holly had thought, *yeah, for you more like!* The photograph was exactly how Holly wanted to remember her friend.

Holly was about to go and ask the guy at the kiosk whether he could frame something for her or whether he only sold paintings already in their frames, when she turned and smacked into a person behind her. And before she could apologise she looked up into the eyes of someone she recognised. 'Mitch.'

But he said nothing, nodded and took the cardboard box he'd been holding against his chest over to the desk she'd been about to go to herself. She could hear murmured conversation with the man behind it and saw the exchange of money before the man took the box, opened it and pulled out a similar frame to the ones Holly had been admiring. Mitch was shoving notes into his wallet and seemed anxious to get away but the man kept him talking a while longer.

Holly backed off but she didn't go far and watched Mitch from behind a display of typical tourist scenes – colourful prints of Times Square, the Rockefeller Center, the Chrysler Building, and the Brooklyn Bridge. And when he escaped from the vendor, minus the box he'd brought in, she timed it well and stepped out in front of him before he could disappear into the crowds.

'Your picture frames are beautiful,' she said simply. 'Different from the frames at your cabin, but wonderful all the same.'

He had on a puffy coat, his beard was the same as it had been that day he'd scooped her up off the ground, but his face was at least clean enough that she could see blue eyes a shade deeper than her own. A glimmer of a smile, if you could call it that, showed on his face before he replaced it with the usual scowl and went on his way again.

'Wait, why won't you talk to me? I slept in your bed for crying out loud!'

He stopped then, and she could tell by his face he was amused she'd yelled those words out in the middle of the crowd. Holly thought about trying to clarify what she'd said but didn't bother, content he'd at least stopped and moved aside from the masses.

'You have a real talent.' She wanted to help this man in the same way he'd once helped her, in the same way Darcy had helped last year and given her friendship at a time she needed it the most. 'I have a photograph I'd like to frame and was about to ask the guy at the desk. Perhaps you'd be able to make me one instead. Cut out the middle man?'

His eyes met hers briefly. 'I sell direct to stores, or sell frames at markets like this one.' He turned to go but this time she blocked his way.

'I'd rather go straight to the source,' she persisted. 'Surely it's easier for you. I could stop by with the photograph, then you'd be able to get the size right. It's a special photograph.'

'Stop by?'

'The cabin.' She smiled in a way that would reassure him, she hoped. 'I know where it is, after all.'

For a moment she thought she had him but then he harrumphed and tried to move on past.

She stood in his way again. 'You know, if you let people in you might be surprised how much you like having their friendship.'

Oh crap. She shouldn't have made it so personal.

'I'm fine as I am.'

'I didn't mean to imply that you weren't. All I meant was... I'm trying to be your friend.'

'We're not in first grade.' He stalked off.

'Would it kill you to be nice?' she called after his retreating back as she followed him.

He stopped again and turned to face her. 'Don't you get it? I just want to be left the hell alone!' His voice rose along with his arms and she reeled with shock at the tone of his voice.

'Fine, you stubborn ass!' she yelled as he turned away again. And this time it was Holly who pushed past him and stomped off, away from the Winter Village, away from a man so infuriating she didn't ease off her pace until she'd covered almost a block.

Maybe some people were beyond help.

* * *

'He's arrogant, rude, and ungrateful,' Holly told Cleo and Darcy at the Little Knitting Box that evening. She'd calmed down when she got back to her apartment and rather than wondering why Mitch wouldn't let anyone in, she decided she wouldn't waste another minute thinking about him. Yet here she was, with her friends, doing exactly that.

Tonight, Cleo was hosting a Christmas party at her store in Inglenook Falls. A lot of the display baskets had been moved into a room out the back where Cleo ran her workshops, shelving in the Little Knitting Box had been cleared, and what was left had been covered. The entire place looked like a little Christmas grotto filled with decorations, from the small tree in the window and snowflake embellishments fixed to the inside of the glass, to the twinkly lights and the glittery pine cones that had been placed all around the store. With a little over three weeks to go until the big day, it was the perfect time to get everyone together before they got too busy with work commitments and family engagements. And Cleo enjoyed hosting. She said she got her best tips, and recipes for tonight's food, from her friend Violet, who'd held the party where Cleo had met Dylan for the first time.

'So our plan to get him back into the community isn't working,' Cleo shrugged after topping up champagne for the girls. 'But it will eventually.' She offered a tray of canapes Holly's way. 'Pumpernickel bite?'

'Thank you.' Holly took one of the little squares topped with smoked salmon.

Darcy took one of the morsels for herself. 'Perhaps Holly's right. Maybe Mitch is beyond help. He said he wanted to be left alone and maybe that's what you all need to do.'

'People who say that rarely mean it.' Cleo smiled at her grandpa

Joe, who'd plucked a pillowy Stilton beignet from the tray Cleo was about to hand round.

'Sometimes they really do, Buttons.' He winked at his granddaughter.

'Don't call me that at work.'

'You're at a party, not work, and you told me I could call you by your childhood nickname. You said it made you feel young.'

She shook her head but smiled and introduced his fiancée, Maggie, who'd come over to join them. 'Holly, Darcy, this is Maggie, Grandpa Joe's much better half.'

'Cheek!' But he roared with laughter as Maggie hooked her arm into his. 'It is true, however. I asked this wonderful woman to marry me and she only went and said yes.'

'That's amazing,' Holly smiled. 'Congratulations to both of you.'

'We hear yours was quite the wedding,' Grandpa Joe said to Darcy.

'Your granddaughter almost stole the show by going into labour, but we pulled it back with the s'mores bar.'

Maggie laughed. 'That would do it. What a distraction, but perhaps a little messy.'

'It was wonderful,' Holly enthused. She took out her cell and showed the other woman the photographs she'd uploaded to Instagram.

'It looks such fun.' Maggie, dressed in a wool dress with long boots, had bobbed grey hair and distinctive, tortoiseshell-rimmed glasses. 'You kids sure are adventurous. We thought we were living on the edge having a lemon and raspberry wedding cake with vanilla buttercream.'

'Now that sounds really good to me,' said Holly. 'Where's the wedding?'

'We're getting married in the spring, in the gardens of our favourite restaurant.'

'How romantic,' Darcy swooned as she slipped her arm around Myles, who had come to join them.

'They don't have a photographer yet,' Cleo whispered as she picked up the tray of mushroom and chestnut samosas plus a little pile of napkins and went to work the crowd.

'We're happy to put out disposable cameras so guests can snap away and we'll get some wonderful, natural pictures that way,' Grandpa Joe insisted. 'We looked into it, but I don't want to sit around for hours plastering a smile on my face, I'd rather be enjoying my girl. I'm not getting any younger.'

Holly wondered whether money was the issue. 'I can do it,' she offered. 'Ask Darcy about her wedding, she loved that I was a friend, and now I've met you, we're friends, aren't we?'

'Oh, we couldn't possibly ask you to,' said Grandpa Joe, and by the hope in his eyes that fell to disappointment, Holly knew it had to be down to budget.

'I'll do it for free,' she said. 'I'm trying to build up my portfolio, get my business running, and weddings are one part of it that I absolutely love. You'd be helping me out, honestly. Nobody wants a wedding photographer without a track record, and if I cover your wedding that's two I've done.'

'Photographers charge hundreds, if not thousands. It wouldn't be fair not to pay you,' said Grandpa Joe.

'How about fifty dollars to cover my travel expenses, and some of that lovely wedding cake to take away with me. Honestly, I need another event to add to my portfolio and I'd be honoured.'

'Well—' Grandpa Joe had his pride but Maggie looked like she was ready to accept.

Holly held out her hand. 'Do we have a deal?'

Grandpa Joe relented. He held out his hand and met Holly's. 'We have a deal.'

The Little Knitting Box was filled with locals, young and old, chatter and laughter bounced off the walls. Talk turned to the wedding plans – small, not too many guests, an informal, cocktail-style reception. And when Holly peeled off to grab another glass of champagne Cleo discreetly joined her.

'Thank you for offering to photograph the wedding,' she said. 'I was going to ask you in private but then they were talking about it and it seemed a good time to drop a hint. Although I was thinking more along the lines of you charging a little more than you've agreed. I don't want to take advantage, but Grandpa Joe is refusing all financial help for this wedding even though Dylan and I have offered to cover something as a gift.'

'I don't mind at all. If I hadn't wanted to do it, I wouldn't have offered. You'll always be his little Buttons,' Holly teased.

'Ha ha.' Her smile faded. 'Thank you, from the bottom of my heart.'

Holly put an arm around her friend. 'You're welcome. Darcy saved me when I felt so alone after losing Sarah. And then you came along too. I kind of look at it as paying it forward.' She took a mouthful of champagne. 'And besides, I meant what I said – it all goes into my portfolio at the end of the day. The more impressive it gets, the better.'

Dylan joined them and they discussed Holly's website, what was working well, what they could change. It seemed freelancers rarely switched off. But Holly didn't mind – in fact she enjoyed it. She left Dylan talking to Myles and after draining her champagne squeezed past a jolly group of locals already talking about Christmas food, what was traditional, what wasn't, what they loved or loathed, including relatives from far and wide.

'Enid's sister-in-law is coming this year,' Cleo confided as Holly stole a goat's cheese choux bun topped with caramelised red onion from the latest platter to do the rounds. 'And she can't stand her. Says she criticises everything from the gravy to the meat and hasn't a nice thing to say about her homemaking skills either. Worse thing is, Enid's won awards for her Christmas cakes and yet the sister-in-law still complains they're bland.'

'Some people are never happy.' Holly was feeling the heat inside the Little Knitting Box and flapped the material of her black and red, floral, twist-hem top. She'd worn it with jeans tonight, knowing that anything warmer would be too hot inside the Little Knitting Box with more than thirty-five guests making an appearance.

'Is Pierre coming along tonight?' Cleo set down the platter for guests to help themselves.

'He said he'd try.' Holly checked her watch. 'I know he was over-seeing a dinner at the hotel and he'll be eager to make sure every-thing is as it should be. He'll possibly make it later on.'

'I hope so.'

'You've got a great turnout tonight.'

Cleo smiled and looked around her little store and the back room where people had spread out. 'I invited everyone in town but I didn't think a lot of people would show. It's a busy time of the year. I hope I've catered well enough.'

'I don't think anyone will go hungry.' Holly looked over to Kaisha, dressed in a purple and bright turquoise knitted dress, belted at the waist, floating around the room plying people with more champagne and canapes. 'Your assistant has it sorted. It's a lot of work for you both.'

'It is, but I'm really enjoying it. Kaisha's boyfriend is minding the stall at the Christmas markets until we can get away and Dylan and I roped in a babysitter so Grandpa Joe could come along tonight. Dylan was most insistent he shouldn't miss it.'

'Well, you look like you're having a ball, despite being the hostess.'

'Talking of which, I'd better go and carry on my role.'

'Go mingle, don't worry about me.'

Music crooned in the background from the docking station next to Cleo's old Singer sewing machine that had once belonged to her grandma Eliza and Holly talked with some of the other locals, but when Pierre still wasn't there half an hour later she was so hot and bothered she made for the door.

'Hold on one second.' It was Dylan.

'It's boiling in here, I need to escape.'

He smiled tentatively. 'I promise you won't regret it if you stay a moment longer.'

She hung around and watched him go up to the counter where Cleo and Kaisha usually rang up orders, measured yarn, chatted with customers about their day, and before Holly could think about going outside, he clinked a knitting needle against his glass. And then, pulling the stepladder out from where it was safely stowed next to shelving, he climbed up so he could be seen and heard by everyone.

'It was handy,' he said of the knitting needle and roused a laugh and murmurs as to what he was up to. 'I wanted your attention, folks, for a short while. Cleo... where are you?'

Cleo emerged from the storeroom, from where she'd been about to bring out more food.

'I want to say,' he beamed over at her, 'to the woman I love, a big thank you for this party tonight.'

Everyone cheered and clapped, chinked glasses, and sipped champagne and Holly stood with Darcy, both wondering what was going on.

'Buying this store for Cleo after I so rudely put her out of business was a risk, but I'm more than glad I took it. Inglenook Falls welcomed Cleo and the Little Knitting Box with open arms. This woman took me and my two kids on – a brave feat for anyone, I think you'll agree – and she's added another two beautiful children to our family. So tonight, I'd like to raise a toast and say, To Cleo.'

'To Cleo.'

Holly watched Cleo in the limelight, smiling but embarrassed, knowing she'd got a lot of things right but not quite ready to be centre of attention.

'One more thing...' Dylan's voice rose above the banter and he deftly jumped from the stepladder down to the tiled floor of the store. He took something from his pocket and in one swift move, lowered himself onto one knee then opened up a midnight-blue velvet box to reveal a dazzling, platinum diamond solitaire ring.

Holly had her hands clasped over her mouth and every single person in the Little Knitting Box held their breath.

'Cleo Jones,' Dylan smiled, 'will you do me the very huge honour of becoming my wife?'

'Well, it's about time!' Tears in her eyes, Cleo let him slip the ring onto her finger. 'I was beginning to think you'd never ask.'

Holly had never seen her friend look so happy and for all the worries Cleo had had over the time she'd known her, this moment eclipsed all of that. Funny how life took twists and turns, sometimes unexpected, but if you followed them, you might very well get everything you ever wished for.

Holly grabbed her chunky knit cardigan, wrapped it across her front, and hugged it in at the waist as she stepped outside. From out here the store was even more mesmerising with fairy lights doing their best to shine through steamed-up windows, made that way from all the voices and laughter inside. She crossed the street to a bench and sat down in the crisp air, the seat cold beneath her bottom but a welcome respite. She thought about calling Pierre, but he knew where they all were; he'd get here when he could. This time last year she would've been exactly the same with her work and when her boss said jump she'd simply ask how high she'd like her to go. Nothing had been too much trouble for Holly, there hadn't been anything that had encroached on her life because work was her life. But it was different now.

As though thinking about him had conjured him up, Pierre's black Mercedes pulled up alongside her minutes later. The wintry air had cooled her right down already so she didn't mind the intrusion.

He got out, locked the doors, and the alarm trilled into the cold air. 'Show me the way to the drinks. I'm staying at the hotel tonight so I'll leave my car if I have to.' He pulled her into his arms. 'Interested? There's a bed and a very nice room.'

'You know, I might have had enough champagne to be tempted.'

He kissed her deeply, taking her by surprise in the middle of the street, and they only broke apart when catcalling came from the Little Knitting Box telling them to either get a room or get inside.

Pierre took her hand and they ran across the street. But as she was shutting the door behind her, she caught sight of Mitch, head down, walking away from the mail box near the café. And she knew he'd seen her too.

Her hand hovered on the door knob. She should be the bigger person, go invite him in. Even after they'd butted horns at the Winter Village, Holly had never given up easily.

But was Darcy right? Should they leave him alone and let him be?

She shut the door and went inside. But rather than letting it go, leaving Mitch to fight his own battles, it only took one mention of the man from the log cabin, when the men were off talking hotels, websites, and business, for the girls to come up with a little idea that may just help.

14

MITCH

The snow was getting heavier and it wouldn't be long before the wooded landscape looked completely different, so Mitch loaded up his tools and drove the track out to the fields where some of the four-footers stood. He shaped some of the branches on the most difficult of trees, did the same in the next field and the one after that. He took in the snow-capped hills at the far edges of the land, then looked back over to where his cabin stood, the only home he knew, smoke reliably drifting out of the chimney from the log burner that kept him warm day and night.

His thoughts soon turned to Holly as he tended to the trees, snipping bits here and there to make them more attractive to buyers when he took this batch out to sell. He felt terrible at how he'd treated her yesterday when they'd bumped into one another at the Winter Village in Manhattan. He'd thrown her kindness back in her face and when most people were scared of him, she'd merely called him a stubborn ass before strutting off. He'd wanted to call out something about her ass looking mighty fine because he couldn't deny it, it wasn't this woman's friendship he was interested in: it was everything about her. And it had been a lifetime since he'd thought of having a woman in his life in that way. Even in the summer when Maisie Roberts from the bar in the next town draped her cleavage on the bar at last orders as he stumbled out to walk the long road home, it hadn't stirred anything in him. Or at the start of December when a woman buying a tree had suggested she put a little zing in his Christmas stocking this year, much to Jude's amusement, he hadn't felt a thing.

But Holly, now she was different. He'd got the invite to the party at the Little Knitting Box last week and had thrown it straight into the trash. But when he'd gone to the mail box last night he'd been surprised at how pleased he was to see her. He'd been about to go over and at least say hello, apologise for his rudeness, when that damn black Mercedes had pulled up and Pierre made an appearance. And Mitch had been jealous as hell to see them together. He wondered again why she hadn't told Pierre about her encounter with him in the woods. Mitch had spent enough time with the man to know he'd have mentioned it if she'd said something. But why had she kept it a secret? Back in the good days, Mitch and Shannon had told one another everything. They'd joked about it, how she had this insatiable need to tell him every single detail. She'd tell him the process the hairdresser followed when she had her hair highlighted, she got him to time her after she taught herself to touch-type, made him try new foods and drinks because she wanted to broaden his horizons, told him about office gossip even though he didn't know those involved. She'd shared a life with him, including all those small moments that would go unspoken otherwise, and Mitch wondered why Holly wasn't doing that with Pierre.

Mitch stepped over a frozen stream and looked at the view from the top of the next field. He could make out the edges of one of the adjacent towns, which looked so small from where he was that it could easily be forgotten. He carried on, his hands cold in the spots his threadbare gloves didn't protect, the rest of him wrapped up warm. And when he was done, he gathered up his tools and returned to the cabin with enough time to eat a hearty bowl of soup before he was disturbed with a call on his cell phone from the post office to say he had a parcel to collect. It would likely be the tree netting he'd ordered and they were getting through a hell of a lot these days. With Jude's superior sales skills and the fact they could fit a decent stash on the pickup that Mitch could leave in his friend's care while he went back to the farm for more, they'd shifted twenty per cent more trees than this time last year.

He trudged down the stairs, layered up again – one of the joys of the winter season – and headed out to his pickup, glad to get the call now before the ground had so much snow he'd have to dig his way out. And when he found himself driving on and past the Little Knitting Box to see if there was any sign of Holly, he did a U-turn in the street, swore beneath his breath and drove back to pull up outside the post office.

He wasn't a teenage boy. He was a grown man, and he needed to get over it.

The girl he usually saw was the only person in the post office when he went in and she searched for the package in a huge pile behind her that looked like Santa had decided to drop everything from his sack through one person's brave chimney. 'It's a crazy time of year,' she called without turning around. 'The holidays mean we can get hundreds of parcels in here in the day, workload is astronomical. It's all the online shopping,' she claimed. 'Means more parcels and when the person isn't at home, which invariably they're not – I mean, we all have jobs to go to, right? – they get left here with us. It's good you came straight away. A lot of folks leave it for days, sometimes weeks!'

Mitch wished she'd hurry up before anyone else came in. He wasn't really here to learn mail-room trivia. But since he'd met and frightened Holly that night he was more aware of how people saw him and so he summoned as much patience as he could. Although if it took much longer, he'd gladly scare her if it meant he could be on his way.

'Hallelujah! Here it is.' She puffed a sigh of relief that sent her ebony fringe up into the air for a brief moment.

He signed for it, took it out to his truck, and dumped it in the back, and when he did spot Holly crossing the street with Cleo, his heart leapt. He wished she was on her own so he could talk to her. He wasn't sure he could brave them both together.

Oh, he had it bad for sure.

As he set off for the solitude of his cabin he realised in a weird way he was very much a part of life out here in Connecticut. Over the last couple of weeks he'd dealt with people amicably enough. He'd looked after a woman he didn't know when she trespassed on his land, sorted the tree for the Inglenook Falls town green, the tree at the library, the big tree at the hotel plus the others they'd called for, he'd liaised with Jude to help him run his business and been into Manhattan twice among the crowds he'd never wanted to see again. Even the brief conversation with a commuter on the subway who'd picked up his ticket and handed it to him after he dropped it could count as social interaction.

Mitch warmed up at the cabin with a cup of coffee as he sat in the rocker on the landing, moving slowly back and forth, his eyes cruising the photographs of Albie. Mitch often suspected the reason he'd framed so many photographs and put them there in the landing where he saw them every day was so that he was forced to face up to his grief, his feelings. He'd brought all this upon himself, after all. If he hadn't let himself fall apart, his son might be here now. The photographs were there to wring out every last bit of pain until there was nothing left, in the vain hope it would help him to move forwards. It had worked for the most part because instead of standing up here and balling his eyes out like a big baby, he could take solace in his memories. His eyes roamed over the photograph of Albie wrapped up for winter, a look of glee on his face as his gloved hands shaped a snowball, squeezing every flake in. Mitch could still remember the day it was taken. He'd been having a snowball fight with his son but took a break to go get his camera. It was the first snow of the season, always a day to relish the change in weather before you got fed up with it and longed for spring to show its face.

He stood, cradled the coffee mug with one hand, and used the other to run his fingers across the carved wooden frames he'd made himself, slightly different to those he made for stores or had taken to the Winter Village in Bryant Park. He wanted to kick himself for not agreeing to look at Holly's photograph for her and frame it. Would it really have killed him to be nice to someone who was trying with him? Jude had told him the other day that it was sad to have a fifteen-year-old buddy, and in some ways he was right. 'You need to play with people your own age,' the boy had told him, making Mitch laugh and tell him to be quiet, eat his soup, and get out there to help load up more trees on the truck.

He looked at the first frame he'd made, maple wood encasing a photograph of Albie kicking a football around on the grassy patch out front of the cabin. He'd drawn the design of tree branches out first and then used a little blade to trace the pattern into the wood, weaving this way and that. He'd used a chisel and a mallet to go all the way along each line, until the pattern was cut deeply into the wood, the grooves on the frame had been sanded back and forth with the grain to rid them of handprints, and then the final stain had finished the piece.

Mitch moved his hand from the frame to the logs of wood behind it, the walls of this cabin he'd seen at all stages. He'd seen the cedar trees growing adjacent to the track he drove down every day, his dad and a couple of friends felling those very trees to get enough logs to build the cabin he stood in now. They'd replanted the cedar trees soon after and the cabin had been here long enough for them to grow tall and proud and frame the land exactly as they had before. Mitch's fingers touched the smooth cedar now, he breathed in the smell of it. He thought about how he'd helped his father debark some of the trees, his patience not lasting anywhere near long enough to complete even a portion of the task. His dad had talked to him about how important it was, how the more care they took now, the longer their home would last. It had been a labour of love and he'd been right, of course. Once the cabin was finished, his dad had started to make other items with the same love and care. He'd start with a completely dry piece of log, its size depending on what he intended to make, then he'd use his electric saw to fashion a vague shape before turning his focus to the intricate work, the skills Mitch admired wholeheartedly.

Mitch settled in the rocker again and shut his eyes as memories washed over him and he must have drifted off easily because by the time he woke, the cabin was cooler than it should be and his half-empty cup of coffee on the ledge beside him was stone cold. He headed for the shower to wake himself up a bit, and chuckled when beneath the jets he found himself humming Christmas carols, something he hadn't done so readily in a long while. He'd whistled a few notes one day when he was out felling trees and Jude had laughed, saying he must have the fun gene buried somewhere inside of him after all.

When he'd finished in the shower he headed downstairs, added another log to the log burner, and picked up the basket to go refill it from the stash beneath the tarp on the side porch. He pulled on his boots, didn't bother with a jacket, and prepared to make a run for it.

But when he opened the door to meet the icy blast, he stopped dead. Because there in front of his cabin was something he hadn't seen in a long while, and he almost fell to his knees.

15

HOLLY

'I hope we did the right thing.' Holly took the glass of mulled wine from Darcy's outstretched hand. Sofia, owner of the Inglenook Inn who shared her time between here and Switzerland where her daughter lived, had been looking after guests in Darcy's absence this evening, their tag-team arrangement working like clockwork. And now, the girls were ensconced in the lounge while Darcy was half on duty, half able to relax now that dinner time had passed.

'I do too. I was terrified Mitch would find us on his land and all hell would break loose.'

They'd just got back from Inglenook Falls, the train whisking them away from the scene of the crime. The snow was coming down thick and fast and Holly felt sure her heart had thudded all the way home. Darcy set her own mulled wine on the side table and tended to the fire, so beautiful it often sold guests on this place as it crackled away near the lit-up Christmas tree by the window that looked out onto the street in Greenwich Village.

'Do you think it'll make him smile or curse?' Holly speculated.

'Honestly? I keep flitting between thinking the man will see that someone cares, then I think perhaps he'll see it as interfering or mocking him.'

'I hope he doesn't think we're mocking,' Holly worried. 'He can't stay in that log cabin forever, he needs to know he could have friends, people who care about him. What, why are you grinning?'

'I heard you on the phone to Pierre earlier.'

'And?'

'And I know he was talking about Mitch because you mentioned his name once or twice. What was that all about?'

Holly sighed. 'You know Pierre wants to make the hotel even more spectacular.'

'Yes, golf course wasn't it? And an ice rink? Impressive.'

'Impressive, yes, but he's told me he's going to approach a local landowner. At the party I overheard someone talking about how many acres Mitch has, so it can only be him, surely.'

'So our poor Mitch is still being gossiped about.'

Holly sighed. 'I guess he is.' She'd once been a victim of the rumour mill herself. She'd had a holiday job at a local bakery when she was fifteen and someone had started spreading rumours that she was sleeping with her boss, a married father of three. She tried to take no notice, let it all blow over, but when the gossip reached her school and family, the looks of disapproval and whispering when she came near got too much. She handed in her notice and in floods of tears told the boss why. He'd reprimanded the girl responsible and fired her on the spot. Turned out she'd made a pass at him, he'd rejected her and out of spite she tried to get her own back and cause problems with his wife. Holly had kept working at the bakery but the damage was done, and ever since then she never wanted to be the topic of local interest again.

Holly sipped her mulled wine, the warm liquid instantly relaxing. 'This is wonderful, so Christmassy.'

'I'm glad you like it. And Christmas Day will be a ball, I'm so excited to have you here again. Are you not even tempted to join Pierre in Munich?'

'No, I want to be here, in New York. I feel like I'm starting to find my feet, and Pierre will be busy networking I'm sure.' She should probably feel sad about not spending the holidays with him, but she needed to use the time to see how she felt about their relationship, because nowadays they seemed to be pulling in opposite directions.

'So, back to Mitch, and Pierre,' Darcy began.

'You make it sound like they're in a competition.'

'Aren't they?'

'Of course not. But I really do feel for Mitch.'

'Oh, I know.' Darcy's eyebrows twitched.

Holly ignored the ribbing. 'I mean in respects to how the gossip mill turns.'

'I get it, you're fighting his corner. I heard you telling Pierre that if Mitch wasn't interested, he was to leave him alone.'

She'd meant to talk quietly, which she clearly hadn't managed. 'Mitch is toppling near the edge and I don't think it would take much to tip him over.'

'And you think Pierre will do that?'

'He's a shrewd businessman who'll go after what he wants. I'm not sure someone like Mitch is prepared for that. I was hoping our plan would bring Mitch back into the community, show him people care. It's Christmas, everyone deserves a little magic, and the plans had a chance of working but if Pierre pushes him too much, we'll be back to square one.'

'I admire your tenacity.'

'And I admire yours too,' Holly smiled. 'But I'm not accusing you of being attracted to the man.'

'I'm married.'

'I think Mitch really needs people to give him a chance to prove himself.'

They both jumped when the fire crackled and spat a burning ember onto the rug. Darcy stamped it out and put the fireguard across the front. 'When's Pierre likely to ask about the land?'

'I don't know, he didn't want to share much. I got the impression he wished he'd never mentioned it.'

'Does he know what happened that day you met Mitch?'

'No, I never told him.'

'And what does that tell you?' But this time Darcy's voice was soft, sympathetic, and she squeezed Holly's hand before getting up to help a couple of her guests in out of the cold, offering hot chocolates all round.

Holly decided to leave her to it when another guest came down the stairs wanting directions to The Plaza, and she walked back to her apartment. She passed by the Magnolia Bakery amazed at how many people still wanted cupcakes at 10 p.m., although she shouldn't be surprised in a city that apparently never slept. She thought about the confetti speciality cupcakes and had no idea if they were on sale tonight, but if they were, she hoped her friend was looking down and smiling at every man, woman, or child who bit into one and lit up a smile like a thousand Christmas lights. 'Stop being so maudlin,' Sarah would say if she could see Holly's face now. Holly smiled, almost hearing her friend's voice in her ear as she carried further along Bleecker Street towards home.

What would Sarah have made of their interference with Mitch? And what would she think about Pierre? Would she have liked him, or would she have had as many doubts as Holly was having right now? Last night, after the party, Holly had stayed at the hotel with Pierre, relishing the plush suite with the fireplace opposite the king-size bed, the bathroom with the television screen in the recess above the tub as she'd sunk beneath bubbles at the end of the evening. She'd slipped in between sheets of the finest linen and woken this morning to a breakfast of eggs Florentine and freshly squeezed orange juice. Pierre sure knew how to treat a woman, but was it enough?

Holly had left the hotel and gone to see Cleo, her mind quickly back on Mitch. She'd chatted with her friend at her stall at the Christmas markets, where Cleo was doing a roaring trade despite her store being local anyway, and they'd chatted with Myles's mum, who was over from England and experiencing her first trip to the markets out at Inglenook Falls. And after a snatched lunch of hot dogs from the Swiss-chalet-style hut near the entrance, Cleo and Holly had gathered together everything they needed for their plan. Dylan was minding the market stall, Kaisha was in charge of the store, and so the girls had gone down Main Street, past the town green and all the way along to where the street met the top of the path that headed down to the log cabin.

'What if he's there?' Cleo trailed behind Holly as they made their way down the same path Holly had followed the day she'd fallen and hit her head. 'It's one thing making an effort to be friendly on the street, but I'm not sure how I'd be if he confronted me out here in the wilderness.'

Holly laughed. 'It's hardly the wilderness. It's less than five hundred metres to Main Street. And come on, we're together, be brave. And if he's there we'll need to be really quiet.' She wasn't about to admit she was a tiny bit frightened too. All they wanted to do was leave a small package for him, wrapped in brown paper and tied off with a green velvet bow. Their plan was to show, in little ways, that the community cared about him.

Snow covered the ground as they followed the left fork of the path between the trees, exactly as Holly had done before. The ground grew slippery underfoot, much worse in some patches that were a mixture of snow and ice. 'Hold on to the trees so you don't slip.'

'I can't believe you got me into this,' Cleo cursed.

'It wasn't only my idea,' Holly batted back. 'Come on, let's get there and hope he's out.'

They were in luck because there was no sign of the bearded owner when they reached the top of the slope that led right down to the clearing in front of the cabin.

'I can see his truck,' Cleo whispered. They watched from behind the copse of trees. 'But there's no movement in the cabin, outside or inside. I think we're good to go.'

'Okay, Nancy Drew,' Holly sniggered.

'Quiet, you. Come on, let's leave the parcel and get out of here. This place gives me the creeps.'

Holly turned to her friend. 'And it's attitudes like that that we're trying to avoid, remember?'

'Sorry, it's just... well, it does, doesn't it? It's so deserted, it's hard to believe the log cabin is anything more than an old shed.'

Holly thought about the inside of the place, the feel of the comforter soft against her skin, the smell of fresh linen on the blanket covering her when she woke, the smooth wooden squirrel on the nightstand with its bushy tail and look of mischief. She recalled the smell of soup served in a clean kitchen with its intricate, wood-carved clock and a handcrafted fruit bowl, the crackling and comforting warmth of the log burner, how he'd dried her scarf, left her boots to warm. The little log cabin was a home in the truest sense of the word.

Holding the parcel they'd put together especially for Mitch, Holly gingerly took the slope down, crossed the clearing, took the two steps up to the porch, and left it to one side of the front door. Was this a crazy risk? A silly thing to do? This man was a virtual stranger, an unhinged individual according to many, someone who was harbouring a lot of resentment, and he might not take too kindly to anyone appearing on his land again.

'I still don't like this one bit, let's get out of here,' Cleo urged. She'd been happy to go ahead with this plan, saying it was time he integrated back into the community, but Holly guessed things were different when you felt threatened. 'The snow is coming down.' Cleo looked to the sky as they walked across the clearing covered in white.

'Did you see the kids building snowmen up on the town green?'

'I did. There's a whole village of snowmen up there.' Cleo was still walking away.

'Why don't we build one?'

'I'm a little busy.' But Cleo turned when she realised Holly wasn't right behind her.

'Here, I mean.'

'Are you serious?' Cleo, hands on hips, looked around frantically for any sign of Mitch. 'I'm not sure that's a good idea.'

But Holly was already bending down gathering snow between her gloved palms. She made a small but solid snowball, then placed it onto the ground and began to roll, covering a length out front and then turning back to pick up the snow in the opposite direction. The snowball quickly quadrupled in size. 'This might put a smile on his face,' she declared, sniffing as her nose ran with the cold, and she stood up for a breather before bending over to get back to it. 'When have you ever known a snowman to upset someone?'

'I guess you have a point.' Cleo relented and took charge of the second ball they'd need.

When Holly's snowball was mid-thigh she moved it so it was facing the cabin and the snowman would be looking up the steps, and when Cleo's snowball looked about the right size, between them they hoisted it up and set it on top of the other one. They packed more snow between the two shapes, patting it down firmly to hold it together.

'We don't have a carrot,' Cleo puffed, flipping her scarf back across her shoulder when it fell down. 'Or sticks for arms.'

Holly went back to where the trees met the path and uncovered some thin twigs from beneath the snow. 'Use these for arms. I'll snoop around, see what I can find for eyes.'

'Holly, be careful.' Cleo's voice rose in panic. 'What if he comes back?'

'Relax, I'll be fine.' She found an offcut of log behind one of the sheds that would do for an oddly shaped nose.

When their work was finished they stood back. 'That's the ugliest looking snowman I've ever seen,' said Cleo. 'He looks like Pinocchio.'

'He does not.' Holly pulled out a bag of almonds she remembered she'd bought from the convenience store to snack on. 'These will do for eyes and a few for the mouth.' She pushed them into the appropriate places.

'Right, now can we get back to the markets?' Cleo pleaded.

Time to put her out of her misery. 'Goodbye, Mr Snowman,' Holly smiled.

'Grandpa Joe said he'd drop off a box of mince pies,' Cleo called over her shoulder as she walked away. 'How about we warm a couple?'

'An English Christmas tradition, yes please.' Holly followed on and as they left the cabin, she hoped Mitch's reaction to what they'd done would be a good one.

16

MITCH

He circled the snowman like it was about to come to life. He'd seen enough of them built in gardens as he drove through towns in Connecticut, or here on the town green in Inglenook Falls, but it was having a snowman built in this very spot that knocked him sideways. Because the last time he'd done that had been with Albie and they'd made a family of three – Mitch, Shannon, and Albie doppelgangers they liked to think, although they of course looked nothing like them. It was the family unit they represented that had tugged at Mitch's heartstrings every time, but in the same way that the snow had melted and disappeared come spring, Mitch's family had fallen apart.

Mitch ran a hand through his beard as he sat on the porch step but his hand didn't get very far, the hair was so matted. It often got food stuck in it, which was revolting even by his own admission, and if Albie was here now he'd probably be too frightened to come within a hundred feet of his dad.

He didn't have time to think much more because he had company and he stood up at the sound of another truck that had come down the same track he used and parked up behind his.

'This is private land!' he yelled. 'Great,' he added under his breath when Pierre emerged from the passenger side, his hand raised in a peculiar gesture of peace. But it wasn't the man himself who made Mitch lay off, it was the look on his face, like riding in a lowly truck rather than his sleek Mercedes had been torture enough. The man looked like he'd suffered the worst experience and it cheered Mitch up no end.

'Been making snowmen I see.' Pierre's smirk when he regarded the snowman out front of the cabin did little to make Mitch warm to him.

'As I said, this is private land.'

'Didn't want to chance coming down the path on foot, didn't want to break my neck.'

Mitch did his best not to smile at the thought. 'What's with the truck?' He could see it was Lionel in the driver's seat.

'Thought my car would get stuck.'

Mitch would have to put a gate at the top of the track to stop this happening again. Up until now, he'd been enough of a deterrent to keep people away. He could keep it locked until he wanted people to come and select their own trees, if that plan ever got off the ground. Jude had suggested having a stall at the Inglenook Falls Christmas markets next year too, and Mitch had surprised him by not completely dismissing the idea.

'What can I do for you?' Mitch was anxious to move the men on.

'I have a proposition. Can we talk?'

Mitch pushed his hands into his jacket pockets. 'We are, aren't we?' He knew full well Pierre was waiting for an invite inside in the warm. But he didn't want the man in his home.

Pierre sniffed and pulled his coat tighter around himself. 'I have a financial offer for you.'

'More trees?'

'Not exactly. It's about your land.'

'What about it?'

'I'm looking to add leisure facilities to the hotel. It's on a good parcel of land with generous grounds, but I need more.'

Men like him always did. Mitch had already heard rumours of the golf course but had hoped the hotel would be using land to the opposite side of it.

'I'd like to make an offer for eighty acres of your land.'

'That's the entire lot. Including the cabin.' He shook his head. 'You've got to be kidding.' He should've added a few expletives in there somewhere. Instead he walked away.

'Hear me out,' Pierre called after him.

'It's not for sale!' Mitch shouted over his shoulder before he reached the porch. For one thing, it was his home. It was where he felt safe, where Albie would remember if he ever came looking for him. And, secondly, it was his source of income. A one-off sum would never make up for it.

Mitch had almost reached the cabin when he heard, 'Four million dollars.'

His jaw almost hit the step up to the porch. He turned back. 'You serious?'

Pierre stepped towards him, his shiny black shoes submerged in the snow as well as the bottom of his trousers, his dark coat tails gradually getting a good dusting from up above as the snow persisted. 'I'm deadly serious. I've already bought a hundred acres adjacent to the boundary of your land, but I want this land too, it'll give flexibility for the hotel development. And I'm willing to pay handsomely for it. Here's my proposal.' He handed Mitch a letter, one of those chunky envelopes you knew contained a lot of information. 'Think about it, you know where I am.' And with that he turned and went back to the truck.

Four million dollars. It was an amount that could set him up for life. He could buy another parcel of land where nobody else knew him, start over. He could pay the PI to find Albie, show Albie he was together now, he was on top of things, prove to Shannon he was worthy of knowing his son. He could give his brother half of that money, his fair share of his inheritance, maybe even begin to form a bond with him again.

When Pierre and Lionel drove away, Mitch took the steps up to the cabin and reached down for a package lying to one side of the door. He must've missed it when he came out earlier. Wrapped in plain brown paper, it was tied off with a neat, green bow. He took it inside along with the envelope containing Pierre's phenomenal offer that had come out of nowhere and, once his gloves were off, opened it to find a box containing items wrapped in red tissue paper. As he unveiled them he found a brand-new, packaged razor with three blades, a can of shaving foam, a packet of Oreo cookies, two pairs of thick woollen walking socks, and a bottle of his favourite Budweiser beer.

When there was a knock at the door he peered out of the window to check it wasn't Pierre, back for round two already. But it was only Jude.

Mitch pointed to the snowman. 'Is that your handiwork?'

'I'm as surprised as you are to see it. Kids messing about I'd say.'

'You're the only kid who dares to come within a mile radius of here.'

'True fact.'

'Come inside.' He stood back and after closing the door asked, 'Do you know anything about this?' He gestured to the opened parcel and the items he'd unwrapped on the side table.

Jude looked at each of them and smiled. 'No, but take the hint, man, you've got last week's dinner in that thing.' He pointed to Mitch's beard.

'Quit goofing around, there's nothing there.' He knew because he'd seen his reflection in the bathroom mirror earlier and hadn't eaten since. He regarded the package contents again. 'So this isn't from you?'

Jude shook his head. 'Wasn't me. Maybe Santa came early.'

'Very funny.'

Jude picked up the blue packet. 'Oreo cookies? Nice touch.'

'Help yourself.'

He didn't need asking twice. Mitch wondered if he ate as much as he should for a growing teenage boy. 'I'll make you some soup if you like.'

'Can't stop, I only came to ask you a favour.' He pulled something from the inside of his coat, a winter coat so thick it had concealed a tube. He opened the end and took out a picture.

Mitch looked at the old-fashioned black-and-white print of a town and realised it was Inglenook Falls. 'Where did you get this?' The shop frontages had evolved, but the café was in the same position as it was now, the grass in front of the bandstand had a couple of kids kicking a ball around, on the sidewalk was a man with shirt-sleeves rolled up, walking alongside a woman in a floaty summer dress pushing one of those old-fashioned, Silver Cross prams with the huge spoked wheels, white engraved body, and dark-hooded canopy. There weren't the cars that populated Main Street nowa-days, but Inglenook Falls looked like essentially it hadn't changed much.

'I found it in Gran's cupboard. She's had it years but the frame broke and she never got around to getting a new one. She would've been a little girl when the town looked like that. I wondered if you'd put a frame on it for me?' When Mitch looked at him he said, 'Yes, I know you make them, I have eyes.'

Mitch had kept that quiet, along with plenty else he did in his spare time. 'There's not much that gets by you.'

'Apart from what's in that second shed out there.'

Mitch roared with laughter. 'You're not going to let that go are you?'

'Never.'

'I'll frame this for you. Is it a Christmas gift?' When Jude nodded he told him, 'I'll have it ready in a couple of days.' How hard was that? Not at all. He could've done the same for Holly when she'd asked, but he'd been stubborn as anything. Instead he'd pushed her away and had regretted it ever since.

* * *

As promised, Mitch had the picture framed for Jude a few days later and the boy came to the cabin to pick it up. Mitch still had no idea who was responsible for the snowman or the parcel. His cynical side said it was someone taunting him, his glass-half-full side said perhaps it was simply a kind gesture. Either way, the snowman was still standing, he'd drunk the beer, and Jude had happily polished off the rest of the cookies.

'Gran's gonna love it.' Jude was pretty happy with the result.

'Let me know if you want me to put it on the wall for her, I'll come over any time.'

'I'll hold you to that. I'll let you know after Christmas, when she tells me where she'd like to hang it. I mean, I can handle a drill. But maybe I'll need your help to get it straight.'

Mitch kept a straight face. 'Of course.'

With somewhere to go tonight, Mitch checked his watch so time didn't get away with him and make him late. 'Come to think of it, why aren't you in school? Bit early to finish, isn't it?' When Jude looked at the floor Mitch added, 'You did go today, didn't you?'

Jude shrugged.

'Buddy, what's this about?'

'Got told off, didn't I?'

'What for?'

'Dunno.' Suddenly the floor beneath him was very interesting.

'Yes you do, out with it.'

'I got hauled into the principal's office and told off about my appearance. Too scruffy, holes in my jumper, trousers are at half mast and my shirt has a tear.'

'I feel for you. I'd never get through school looking like this.' Mitch tried to make the boy laugh but it didn't work this time. And so he went to the kitchen, opened a drawer, and pulled out his wallet.

'What?' Jude saw what he was doing. 'No way.'

'Call it a loan.' Mitch handed him a hundred bucks. 'Should cover some new gear. You can work it off, starting with another haul of trees tomorrow. *After* school,' he added in case there was any doubt. 'Check with the council who run the Inglenook markets and maybe flog a few out front there.'

He took it reluctantly. 'Thank you.' He shook Mitch's hand, the proper young businessman, and, Mitch suspected, embarrassed at revealing his plight. But Mitch didn't miss the threadbare sleeves beneath his coat either. His jumper needed replacing, but Mitch knew he'd use the cash for his gran or for food, not for himself. So the second he left, Mitch did something he thought he'd never do again. He went Christmas shopping.

* * *

Okay, so it wasn't exactly a shopping expedition. It was only the local knitting store. And the owner, Cleo, seemed harmless enough. Although when he went inside he could tell she was making the effort to not look frightened.

'Hello, Mitch.'

He might've guessed she knew his name despite them never

having met. He'd been the subject of town gossip long enough. 'Afternoon,' he managed before turning to flip through the small rail at the front of the store. Thankful for a lack of other customers – although he suspected Cleo didn't feel the same way – Mitch took out each sweater in turn to assess its suitability for a teenage boy. The first was cream: definitely not, it wouldn't last five minutes before Jude spilt Coke or sauce down the front. The second was pale blue, or baby blue in Mitch's eyes, and the boy wouldn't touch it, he was sure. Maybe he'd do better to ask for something to be knitted. He'd seen the sign in the window that said garments could be made to order.

'Can I help you?' Cleo had braved coming much closer.

He kept his eyes on the sweaters. 'It's for my friend, Jude.'

'I know him. He's a sweet boy.'

'He is.'

She shook her head when he pulled out a red sweater with a white trim. 'Right size, totally wrong colour; although you seem close so Jude would probably wear it without a fuss.'

He gave a wry smile. 'I expect you're right. But I couldn't put him through that.'

She relaxed a little. 'We don't have much in, I'm afraid. A lot of our sweaters are over at the market stall. Let me see what I have out the back. Kaisha, my assistant, was teaching a workshop last night and I'm pretty sure she was knitting a sweater as demonstration.' She disappeared for a moment.

Mitch was tempted to do a runner but he'd come this far. He could sweat it out a few more minutes.

'What do you think to this?' She came back with a peculiar-looking, navy thing.

'It doesn't have sleeves.'

'It will have, it's not finished. But I know this was going to go in the store front for sale and we could have it done in a couple of days. I think it would really suit your friend. Navy-blue brick stitch with a crew neck is trendy right now – and if he really doesn't like it, you can return it.'

Mitch asked the cost and when she quoted he agreed he'd pick it up in a couple of days.

'Any plans for Christmas?' She looked awkward, perhaps realising her faux pas, her typical customer-friendly conversation piece that wouldn't work with him.

'I'm heading out of town.' No extra explanation was needed. Jude had invited him to spend the day with him and his gran, but Mitch had declined in favour of getting away. He was going hiking. Anything to avoid the whole jolly holiday season that only reminded him of all that he'd lost.

'You can pay on collection,' she said when he took out his wallet.

'I'd rather pay now.' That way all he had to do was come in here and pick it up, without engaging in unnecessary small talk.

She took the notes he handed her and gave him back his change. 'You can collect it Tuesday, it'll be ready by then.' Before he could escape she said, 'Nessa is really pleased with the tree at the library, said it's the most beautiful one they've ever had.'

He managed half a smile. 'Glad to be of service.'

'I wondered, do you sell offcuts of your trees?'

'Offcuts?'

'You know, scraps. I want to make a few holiday wreaths this year, so would need a good supply of spruce. I'll add holly, winter berries, you know the sort of thing.'

Actually, he did. Shannon had always had a holiday wreath on the front door to their home, but since she and Albie left and his father passed away he hadn't bothered again.

'I'm happy to pay you,' she added. 'I wasn't asking for a handout.

I'd need, say, one garbage bag full of spruce. How much could I pick that up for?'

'It'll cost you nothing. I'll bring it by on Tuesday.' He turned to leave.

'I insist on paying. How much, Mitch?'

She probably assumed, because he looked so terrible and lived in a cabin, that he had a hard time making ends meet. He wanted to laugh. Pierre had offered him a ridiculous amount of money and he was still trying to get his head around what it could mean. Four million dollars would cover the cost to find Albie. It would pay for a house and land somewhere far, far away from here once his son was back in his life. With four million dollars he'd never have to fell another tree again – or freeze his ass and fingers off trying to fix a clogged irrigation system as he'd done last month. With four million dollars he wouldn't have to haul trees from town to town. With four million dollars he wouldn't buy Jude a sweater for Christmas, he'd buy him his first car, pay for a full-time carer for his gran.

'And I insist it's free.' He nodded firmly to make his point and she put away the change purse she'd picked up. At last he could get away.

Not so fast. The bell above the door tinkled and in came a man with a kid in a stroller, another baby strapped to his chest and two older children, one of whom looked to be around Albie's age now, perhaps a little younger. Mitch went to step past them but the man and his tribe were blocking the door. He waited but the man held out a hand.

'Mitch, isn't it?' The guy waited for Mitch to meet his handshake. 'It's good to meet you, I'm Dylan.'

The girl at his side headed for the counter and the safety of her mum. He certainly had an effect on women, and not the right one.

'Nessa at the library loves her tree,' said Dylan before Mitch could escape.

'Your wife already told me.' What was this, engage-the-local-freak-in-conversation day?

'We're not married,' Cleo smiled at him, her arm draped around the little girl's shoulders. 'But we will be soon – Dylan proposed at the party the other night.'

'Congratulations... and, uh, thank you for inviting me. I'll see you Tuesday.' He was doing his best to leave.

'About those trees...' Dylan stood in the doorway. 'When I found out you supplied that beauty to the hotel and the tree to the library, I looked at your website. You know, with a revamp you could bring in a lot more business.' Four million dollars' worth? Mitch doubted it. 'Here's my card.' Dylan pulled it from his jeans pocket and handed it to Mitch. The older two kids still seemed wary despite their parents' ease with him, the younger child in the stroller was cuddling a teddy bear against her face and looked like she was five minutes away from a long snooze, and the baby in the carrier strapped to Dylan's chest was oblivious. 'No pressure, but if you'd like some help, let me know.'

Mitch had been meaning to sort his website, but it was one of those things that moved further and further down the list. He nodded to Cleo, then Dylan, but before he could escape, the boy who must be about Albie's age asked a question.

'Does Santa come to your cabin in the woods?'

He could answer it with a gruff 'What do you think?' or an impolite grunt and walk off, but these people were being nice rather than assuming he was about to rob the store – he'd had that reaction in many a place before today.

'Santa goes to every house. I have a chimney.' The explanation would hopefully suffice.

'But you don't have any children. Why would he visit the cabin?'

Cleo's eyes widened and she mouthed the words 'I'm sorry' in his direction but he looked the boy in the eye and said, 'I think

Santa goes everywhere, he cares about everyone.' He remembered Albie's tricky questions from an early age, how it was difficult to answer most of them and sometimes when you did you dug yourself an even deeper hole.

'But you're old.'

At this Cleo and Dylan reprimanded the boy gently but Mitch laughed. 'I'm not that old, but you're right, I'm not a kid any more.' He suspected he looked twenty years older than he actually was with this beard. If it was grey he could probably pose as a realistic Santa.

'So why does Santa come to your cabin?' The boy sat down on the floor of the store cross-legged as though this were part of story time and Mitch found himself crouching down onto his haunches to address him.

'I think he likes to check whether my son has come home.' Albie, the boy who always left Santa three oatmeal and raisin cookies, a tall glass of milk, and a bag of carrots so no reindeer missed out. The four-million-dollar price tag for what had been his life was pressed down on Mitch's shoulders forcing him to see the need to change, which started here, by acknowledging his part in this community and talking to these people.

'You have a son? How old?' The boy was in this for the long haul.

'He'd be eight now. He lives with his mom.'

'When does he visit?'

'He hasn't, not for a very long time.'

'What's his name?'

'His name is Albie, short for Albert, after my dad.'

'That's cool. I'm Jacob, that's Ruby, she's Tabitha,' he said pointing to the kid in the stroller, 'and my youngest sister is called Emily. Dad says our house is overrun with girls. Sometimes I'd like a brother. If Albie visits, I could hang out with him.'

'I'm sure he'd like that.' Mitch pushed himself to standing, overwhelmed at the frank exchange. 'Good to meet you folks,' he said to the room and this time Dylan moved to the side, out of the way.

Mitch pulled open the door and met with the cold, completely at odds with the cosiness of the Little Knitting Box. He turned to Cleo, who'd scooped the baby from the carrier into her arms. 'I don't suppose you know anything about a snowman and a parcel, do you?'

When she said nothing and her cheeks coloured, he had his answer.

And rather than resent the interference, he began to think that this town may not be so bad after all.

* * *

Darkness blanketed Inglenook Falls and, back in his cabin, Mitch headed up to the shower. He stood beneath the jets letting the warm water cascade over his body.

Sometimes reminders of Albie floored him; he fell apart, he didn't surface for days. But, instead, Jacob's curiosity earlier about the boy who'd once been a big part of Mitch's life had given him a sense of inner peace. A sense that he could still relate to his son, he knew things about him that could never be forgotten – the way he'd always liked his bedroom door to be left with the tiniest part open at night so he could get light from anywhere else in the house, the way Albie hated baked beans touching his toast when it was served and how Mitch had to fashion a dam of sausages in the middle of his plate to prevent liquid seeping towards the bread. Mitch could still remember snipping the tiniest of fingernails when Albie was a baby, how he'd scream as though you were cutting his skin rather than a part of him without nerve endings, and the way his hair smelled after a bath as he lay against Mitch's chest and drifted off to sleep.

Those were the memories that kept Mitch going, and seeing that family today made him realise how important it was for him to become a real part of the world again.

He washed the day away, preparing for an evening different from the usual sitting in front of the log burner or kicking back on the front porch with a beer if the weather allowed. Thoughts of Pierre's crazy offer churned around in his head. When he'd first started dating Shannon, they'd watched one of her mum's favourite movies. He couldn't remember what it was called now but the man had been offered a million dollars for some very handsome actor to have a night with his wife. The couple had desperately needed the money and so agreed. But the money had brought turmoil, pain, not the happiness they'd envisaged.

He could do so much with four million dollars if he were to sign on the dotted line. If he found Albie, this could be the start his son needed. Money to put him through college, take him on fancy vacations; his son would never want for anything. But Mitch couldn't let go of the facts. This was his home and he loved it more each day. He had memories here, he loved his work with the Christmas trees, he was selling wooden frames so regularly it contributed to his income and he had another passion that recently had started to take hold in a way he'd never predicted. Hidden away in the second shed was the solace he'd found in the darkest days and was very much connected with the way he lived his life out here. It had helped him to find meaning when everything around him seemed impossible to make sense of.

He finished up in the shower, dressed, and grabbed the keys to his truck. He had somewhere he had to be, but not yet. First, he needed to go see Pierre about his offer.

Driving slowly on account of the snow that meant his snowman was still standing outside the cabin, he pulled up at the hotel twenty minutes later. Last time he'd been here he'd brought those trees dotted along the front now, dusted with snow and glistening proudly with their twinkle lights as though all was right with the world. He crossed the parking lot, the woman at reception hurried off to get Pierre almost the second he stepped into the foyer and made his request, and with his unkempt hair and the beard, all the parts that kept him hidden from the real world, Mitch stood next to the tall tree that had once been a part of his land until it was taken away. And now the tree could be witness to what he was about to do.

Pierre appeared on the polished floor in a sharp suit and collars and cuffs that wouldn't dare be out of place. 'Mitch... good to see you.' He glanced at his rather expensive-looking watch. 'You just caught me, I was about to leave for a meeting in the city.'

The man was no doubt being friendly because he thought Mitch had come with signed documents. Instead of returning the handshake Mitch thrust forward the documents in their original envelope and came straight to the point. 'Thank you for the offer, but it's a no.'

'It's a what?'

'I'm saying no. I don't want to sell my cabin or my land. Not to you, not to anyone.'

Pierre cleared his throat and lowered his voice. 'Mitch, think about this. It's four million. It's the best offer you'll ever get.'

'No thank you,' he added again, firmly. 'It's not for sale.' The way Pierre's jaw twitched in annoyance was all the reassurance Mitch needed that this was the right thing to do. He'd lost control of his own life, but working the land and living in the cabin gave him a little bit of that back. And he'd still be able to raise money for the PI if that was the route he chose, rather than waving money around here, there and everywhere with no real thought about what it meant, what it could do. For once, he had all the power, and it felt good.

'You'll regret it.' Pierre staunchly delivered his opinion much like a child used to getting his own way.

Mitch said nothing, raised his hand in farewell without turning around, pushed open the front glass doors and left the warmth for the freezing cold without looking back.

17

HOLLY

Sitting opposite Pierre in a quaint bistro nestled in the West Village, Holly felt her spirits lift. She'd had two rejections this morning, both from major periodicals. But she figured this was all part of freelancing and so when her boyfriend had called following his business meeting in the Financial District, she'd been very happy to meet him before she went along to the art gallery to cover the exhibition.

'How's the pizza?' Pierre had gone for a panini with its filling neatly tucked inside.

Holly looped a piece of mozzarella up onto the crust. 'Really good.' She bit into the chicken and bell-pepper topped pizza as they sat beneath holiday decorations strung from the ceiling on one side of the bistro to the other. When Pierre had come in he'd had to duck so he didn't end up with lights, foliage, or baubles in his hair.

'I'd have rather taken you to Malaparte. They do the best spaghetti.'

'Here's fine,' Holly smiled and went in for another mouthful. 'And I can't be too long as I need to get to the gallery.'

'Kind of sucks working evenings, doesn't it?' he asked when he saw her stifle a yawn. 'You could've come to a cocktail party at The Plaza with me tonight, worn that sexy party dress, the one with the low back.'

'Work comes first.' He should know that. But she smiled, remembering what had happened with Pierre the last time she'd worn that particular outfit. They'd been to a work function for her that night, the reason she'd bought the dress, but it hadn't stayed on very long after the party.

'Talking of your work, Lucy contacted me yesterday.' He finished his last mouthful of panini. 'She asked about your availability.'

'She knows I'm freelance, would she like me to work on something for her?'

'She would, but she's also hoping you'll consider coming to work for the company full time.'

'We've talked about this. I want the freedom of freelancing, I enjoy it, especially the photography and choosing what I work on.'

'But this role is career-changing. You'd progress quickly, the salary is amazing.'

She stiffened. 'I'm not bringing in a huge amount of money right now, but I'm doing fine. I'm starting from scratch with this, Pierre. It would be nice to have your support.'

He reached out and took her hands in his. 'And you have it, which is why I'd encourage you to at least talk to Lucy. See what she's offering. The decision will always be yours, I just don't want you to ignore a possibility. It's a change to the work you were doing with the magazine, but with more security than you have now.'

'Pierre...'

'Think about it.'

'I've only been freelancing a couple of weeks.'

'And you're exhausted.'

'I yawned a couple of times,' she laughed. 'And it's coming up for Christmas, it's always a busy time.'

'You'd be paid for holidays with the company, remember. They give generous annual leave – we could go away somewhere exotic, really relax.'

'We can still do that.' She squeezed his hands. 'But I've done so much in a couple of weeks, imagine what I can do in a few months, years even. If Lucy wants me to do some freelancing I'll jump at the chance, but anything else... I'm not interested.'

'It seems that no is the order of the day.' He took his hands away and leaned back in his chair.

'What's that supposed to mean?'

'The owner of the land I had earmarked for the golf course said no too. Damn fool.'

Mitch said no? Good for him! It took a lot to stand up to Pierre because the man was persuasive, went after what he wanted, and no doubt would've offered a hefty compensation.

'Maybe the hotel doesn't need a golf course,' she suggested.

'Are you kidding? It'll be a great addition. Not to mention the jobs it'll bring to the area. There'll be landscaping, forestry operations, horticulture, maintaining walkways, and then all the additional facilities that'll go with the club aspect of the course. It's not going to impact the view from the towns nearby, Inglenook Falls will look exactly the same, and locals are in support of this.'

'I kind of got that impression at the opening,' she admitted, 'and again at the party at the Little Knitting Box. Even Cleo's grandpa said he was thinking of joining up, something to keep him moving in his old age.'

'There you go.' He braved taking her hands again. 'It's a positive move for the area. We need that land.'

'But he said no.' And it was his home, where she'd trespassed, twice. Cleo had texted earlier to say that Mitch was onto them.

Apparently he'd been into the Little Knitting Box to buy a gift for the boy who worked for him, and Cleo had been flustered when he asked whether she knew anything about a snowman and a parcel. But between them Holly and Cleo had decided that, firstly, he hadn't stomped into the store and yelled at Cleo, which was a good sign, and that, secondly, he'd gone out of the cabin and interacted with locals. Maybe their plan was actually working.

'Like I said, he's a fool. I offered him a great deal of money.'

'I guess money doesn't always buy happiness.'

Pierre harrumphed. 'This guy definitely doesn't look happy. And if he is, I'd hate to see him when he's down.'

Holly was hoping the next time she saw Mitch he'd be a lot happier. And saying no to Pierre? Well, that could only be a good sign.

* * *

Holly made her way straight to the gallery from the bistro, her big coat and scarf keeping her warm over a part-sheer, laced, inky-blue and white top with a scalloped hem, her favourite Abercrombie & Fitch jeans, and a pair of knee-high, suede boots. And the second she arrived at the door, Nikita hurried over to let her in.

'I'm so nervous.' Nikita was in a flap already. 'I'm always apprehensive when it's a new artist, I want this to go well for them and me.' She looked set for a good show with glasses lined up, bottles of wine, trays of canapes laid out on a central white high-gloss table.

Holly shoved her gloves in her pocket and took off her coat. 'It's going to be wonderful, and the article I have published will help get both your names out there. And you look gorgeous tonight.' The belted, ruched, pale-blue dress with detailing on the sleeves came to a little above her knees and was tied flatteringly at the waist.

'Enjoy every moment, and I'll be sure to get some wonderful photographs.'

While Nikita hung up her coat, Holly took out her camera and stowed the bag out back. She hung the camera around her neck and clicked away to grab some formal shots of the paintings in the exhibition by Campbell Baldwin. His work was on display in the same area but lighting had been changed subtly to throw the focus towards the artist coming here tonight. When people gathered and milled around discussing the artwork she'd change her shutter speed to create motion blur thus giving the impression of busyness and interest surrounding the artist.

Nikita opened the doors at 7.30 p.m. sharp and half a dozen people filed in. The gallery owner turned her attention to looking after guests, offered canapes, drinks, creating an easy-going atmosphere. People were relaxed and by the time they went over to the paintings, they would linger, talk freely, enjoy tonight. Holly hung back and observed, listened in on snippets of conversation. She heard an elderly couple debating why the artist painted mono-chrome scenes but added a small splash of colour to each. Their faces were so animated, Holly wondered had they a passion for art, did they collect it at home?

She captured a couple of pictures of Nikita offering round nibbles, pointing to paintings, and chatting with her guests before her attention was needed at the front door when the artist arrived. Holly would let him settle in first then get some good quotes when she could have his attention to discuss at least one of his paintings in depth. Through the thick crowd she could just about see the top of his head. He was facing away from her. He had distinguishing dark hair, cropped neatly at the base of his neck where it met the collar of his shirt. As he turned she could make out his profile, the smooth-shaven jaw, the strong shoulders in a deep-red and black plaid shirt, and when the crowds parted her eyes fell to his rear, which looked far too good in a pair of well-fitting jeans. As an artist, maybe he stood up to paint, because from where Holly was standing it didn't look as though he spent much time sitting on that butt.

She giggled to herself, especially when she realised she wasn't the only one admiring more than this artist's paintings. She moved to another work of his. This one was called *Ragged*. On the canvas was a mountainous landscape with water trickling through a creek left of centre. A splash of colour had been added in the bottom-right-hand corner and, peering closer, she could see it was some kind of bird perched on one of the cliff faces. She was about to move on when she sensed someone behind her.

A subtle waft of a clean, fresh, and very masculine aftershave drifted gently her way. 'You like it?' the deep voice asked.

Actually, she really did. As she'd told people long before now, she liked art that looked like art. The piece was brooding, melancholy, and could do with a little more colour, but she started with a simple question. 'Can I ask, why the name *Ragged*?'

'Ragged Mountain. Hiked there once.' The deep voice came closer.

Holly almost turned but her focus was still on the painting. 'Why the splash of colour, with the bird? I mean, the entire piece is black and white, why add a tiny bit of something else?'

'Everyone needs a bit of colour in their life, Holly.'

She drew in her breath, because in an instant, she knew who he was. And when she turned and the man smiled back at her she saw colour in the depths of his eyes, something beyond the pain that had been there before.

18

MITCH

Her face was a picture, far more powerful than anything else in this gallery. He hovered by her right shoulder, so close he could smell her sweet perfume mingling with the aftershave he'd found in his closet. He'd dabbed it on hoping it still smelled as good as it should.

'Thanks for the razor, by the way.' He kept his gaze on the painting, as did she. 'I used all three blades – took a while, but it's all gone.'

She briefly turned around once more to take in the change and her gaze roamed his face before flicking to the little red scratch below his bottom lip where he'd tried to perfect the finish and gone one step too far. She turned back to the painting again. 'We wanted to help.'

'It sure seems that way.'

Nikita swooped in. 'Holly, I see you've met the artist. Campbell, this is Holly, she's the journalist covering tonight's exhibition for *Contemporary Edge* magazine. You both look like you're already working well together. Campbell, can I get you a champagne, a beer?'

'No, thank you. I'm driving, but Holly here looks like she could use something.' He couldn't resist. She was squirming and he didn't want her to. If it wasn't for her, he may never have been brave enough to step out of his comfort zone. Last month when Nikita had suggested an exhibition at which he was present, he'd resolutely refused. Then he'd agreed because she kept harping on about how it could generate not only a lot of sales but possibly some commissions. He'd planned to cancel, send an apologetic email on the night along with an artist's statement that would tell everyone everything they needed to know. But Holly coming into his life had ignited something in him, made him willing to try or not give up, he wasn't sure which of the two it was. Did she even realise the effect she'd had on him?

'Nice to meet you, Campbell.' Holly grinned when Nikita scooted off to get that champagne.

'I wanted to keep my anonymity, you know, if I hit the big time.'

She was still smiling. 'Does Nikita know your real name?'

'She sends cheques to MC Baldwin and never asked what the M stood for. Campbell is my middle name.'

'How did you get your pictures into the gallery?'

'I was selling my frames at a store and one of my paintings was inside it. The store owner knew Nikita, told her about me, and it all went from there I guess. I never thought I'd ever have an exhibition; I was painting for myself rather than anyone else.' Conversing was surprisingly easy when you'd come into a city where nobody knew who you were. Or maybe it was Holly, because she was somehow different from anyone else.

Nikita returned to give Holly her champagne and steal her artist away, and Mitch had to leave Holly to meet more guests. He got a little tongue-tied when the first gentleman asked him was he a family man and, if so, how did he get away to paint these beautiful outdoor spaces in the middle of nowhere? If this man had seen him a couple of hours earlier, with the beard that covered up most of his face, the scruffy clothes, the hair that was all over the place, he would've avoided him like the plague. After the hotel he'd gone back to the cabin, cut and then shaved off the beard and scrubbed himself up as best he could. He'd also made a slight change to the snowman in front of his cabin, before driving towards Manhattan. He'd stopped in a town along the way where he'd found a barber's, had his hair cut from shoulder length to the nape of his neck, over his ears and no longer than a couple of inches on the top section. He'd left the barber's and quickly understood the need for a woolly hat in these kinds of temperatures. Up until then his hair had kept out the cold more than he'd realised.

As Nikita brought him round more people he relaxed into conversation, surprised at how easy it became the more he did it. He talked to a young couple about how he'd used art as an escape – they hadn't asked for details. He talked with a retired couple from London, England, and sold them his painting of the Rattlesnake Mountains in Montana, which was on their bucket list before they grew too old. Listening to them talk about all the things they'd seen and done in the last couple of years showed Mitch how closed off to life he'd become, how he'd been existing rather than living. And that had to change. From now.

'I've spoken to more people tonight than I have in the last year,' he told Holly when Nikita took him her way. Seeing Holly tonight had been the biggest and best surprise of all. He could talk to her, perhaps because she'd once been so vulnerable in his care.

'And how does it feel?'

He let out a long sigh. 'Better than I thought it would.' The canapes had been eaten, the wine and champagne had gone, and he was spent.

'Tell me about this painting.' She was standing in front of a canvas he'd worked on three months ago, using an old photograph he'd taken during a lightning storm.

'I took the photograph a few weeks after my ex left with my son.' His jaw clenched and he almost forgot where he was for a moment. 'Forecasters were telling people not to venture out unless absolutely necessary, but I ignored them. I hadn't been out for weeks and I'd reached saturation point.' Getting outside had been necessary for his sanity.

Holly looked at him briefly but then turned her focus back to the art. 'It looks like the sky is short-circuiting, it's incredibly powerful. I once took a similar photo, everyone thought I was crazy.'

He smiled and sneaked a look at her, glad to find she was genuinely interested in the work and seemed comfortable around him. 'I disregarded all the warnings that day and took my camera out into the fields surrounding the cabin.'

'I was never much good at physics, but isn't it dangerous to be near trees during a thunderstorm?'

'It's very dangerous, not to mention stupid. Sheltering under a tree is crazy. Lightning strikes the tallest object and the strike travels down the tree to where you're standing. Open air is deadlier, and I braved both. But I wasn't thinking straight that day. I stalked out there as though I was invincible. I took photographs of the fields, the torrential rain, waited for thunder to rumble and let it shake my body awake. This canvas is painted from one of those photographs.'

'It's an amazing scene, really intense.'

They talked about the deeply bruised violet sky with clouds billowing behind and the lightning strike that had shot down to a single tree on an otherwise deserted landscape.

'You think I'm antisocial and hide away now, but I was far worse back when this was taken,' he admitted.

'Really?'

He allowed himself a small laugh at her surprise. 'I needed a close bolt of lightning and a clap of thunder to make me feel alive again. It awoke my senses. The unpredictability of a thunderstorm was how I felt in myself, like I didn't know what could happen in my life, didn't know what I was capable of.'

'I didn't see any sign of painting in your cabin,' she noted.

'You should've tried the shed.'

'Ah.' She absorbed his last statement. 'Can I ask you a question?'

'Go on.'

'In some of your black-and-white paintings, like this one here, you use a splash of colour that seems a little out of place. Why?' She'd tried this question before, but he hadn't really given her a proper answer.

Part of the escapism he enjoyed was that he could bring new meaning to his life through paintings and if he didn't want anyone to muscle in on that, he didn't have to let them. But this time he would. 'This is one of our fields that doesn't have Christmas trees in it, at least not yet.' He looked at the scene, the land blanketed in mist, the stream snaking through the grass that lay in clumps after its first mow of spring. 'That's the old hay barn,' he said of the wooden structure bathed in a soft glow as the sunshine had fought the mist that day and won, 'and the little dot of colour...' His voice caught.

'You don't have to tell me.'

He cleared his throat. 'I'm out of my comfort zone tonight, but I'd expected questions.' He gathered himself. 'The blue represents my son, Albie, and him coming back into my life. I paint tumultuous pictures like this, I can paint haunting and bland scenes, because my life has been a lot like that, so it's the way I've dealt with it. All my frustration and anger transfers onto the canvas. The first time I got the urge to add some colour, it was like Albie was there, pushing me on, daring me to be different, making me take a chance. And once I'd added it the first time, I started doing it all the more. It sounds crazy, but it's like there's a little bit of Albie carried in each of these paintings.'

'It's not crazy.' Her voice came out soft but she didn't say anything else because yet again he was whisked away to talk to some latecomers. And by the time he'd sold four of his paintings that evening, he was about ready to drop.

'Are you heading back to Inglenook Falls tonight?' Holly asked as she packed up her camera beside him. He'd already thanked Nikita for this exhibition and they'd discussed what he was working on now, when he could get the paintings to the gallery.

'I am, do you need a ride?' Another thing out of his comfort zone. He wasn't sure how ready his truck was for a woman to climb into it.

'No, my apartment is in Manhattan, not far from here actually.'

He nodded his head to her and moved to go. 'Goodnight, Holly.'

But she was quick, she was right behind him at the door. It reminded him of the time in Bryant Park when she'd done everything she could to make him talk. 'We got some good shots tonight, I could show you if you like.'

They stepped out onto one of the many tree-lined streets in Greenwich Village where the art gallery stood in the eclectic neighbourhood. 'I was there tonight, remember, and I painted the pictures myself.' He didn't need to see the photographs but he feared driving back to Inglenook Falls, reaching the sign to town, heading down to his cabin and it would be as though all of this had been an optical illusion and hadn't really happened at all.

'I guarantee you'll want to see these shots.' She took out her camera, tugged off her gloves. 'Seeing people's reactions to your paintings will be incredible for you.'

'You'll get frostbite if you don't put your gloves on,' he warned. It had dropped at least five degrees since he'd been in that gallery and even he wished he had another layer. Dressing smart didn't do much for keeping warm, especially when you'd also lost your facial hair and a large proportion of what had been on your head.

But she ignored him and not only did he admire her determination, but it turned out she was right. It was quite something to see people's faces as they studied his work, as they moved around the gallery eager and anxious to discover what this artist, him, was all about.

When he noticed her shiver and her fingertips turned pink he said, 'I think that'll have to do.'

She reluctantly put the camera away and pulled on her gloves. 'Maybe I could send you a copy of some of them. The article write-up won't be for a while, but I don't mind.'

He was about to do something risky. About to take a chance. 'Or we could find somewhere to eat and go over them there. I don't know about you, but the canapes were only tiny and I didn't like to shovel in too much when I was supposed to be working.'

A smile spread across her face. 'You're on. Where shall we go?'

'Hey, this is your neighbourhood, I follow you. But I'm parked in a garage near Washington Square Park, so not too far or you'll get me lost.'

* * *

They ended up in a café nestled amid the brownstones synonymous with Manhattan. Low lighting, a mishmash of tables, frantically busy yet you felt as though you could take a tiny slice of it for yourself when you sat down. The place had sent his nerves all over the place when they'd first arrived but Holly had a bizarrely calming influence on him and it wasn't long before he felt comfortable again.

'You have quite a talent,' he told her when she finished scrolling through the rest of the photographs, this time her fingers warming to the inside of the café, the open fire burning at one side as waiters buzzed about taking and delivering orders.

'Thank you.' She sipped from the Diet Coke she'd ordered after they were seated. 'It was a hobby at first but I'm starting to make it part of my job.'

'Working for yourself has so many perks, I don't think I could ever go back to what I did before.' Wow, he'd never actually said that out loud. It was kind of a given, probably an assumption that many made, most of them wildly unable to reconcile the image of Mitch as a top retail manager.

'What did you do before?'

He filled her in and as he enjoyed a root beer she, in turn, told him about her high-pressure job, the position that had brought her to Manhattan in the first place. 'I got to the point where I thought, where do I want to be in ten years' time? Would I be happy doing exactly the same? A couple of years ago I would've said yes, but not any more. I love writing, editing, being part of the media side, but I wasn't doing much else apart from work. My friend, Sarah, she was at the top of her game as a financial analyst, loved it, worked sixty hours a week, but she'd started to question whether there was more to life.' She smiled. 'I guess it was her who put the thought in my head and I did my best to ignore it for a while.'

'Did Sarah stop too, find something else like you've done?'

Her voice wavered. 'No, she didn't.'

'She's still working those hours?' He whistled through his teeth. But then he looked at Holly. 'She's not, is she?'

Holly shook her head and swiped away her tear. 'Oh, would you look at me?' She took the napkin he'd pulled from the dispenser and passed to her. 'I'm usually fine, but it's coming up to the anniversary of when she died.'

'What happened?'

'She had liver disease and her illness came out the blue, but with a transplant she had a new lease of life. She left the high-pressured job and found work with a small accounting firm and for a while everything was good. But then her body started to reject the liver. We planned to have Christmas in New York together, ice-skate in Central Park, go to the top of the Empire State Building on the coldest day, watch the lighting of the tree at the Rockefeller Center. I came to New York to visit her as well as check out whether I wanted to move with my job. I hadn't expected her to be quite so sick, nobody had. But by December she was going downhill fast. She was confused a lot of the time, sleeping so much. She passed away right before Christmas.' She swished a hand in front of her face, looked up to stop the tears. 'She was only my age.'

'Doesn't seem fair, does it?' And there was he, wasting his life until now. 'I've not lost friends but I've lost people I love and the grief doesn't go away, but you do learn to cope.' He started to laugh.

'What's so funny?'

'Me, telling you that you'll learn to cope. I've alienated an entire town, hidden away in a cabin, I grew a beard my dinner used to land in most nights, had hair worthy of Forrest Gump. Who am I to give advice?'

'Actually, you've got a good point there.' Her tears of sorrow were replaced by those of amusement. 'Sarah would've appreciated your humour.' Holly got the feeling Sarah would've been charmed by Mitch far more than Pierre.

The waiter came over and they ordered a plate of curly fries to share. 'Another Diet Coke for me, please,' Holly added when Mitch grabbed another root beer and asked what she'd like. 'So what are you going to do?' she began. 'My way forward is this new branch of work to get a better work–life balance. But what's your plan? Are you going to stay hidden away in that cabin of yours after tonight or is this the start of something more?'

Her words floated on the air along with the steam from the coffees carried past on a tray to the next table. 'I know I need to make a change, and you tumbling into my life that day, well, you instigated it.'

'Me?'

'Yes, you.' He met her gaze but it was broken when the waiter delivered the drinks and fries. 'Eat up,' he told her, unsure of how to continue the conversation, anxious to gather his thoughts. He hadn't been with another woman since Shannon left, he hadn't wanted to, hadn't thought himself capable. Yet here he was, opposite someone who was not only beautiful on the outside but all the way through to the inside too.

'Pierre told me about the offer to buy your land.' She blew across a curly fry, its golden crisp finish balancing between her fingers.

So the man did tell her some things. 'Did he say how much he offered?'

'No, but I can imagine it was quite a bit.'

He leaned forward so much he caught another waft of her scent, something he'd enjoyed at various moments this evening, first at the gallery when he'd stood behind her and taken her by surprise, then as she'd cornered him at the door, again as he'd opened the door to this place to let her go inside first. 'Four million.'

The curly fry hung in the air. 'Are you serious?'

'Yep.' He dipped a fry in the BBQ sauce, then bit it in two. Now and again he moved to check nothing had landed on his beard, totally forgetting the facial hair was already a thing of the past.

'I'm curious... why did you turn it down? That kind of money could buy you a house, you could start over.'

He dabbed the sides of his mouth with a napkin and was catapulted back to when he'd once done this on a regular basis, dining out with co-workers, business associates, the board of directors. And all for what? So they could give him the push? Nobody had

had his back apart from himself, and that hadn't counted for much because he'd fallen apart and lost his family.

'The log cabin is the only tie I have,' he told her.

'To your son?'

'My son, my parents, everyone. I never ever thought I'd live anywhere other than a palatial house with a neat garden, in a friendly neighbourhood where my kid could cycle, you know. When my father died, I'd already hit rock-bottom, I was already at the cabin. I loved that I felt closer to him when I was in those four walls, but gradually it became more than that. It became my anchor, what kept me from losing the plot completely. Your boyfriend could offer me three times the amount he did and my answer would still be the same. I love living there. I know I need to make some changes but losing the log cabin isn't one of them.'

They ate the rest of the fries without talking much, but Mitch hadn't missed the look of doubt on Holly's face at his use of the B word. Boyfriend. When they were done he ordered two coffees and waited until they came to the table before he carried on.

'I never did much with the Christmas tree business,' he admitted as he stirred a black coffee and set the teaspoon down. 'But I kept it ticking over when I came back to Inglenook Falls.'

'Back?'

Was this really all going to come out tonight? He blamed his shave, his haircut, and his foray into socialising, for what he was about to admit. 'I'd been in hospital for a while. A few months.'

'A bad accident?' she enquired.

'Not exactly. I was in Bampton Lake Lodge. You heard of it?' She shook her head. 'It's a residential treatment facility.' When her expression remained neutral he expanded his description to, 'They treat mental-health conditions.'

Her eyes met his. 'Why were you in there?'

He toyed with the idea of making a joke but he knew enough

about this woman to know she wouldn't appreciate anything but the truth, and anyway, a joke would only mask his shame, his embarrassment at having to reveal this part of him. 'When Shannon left with Albie, I fell apart. I crashed at the log cabin with Dad but he was on his own, trying to run the Christmas tree business without help from either son.' He took a deep breath. 'When Dad was diagnosed with cancer I picked myself up enough to help for a while but it didn't last long. I wouldn't get out of bed some days, I wasn't washing, shaving. I was disgusting. Dad's carer, Beryl, came to the cabin every day to help out and it was she who handed me a leaflet about Bampton Lake Lodge. "You need help" was all she said before she got back to the business of caring for my father. I knew I had to sort myself out before it was too late. My father funded it, for which I felt terrible, but he'd pleaded with me to let him and I did because I couldn't ruin his last days on this earth. He deserved to go in peace, knowing his son was doing okay.'

'That takes a tremendous strength, Mitch. Not everyone would be able to do it.'

'I can't believe I'm telling you all this.' He sat back to get some distance but found he didn't really want it.

'Sometimes it's easier to tell a stranger our deepest thoughts.'

'You're not a stranger.'

'What was it like?' Her eyes never left his.

He took a deep breath. 'I admitted myself to the lodge and they were able to closely monitor me, prescribe medication, and slowly I got better. Beryl would bring Dad most days and after a couple of months I went back to Inglenook Falls to take care of him alongside her. We even had some laughs. That man loved cribbage, hated losing too.'

'It sounds as though you made his last days his best.'

'I wish I'd sorted myself out sooner, then Albie would've been in his life. He loved that boy almost as much as I did. They'd sit together for hours out on the porch talking about the Christmas trees, how they grew, how they got their shape. Dad made the best pot roast known to man and Albie couldn't get enough of it, he'd always help in the kitchen. They'd cook other things together – Christmas cookies with fancy designs on top, and these funny little Santa-like strawberries with cream filling and decoration. Both of them filled the cabin with joy and laughter and I miss it so much it hurts.'

'I think your father would be proud of you for keeping the Christmas tree farm going.'

'I hope so.' This conversation was too miserable, dragging down the good mood he'd had all night. 'Running the Christmas tree farm was how I met Jude.' A warmth settled through him at the thought of his unlikely friend. He'd collected the sweater for Jude from the Little Knitting Box yesterday as well as dropping off the bag of offcuts for Cleo.

'Tell me about him.'

Mitch told her all about how they'd met, how they'd formed a bond, the strength he'd drawn from their friendship. 'I'd do anything for him,' said Mitch. 'I'm not trying to replace Albie, but at the same time it's almost like Jude coming into my life was meant to be. And I think that works both ways.'

'It sure sounds like it.'

'When your boyfriend offered—'

She held up a hand and put down her cup. 'Hang on, just for a minute, could we not call him that? Can we call him Pierre?'

Happy to. 'When Pierre offered the money my first thought was to go ahead with hiring a private detective to find Albie. But after talking to Jude about his own history I realised I could do more damage than good. And now, well, I don't know what to do.'

'You said I instigated a change for you.' She looked down at the table briefly as though this was getting too personal. But she couldn't forget what he'd said when they first arrived at the café. 'May I ask how?'

'On that day we first met, you asked me who the boy was.'

'I'm sorry.'

'Don't be. I needed the jolt. I needed something to get under my skin again. Somehow after losing him I'd gone numb. A protective coating had grown over the hurt I was feeling but you broke into that layer. Asking me about my son was exactly what I needed.'

'You say you were worried about searching for Albie not being the best thing, in light of what happened to Jude, but why not take the money so at least you're financially secure for when he does come back?'

He appreciated her saying 'when' rather than 'if'. The coffee, bitter to his palate, burned its way down his throat. 'It's true. If I took the money I would never have to worry about finances again. I could shower Albie in gifts, it would be like when I'd had the big job – but I've changed. I began helping out with the Christmas tree farm for Dad's sake, but after a while I saw a different kind of life, I saw the start of a way through. And I don't want to give it up. I want it to be a part of me when Albie sees me again.' He had to stay positive. 'You know, my brother thought I was mad to take the business on. He wanted to sell up right away, be rid of it all. Probably rid of me too. No, I mean it,' he insisted when Holly tried to disagree. 'After my stint in the Bampton Lake Lodge I didn't see much of him. I don't think he knew how to handle me. I saw him for Dad's funeral, but that was it.'

'Doesn't sound very supportive.'

Mitch shrugged. 'In a way I get it. He'd nursed Mom through her illness and then watched his dad die. I think his way of coping was to run away.'

'I think you need to consider Pierre's offer.' She held up a hand before he could protest. 'Tell me, do you object to a luxury golf course being anywhere near Inglenook Falls?'

'I do if they take my log cabin.' He thought she'd understood.

'But do you object to the course?'

'I don't suppose I do. I know it'll create jobs, the folk in town would welcome it; the nearest one is too far for some to travel to, and they're pretty tranquil places, I guess. Even played a few rounds myself once.'

'I don't know much about land, golf courses, or business. But how about you meet Pierre halfway?' she suggested. 'You could sell part of the land – most, or half, whatever you could both agree. You could keep the Christmas tree farm business – maybe ask him to wait until after next Christmas so you have a chance to sell on as much of what has been grown as you can – then he can get going on his golf course. He'd probably pay a decent amount of money still and perhaps even some in advance when the contract is signed. You'd be able to hire the private detective, if that's what you decide, map out a secure future, and stay at the cabin too.'

'You've given this some thought.'

'Well...' she smiled sheepishly.

He leaned back in his chair, ran a hand across a strange smooth chin. 'I don't know. It might encroach on my land, I like the wilderness feel to it how it is, I'm not sure I could get used to anything different.'

'All you have to do is meet with Pierre, talk about it. And then if you still don't want to do it, walk away.'

He exhaled. 'You're quite the businesswoman.'

'I want to help, that's all. Now, how about you do something for me?'

'What's that?'

'I'd really like that photograph framed, the one I mentioned.'

'Consider it done. When are you next in Inglenook Falls?'

'I'm a freelancer, so anytime.'

'Then how about tomorrow? You can come and choose the kind of frame you'd like.'

'It's a date.' She looked embarrassed at her choice of words and it tickled him. She was beautiful already, even more so when she got flustered.

They settled the bill and he walked her home on the way to collect his car. And after they parted ways he realised how far he'd come. He'd cleaned himself up, he was falling for someone, and a possible deal with Pierre could see him financially secure and able to get Albie back.

But how did the saying go? Sometimes things were too good to be true?

19

HOLLY

Holly woke before the sun and looked out of the window, hoping the snow hadn't come down so heavy it would stop her going out to Inglenook Falls today. But it hadn't. A light dusting had settled over Manhattan, main roads were clear again and, more importantly, the trains were running. She'd texted Darcy and Cleo before she fell asleep the night before to fill them in on the events of the evening and they'd both been excited as well as a little dumbfounded to find out Mitch was the mystery artist.

When Holly had realised who was standing behind her at the gallery last night she'd been stunned, not only with the physical transformation but also by the guts and emotional change that must've been behind it. And when Mitch had spoken to her she'd had a hard time reconciling him with the same gruff character who'd scooped her up that day. He'd walked her home from Greenwich Village to West Chelsea as the snow started to come down again and he'd been like any normal guy.

'I meant to ask,' Holly had enquired after they'd crossed the street that led to hers, 'how's the snowman?'

He grinned. 'Your snowman? He's doing well, I'm looking after him.'

'Is that so?'

'He had to have a bit of an operation.' Her laughter echoed through the street, past the young couple running to meet another twosome waiting outside the laundromat. 'Those arms you gave him were terrible, and that nose!'

'I didn't have a carrot in my pocket unfortunately.' She didn't add that her accomplice had been petrified he'd come outside and catch them in the act.

'I fixed his arms and gave him a proper nose. I felt sorry for him.'

They reached the entrance to her apartment building. 'This is me,' she told him. 'Thank you for bringing me home.'

'Thank you for tonight, for the gallery and for the dinner afterwards.'

'Yeah, to anyone else you look almost normal.' She braved teasing him and thankfully he took it the right way. 'I had a good time, and I'm glad you did too.'

'When will the article appear?'

'Should be early February. Would you rather I used the name Campbell in my write-up?'

He shook his head. 'There's little point when I'll be in the photographs.'

'Fair point. So I can call you Mitch throughout?'

'Go ahead, happy for you to.'

'And how much of the details we shared can I include?' Why hadn't they discussed this at the restaurant where it was warmer? She cuddled her arms around herself.

'You're freezing, you should get inside.'

'I'm serious, Mitch. I don't want to include anything you'd rather was kept between us.' Between us. The phrase brought unexpected feelings to the surface. She'd stayed in this stranger's cabin, he'd put her in his bed, and now he'd bared his soul.

'I think it's time I stopped hiding but keep it about the art rather than Albie if you can. I sometimes can't detach the two – painting was my solace for a long time, but...'

She put a hand out and touched his arm. 'Mitch, I'm good at writing and editing, I'll keep it about the art with enough insight into the artist that the piece works, not so much it makes you uncomfortable.'

'I appreciate it. Now get inside and get warm. I'll see you tomorrow?'

'Of course. I'll bring the picture.' Her heart soared. 'Goodnight, Mitch.'

'Goodnight,' she heard as she took the steps up to the front door of her building.

She turned and waved at him, although he was fiddling with his cell phone so she closed the door and went up to her studio apartment. She didn't even remove her coat or boots before she dashed to the window overlooking the street. She could see him walking away, his feet trying to hold him steady on the slippery sidewalk. She watched him cross the street, his physique a sign he was no stranger to hard physical work.

Now, with thoughts of last night churning around in her mind, she grabbed her things and took the train to Inglenook Falls at midday, escaping the holiday crowds of Manhattan and swapping them instead for the tranquillity of a quiet town. She would be meeting Pierre for dinner tonight as planned, but first, she couldn't wait to get to the cabin and talk to Mitch about a frame for her photograph. Although deep down she knew it was so much more than that, at least on her part. They'd connected in a way she hadn't expected, and as the train pulled in she was already counting down the time until she'd meet him at the cabin in an hour.

It had snowed out here, more than in the city, and after dropping her overnight bag at the Chestnut Lodge, Holly snatched the chance to browse the markets. A scent of chestnuts, chocolate, cinnamon, and spices hung on the air, people laughed their way along the Swiss-chalet-like stalls and the Little Knitting Box stall didn't disappoint with its bright yarns and colourful knits that Kaisha was doing a great job of selling. Holly tasted cheeses, chocolate, and had a hot dog as she watched kids trying out the make-your-own-bauble stall and then finally meandered back into town to see a line of children on the town green snaking along towards the steps of the bandstand as they waited to see the Santa Claus who was sitting on an enormous red-and-gold throne at the top between the twinkly lights on the posts. She followed Main Street and dropped a few coins in the collection tin for the hospice in Bampton, and another few dollars in the collection for the care home nearby, before admiring store windows decorated in bright colours, lights strung between streetlamps creating a magical world to wander through, and finally crossing the street to meet the top of the track that would lead her to the log cabin.

As she made her way down into the woods she could see why Mitch wanted to protect this land. It was close enough to Main Street to be a part of the community yet far enough away that it could offer solitude. She reached the fork and took the left side, surprised at how quickly she'd learnt the lie of the land. She took care as there were a few patches filled with ice and snow, and at intervals she hung onto branches to guide her way and prevent sliding. At least she'd chosen flat, grippy boots for today, knowing this would be what she was up to. Mitch had advised it was better to follow the road he took with the truck in winter because he kept it as clear as he could and gritted it most days, but she wanted to come this way and approach the quaint log cabin and the man she'd once feared from an angle she was familiar with. And when the cabin finally came into view she had no regrets. Smoke curled from the chimney into the crisp yet sunny afternoon air. A dim glow came from where she knew the log burner sat in the living room beyond the window. She could almost smell the mixture of timber, wood smoke, and the leather couch she'd sat on, the unlikely sense of home. She smiled as she got closer to the snowman. Mitch must've packed more snow onto its body to keep it sturdy, and he'd given it fat twigs for arms, both round about the same length, and a long carrot for a nose as well as pieces of coal for its eyes.

She didn't get to knock on the door because Mitch emerged first. He must be so used to being alone out here that he sensed when he wasn't.

'You came,' was all he said, one arm hung loose by his side, the other resting casually on the door jamb. His sleeves on the checked shirt that hung outside his jeans were rolled up, exposing hard-working, muscly forearms, and when she made her way up the porch steps and got closer she could see stubble beginning to push through on the clean-shaven jaw that still seemed at odds with the man who lived here, but it was like a combination of the old Mitch and the new.

'I told you I would. I worked on my article this morning, it's all finished.'

'That's good.' He couldn't stop looking at her.

'I brought the picture.' She lifted up the document carrying case, big enough to take the picture once it was framed too.

'Come in out of the cold and show me.'

'Snowman looks good,' she smiled as she stepped over the threshold. The inside of the cabin looked exactly the same as it had been that day, yet so much had changed.

'He's not bad, is he?' He shut the door behind them and she pulled off her boots, hung her coat on the hook next to his along with her scarf, and cut through the lounge to the kitchen counter where they looked at the photograph together.

'It's a stunning shot.' He admired her photography, his eyes not leaving the print. 'The way you've captured the light, the changing colours of the season, the orange from the pumpkin your friend is carrying. Is it Sarah?'

He'd remembered. 'It is. I have a ton of photographs of us together, but this one's special. The way she's smiling is Sarah all over. She was the funniest, kindest, most persuasive woman I've ever known. I really miss her.'

Holly hadn't realised until now that her skin was touching Mitch's as they looked at the picture together. She let the warmth of human contact seep into her but this time she didn't cry about Sarah, she remembered the good, the funny and the kind.

He was the first to step away. 'Coffee?'

'Not for me, thanks.'

He abandoned the idea and moved back towards the photograph. 'What sort of frame and mount were you after?'

'I thought you'd have more of an idea than me.'

He seemed glad to take over and his brow creased in quiet contemplation. 'You've got plenty of colour in the picture, you don't want to detract from it, and you've captured your friend so well. You want the focus to remain on those things. And the frame isn't dictated by the style of photograph, it's always individual.'

'I really loved what I saw at the Winter Village.'

'They're popular. I make those mostly from cedar or oak.'

'I actually prefer the ones I saw on the landing upstairs.' She wasn't sure whether her comment would be too much. Thankfully it wasn't.

'I sell those out of town, they're very popular too. The stall-holder at the Winter Village wanted something with a sleeker finish though.'

'I disagree, it's the markings in the wood that make those frames so beautiful.'

'Come on.' He cocked his head and led her through the lounge room and she assumed they were going upstairs to look at the frames, but he paused at the bottom of the staircase and pulled on his boots and coat again. He plucked a key from the open-fronted wooden storage box with butterflies and flowers etched into the dark wood and fixed to the wall.

'That's beautiful.'

He smiled. 'Dad made it, like many of the other things in this cabin. The clock on the kitchen wall, the bannisters and treads on the stairs, the squirrel figure beside my bed, the rocker on the landing and the one out on the porch.'

'He was very talented.'

'He sure was.' He waited for her to dress for the cold again.

'Where are we going?'

'Not far.' He stepped out onto the porch and led her over to the two sheds, opening the farthest one from the cabin.

The wind was howling by now, whipping up some of the powdery snow from the ground, and she was grateful to step inside the wooden structure. But this was no ordinary shed. All windows but one were covered with curtains to stop anyone peering inside and a strip skylight was the main source of light as well as lamps placed at various spots around the walls.

'Dad made this shed.' Mitch briskly rubbed his hands together after flipping on a fan heater. 'Mom wanted him to get his hobby outside. The house wasn't the place for wood chippings, she'd say, although she let him in there in the winter months as it seemed cruel pushing him out here. Then she let him in when it was too hot because there's no air conditioning in the shed, then she'd let him in when it was stormy because she was scared something would happen to him, then again when bears were around in case he stumbled into one on his journey back to the cabin.' He laughed softly as though he didn't want to disturb what was happening inside. 'I think he only really came in here when he wanted some time to himself, some peace and quiet.' He took off his coat as the heat circulated around them. 'I came in here a lot after he died, started making picture frames and then couldn't stop. I attempted a few other bits and pieces too, something for Albie on every birthday and Christmas he wasn't with me. Unfortunately I'm nowhere near as talented as my father.'

'And where are all these things?'

He pulled out a plastic box and lifted up the lid. 'They're all waiting for him.'

She looked at the carvings as he took out each piece in turn, the intricate details made by the hands of this man who kept surprising her. There was a wooden pot to store pens and pencils in as Albie did his school work, a sign for Albie's bedroom door with his name and a baseball bat, glove, and ball etched at the bottom-right-hand corner. There was a keyring that Mitch told her was for when his son first got responsibility for a house key, something that would mark a turning point in his life. And there was a wooden bowl, because every boy needed somewhere to throw his crap apparently – a dime from his pocket, a button that fell off his shirt, a baseball card he'd traded at school.

'They're so beautiful.'

He cleared his throat and veered away from the topic by turning and pointing out the easel behind another plastic box, which was full of paints – oils, pastels, acrylics. 'I use that to do all my canvases.' He turned off the fan heater that had sufficiently warmed up the enclosed space. And then he turned the easel so she could see what was on the front right now.

'It's your cabin.' She smiled up at him. She wanted to run her fingers across it, feel each brushstroke, smooth or rough. He'd captured the cabin in the summer months, a contrast to how it looked now. Lush green grass grew out front, the porch a welcome respite with its shade, the rocker half in and half out of the heat, some of the surrounding trees overhanging the roof.

'It needs a little bit more work but it's almost finished.'

She looked at him again. 'Have you thought about what we discussed? About selling part of the land to the hotel rather than all of it?' She referred to the hotel, but they both knew she meant Pierre.

'I thought about it all night, and I think you're right.'

'Really?' She hazarded a smile.

'You kind of made sense. I'll go talk with him tomorrow. Will you still be around?'

'I'll be staying at the guesthouse.' She didn't miss the smile that sneaked onto his face. She'd told Pierre that Lisa and Christopher had asked her to visit again. They hadn't, but she needed the head-space, the chance to think about the relationship she'd run with since earlier in the year, the many things that had changed since she'd arrived in New York.

'I guess I might see you around then,' he said.

'I guess you might.'

She took in another corner of the shed, this one with a stash of offcuts of wood in a basket beneath the worktop and a partly assembled frame on top. Next to it was a tin of varnish, a brush at the ready. 'Don't you ever work inside where there's more space?'

'Old habits die hard. Mom never wanted me or Dad to work inside, even though she relented enough times, so it kind of feels wrong to do it now.'

'Like she's watching you.' Holly smiled. 'I get that. You know, on Halloween I carved a pumpkin because I thought Sarah would be looking down on me, shaking her head saying I should embrace life, join in, live a little. I set it outside on the steps and hung around in the lobby with a basket filled with candy ready for anyone who stopped by. I'm not sure everyone in the building approved, but I had had fun.'

'Did anyone come?'

'You know what, I saw more trick or treaters than ever before. It was as though Sarah was watching from above and purposely sending everyone my way.' She looked at a partially finished frame. 'Do you use the trees on your own land to make these?'

'Sometimes, but mostly I source from elsewhere. The frames on the landing that you like the best, they all came from timber that once existed as something else.' He reached into the basket and pulled out a piece of dark wood, naturally occurring marks characterising its surface, the scars from nails that had once given it purpose. 'This piece came from the old dance hall in Bampton that was demolished earlier in the year.'

'How did you get hold of it?'

'I'm always on the lookout for reclaimed wood, I heard they were tearing the place down, I approached the owner and I think he thought I was nuts when I offered him cash for it. He said he was only going to burn it, but when he realised who my father was he said, "Like father like son."' He swallowed hard.

'But that's a wonderful thing to say.'

'I know, but it only reminded me how disappointed my father would be in how I've hidden myself away, failed my family.'

'Tell me more about how you work.' She wanted to get him onto a subject that didn't fill his face with sadness.

He took her through some of the tools he used: a table-mounted saw, a special chisel, a planer. 'I love how reclaimed wood tells a story. Take this piece as an example. How many couples fell in love dancing on top of this when it was part of the dancefloor?' He grinned. 'Or how many couples fought and split up? I like taking something that seems past its expiration date and turning it back into something beautiful.'

'Could you frame my picture with this wood?' She reached out to touch the piece he still held in his hand, the grain smooth in parts, rough in others.

'Of course, it'll go perfectly.'

She watched him carefully lay it back in the basket. 'Why did you show me all this?'

He kept his back to her. 'Because you're the first person to see the real me in a long time, and I feel comfortable with you. I wanted to show you.' He turned then. 'And now I'm talking like some flamboyant artist who wouldn't know one end of an axe from another, let alone be able to slice a log of wood in two or build a fire.'

'Don't do that.' She put a hand to his forearm and he looked down at her skin making contact with his. 'Don't judge yourself so harshly.'

Before he could answer they heard a voice outside. 'That's Jude. I'd better get out there. I need to keep up the pretence that I'm harbouring a dead body in here,' he winked. He put the lid back on the wooden objects, picked up the keys, and let them both outside when he saw the coast was clear. Jude must have already disappeared in the direction of the field judging by his fading voice calling Mitch's name. Mitch locked the shed door behind them. 'I have to go after him. He'll walk the entire land if I don't, I told him I needed his help today.'

'Go, I'm fine. I know my way back to Main Street.'

'I'll frame the picture and be in touch soon.'

'I'll send you my number, you know, via your website.'

He raised a hand, already running off in the direction of Jude's voice, and Holly took the path back up towards the town, back to another type of reality altogether.

* * *

Holly had only just reached Main Street and turned in the direction of the Little Knitting Box, where she was going to say hello to Cleo and hang out before she met her boyfriend, when Pierre pulled up alongside.

'This is a nice surprise!' He stepped out of the car and wrapped his arms around her. 'You smell of wood smoke, where have you been?'

Momentarily flummoxed, she quickly got her head together as delicate flakes began to come down from the sky. 'The Chestnut Lodge has their fireplace going all day. I was early so I've already dropped my bag off and I sat in the lounge chatting for a while.' She felt terrible lying but how could she admit where she'd really been? It was time for them both to talk; she didn't want to lead him on. And being with Mitch today had confirmed it. She was falling for him, more than any man she'd ever known before.

'I'm glad you're early,' he said. 'Come on, hop in the car, it's freezing.'

She climbed into the passenger seat and when he switched on the engine so they could run the heat, told him, 'We need to talk.'

He leaned in and kissed her, more passionately this time. 'How about we talk back at my apartment? I want to be in New York, return to civilisation for one night. I'll take you for a fancy meal, great wine.'

'I told you, I'm staying at the guesthouse.'

'I'll buy your favourite champagne,' he grinned. 'Two bottles if you're lucky.'

'What's got into you? Do you have a new project?' Every time Pierre started something new, he'd told her it gave him a buzz akin to being on drugs. Not that she'd know what that was like and she didn't want to think about whether he did or not.

'Of sorts.'

'Tell me what's going on. A new site for your next venture? A promotion?' She'd have to humour him because while he was in this mood there wouldn't be any getting through to him.

'I'm still working on this venture. And I think I'm one step closer to getting what we need. I promised this golf course, the company expects it now.'

'Not much you can do without the land.'

'Everyone has their price.'

'You're going to offer more? But Mitch doesn't want to sell.'

His eyes met hers. 'How did you know it was Mitch?'

She hesitated. 'You know the local gossip mill, I heard about it, that's all.'

'Actually I do know the local gossip mill and I think when I send Mitch a copy of the blogpost I intend to run, the blogpost that'll reach thousands, he'll be happy to do the deal.'

'What's in the blogpost?' She had a bad feeling about this.

'I'm only telling the truth.'

Then why did a shudder course all the way through her body?

20

MITCH

After Holly left, Mitch had taken a call from Nikita and it left him with a big smile on his face, a rarity in these wooden walls of the cabin until recently. She'd called to tell him he'd sold another two paintings and they'd agreed he'd supply more in a similar realm. After so many months of heading down a road to pretty much nowhere, Mitch finally felt as though he had direction.

He spent the next half an hour at the kitchen table with a pad and a pen, working out a way forward. He estimated he could sell off plenty of the trees early next season, he could move some of the others that were spread out across his land so they were closer together, and he'd keep the Christmas tree farm to within thirty acres, meaning he'd still have the space that made these woods and the cabin so special. Pierre could purchase the remaining fifty acres, build his golf course with the land he already owned, locals would get the employment and the facility, so everyone was a winner.

He set down his pen, happy with his plan, which he'd take over to the hotel today. He was rather looking forward to it, especially seeing the look on Pierre's face when he showed up clean-shaven – almost – and ready to do a deal.

He washed his breakfast dishes, wiped down the counter, and glanced briefly at the log burner. He'd purposely not built it up too much this morning, knowing he'd be out. But he needed to chop more wood and then later on, when the deal was done, he'd be able to stoke it up as much as he wanted. Maybe he'd work on the frame for Holly, and after that he'd kick back inside his cabin with a cold beer knowing his future was about to change. With the money coming his way, he had every chance of getting Albie back into his life, and soon. He was about to take his proposal out to the hotel when there was a knock at the door.

The man himself. And Pierre's face was priceless when Mitch opened the door. The location hadn't been what Mitch had had in mind, but the shock sure was. He chuckled inwardly.

'Mitch?' Almost dumbstruck at the difference in the cabin owner's appearance, Pierre stuttered out his next words. 'Can I come in?'

'I need to chop wood.' No way was he letting this man inside his home. So he unhooked his coat and the key to the shed. 'What can I do for you?'

'I wondered if you'd had a chance to rethink my offer.'

'As a matter of fact, I have.'

Pierre's face showed a second blow of shock as they stood on the porch. 'Well, that is interesting. You won't regret this. I'll have my lawyer draw up a contract, get things moving.'

Mitch pulled on his jacket. 'You misunderstand me. I don't want to do the deal you suggested. I'm willing to sell you fifty acres, but the rest will stay mine.'

'That's not what we discussed.'

'It's not, but it's what I'd be happy with.'

'I want more.'

Of course he did.

'Mitch, four million can... no, *will* change your life.'

'And so will the price we agree. I'd suggest three million.' He may as well be cheeky about it. 'It's over half the land after all.'

'No deal. I won't buy less than the entire parcel of land.'

'Ever heard of the phrase cutting your nose off to spite your face?'

'Of course I have.' He turned, looked out beyond the cabin, then turned back to Mitch. 'I want the land, five million, final offer.'

When Mitch ran a hand across his jaw he still wasn't used to not finding a grizzly beard there. This man was offering way over the odds, but then again, its proximity to the hotel was ideal for him and the closeness to Inglenook Falls and Main Street had another appeal. 'What are you playing at?' he asked outright.

'I want to build the golf course.'

'And you could with the land I'm offering, plus what you already own.' And then he got it. 'You want to build residential properties, don't you?' He'd seen it with too many towns close by, Inglenook Falls being one of the few that retained its unique small-town America charm. He should've known. And Pierre's lack of immediate response confirmed it.

'It's none of your business what I do with the land. But for your information the buildings would be an extension of the hotel's accommodation to cater for guests with varying tastes.'

Mitch could see how much Pierre hated having to explain himself, but he needn't have bothered, because the retort fell on deaf ears.

Mitch went over to the shed and undid the padlock. A good swing with the axe would do wonders right now and Pierre would be wise to stand well back. 'Fifty acres, take it or leave it,' he said simply. 'And I want your word there'll be no residential development.'

'You're a stubborn fool.' Pierre glared at him.

Mitch couldn't care less. If Pierre didn't want to do the deal, he'd just have to push on with the Christmas tree farm, the paintings, the wooden pieces and frames he made. He'd get there eventually, make something of himself and get Albie back, with a lot more scruples than this man had. 'Inglenook Falls won't thank you for building any residential places out this way, regardless of whether they're for vacation rentals or not.' He grabbed a chunk of wood and put it end-up onto the upturned old log and went back for the axe. 'I'm doing you a favour. You don't want to fight with the people of this town, believe me.' Because they'd stand up to this man, he knew they would. He'd heard many a time that surrounding woodlands and hiking trails were what made Inglenook Falls what it was. He positioned his hands on the axe.

'And you'd know all about that, wouldn't you?'

Mitch stopped. 'I've never fought with the locals. I keep myself to myself, that's all.'

'Not what I've heard.'

'Yeah, and what have you heard?' He geared up, ready to swing the axe up overhead and down onto the wood to split it in two.

'That your wife did a runner, took your son, and you had a mental breakdown and took it all out on the locals, charging about and threatening people.'

Mitch stopped. He didn't appreciate the unwelcome insight by an arrogant stranger. 'I'd say that's none of your business.'

'It's my business if you're getting in the way of my hotel.'

Mitch regarded him. 'Haven't you made enough money here? Perhaps it's time to move on.' He swung the axe through the air and down it came with such force he felt Pierre shake beside him and saw him visibly take a couple of steps back from the log that had become two with one clean hit.

'I like to finish what I started.' Pierre braved moving closer and handed him a few sheets of paper, stapled together. 'You leave me no choice. That's copy for a press release I'm going to send out in the New Year, show people our plans. The Hatherleigh Group like to keep locals on side. We're also about to run it as a blogpost from the company website as soon as I make the call to my communications people. We have more than half a million followers, you know.'

As if he cared. But Mitch took the papers and flipped through. There was a short spiel about the hotel, the proposed golf course, and another section outlining a log-cabin development. 'You want to build log cabins, here, cabins like mine?' His laughter peeled into the snowy air as a soft, glowing sky brought twilight their way.

'Like yours on the outside, but modern on the inside, bright interiors.' How the hell would he know what Mitch's cabin was like inside? 'Tourists will love them, they'll be enormously popular, you wait and see. And initial market research tells me locals won't object as long as they're developed tastefully. I'm not destroying existing homes – apart from one of course – so I can't see any problem with the project.'

Mitch pushed the papers back at him. 'Never going to happen. You're forgetting a little matter of me not selling you the land. No golf course, no log-cabin development, you can stick it where the sun don't shine.' He positioned another log and swung the axe up and brought it down, cutting the wood clean in two. 'Go ahead and publish the information, won't make any difference to me.'

'But you didn't read to the end,' said Pierre.

'I don't need to.'

'Oh, I think you do.'

Mitch snatched the papers back and flipped over after the page depicting the proposed log cabins on the parcel of land where his own stood now. All very idyllic, but all a pipe dream as far as he was concerned. 'What's this?' he asked when he reached the second to last page. At the top was a photograph of him, his beard straggly, his clothes muddy and torn. He was swinging the axe high in the air.

Then at the bottom was another shot, in profile. He looked drawn and lost, a sad, sorry excuse for a man. And his insides swirled, because he knew who must've taken this picture. Which could only mean one thing. This man and Holly had planned this all along. She'd made Mitch think she was on his side when she wasn't. He'd trusted her and look what she'd done.

'Read on,' Pierre urged and Mitch read every painful word on the last page. He read all about the local man who'd had a breakdown and been in an institution for a time, something he'd only shared with one person around here. His father had assured him he had never breathed a word to anyone outside of their family, so the source of the information was obvious. The words swam in front of him. Phrases about a man locals 'feared', his behaviour described as 'aggressive' during the hotel's development, which was bullshit. The only time he'd been remotely aggressive was when he'd found that man Lionel trespassing on his land. And of course when his wife had first taken off he'd had a go at her friend Nessa, trying to track her down, but he knew that Nessa was discreet and certainly wouldn't have mouthed off about this to Pierre. And besides, that happened long before the development started.

All the words in this article, the pictures, they were all exposing him at his worst. He shoved the papers back at Pierre. 'You must be really proud of that piece.' He locked eyes with his nemesis and swore he saw a muscle in Pierre's jaw twitch in frustration. 'Run it, see if I care, I have nothing to lose.'

'Oh, but you do.'

'What's that supposed to mean?'

'This piece will run locally and over the internet, it'll have a far reach, could even make its way to that wife and son of yours, wherever they are.'

He was bluffing, had to be. Mitch lined up another log. The axe came down but barely cut through half the log and it stuck there.

Pierre stepped closer, braver now the axe wasn't free. 'Sell me the entire land, the five million is yours, and this document will be destroyed. Your whole sorry past can stay with you and you can start over. I can't be more reasonable than that.'

The word reasonable was what did it and Mitch flew at Pierre, knocking him to the ground. They wrestled in the snow, Pierre's coat covered in white powder mixed with the mud that lay beneath. His fancy shoes left grooves as he tried to get purchase on the slippery surface while Mitch's boots did their job and gripped well. Mitch shoved his face into the snow and the dirt beneath. He thought about punching the man, he had it all lined up, Pierre beneath him, his arms trapped, but instead he stood up. 'You're not worth it.' He'd never seen his father punch a man in his lifetime and he'd be damned if he'd ever stoop that low either.

'I could have you charged with assault!' Pierre got to his feet and brushed himself down. 'I'll add it to the press release, shall I?'

A figure emerged from the track leading down to the cabin. 'You'll do no such thing!' It was Holly, watching her footing carefully.

'Stay out of it, Holly, this doesn't concern you.' Pierre had dirt and blood on his jaw – he must've bashed it as he went down. He looked like a character in an action movie, testing whether he could still open and close his mouth. Mitch hoped he'd shut it permanently.

'Are you okay?' Holly was at Mitch's side. 'Mitch?'

'Go away, leave me alone.' He stalked off to the cabin. 'And both of you get the hell off my land before I use that axe over there to do more than chop wood.'

He slammed the cabin door behind him. He didn't want to watch the pair of them any longer. He leaned against the wood, slid down its smooth surface to the floor. This morning he'd been on a high, and now look at him. He was plummeting towards a low he hadn't felt in a long time. A stranger, a man he didn't think much of anyway, had proven himself to be one of the most evil-minded men he'd ever had to deal with. He wanted to build his own log cabins here on Mitch's land? Not a chance.

And the blackmail? Mitch would never succumb to it, no matter how much it hurt him.

But the worst thing of all was Holly's betrayal. A woman he'd thought a friend, someone he cared about and to whom he had opened his heart.

Never again would he be taken for such a fool.

21

HOLLY

She rapped on the door again. 'Mitch, Mitch, answer, please. Pierre has gone.' She had no idea whether he could hear her or not. 'Mitch, please let me in. I know what he tried to do, the blackmail, and I won't let him, do you hear me?'

The door flew open but rather than the forlorn Mitch she'd expected or the man who'd kindly walked her home to her apartment, aside from the scraggly hair and matted beard he was back to the man he'd been before, his eyes wild with fury, a look of hopelessness on his face.

'Go away, I won't tell you again, I don't want you here,' he spat.

'Mitch...' But he'd shut the door. She thumped on it this time. 'Get your stubborn ass out here now!'

He opened up again but all he said was, 'Holly, we're done.'

'What are you talking about?' Her breath came out in gasps, white against the air. She could feel a hit of warmth from inside drifting onto the porch.

'That man is sick in the head, and you're not much better.' He moved to slam the door and she risked putting her foot in the way. 'Move your foot, I don't want to hurt a woman.'

'So talk to me then!'

'Oh the irony. Look what talking did last time.'

Holly had no idea why he was being so ridiculous.

'I trusted you!' He yelled now and stepped out onto the porch, advancing on her, confronting her. She could feel his breath on her face. 'Get the hell out of here, Holly!'

'No.'

'I'll pick you up and take you up the hill myself if I have to.' He leaned even closer. 'Don't ever come here again, do you hear me?' And with that he leapt down from the porch and the snowman bore the brunt.

He didn't stop kicking until the entire snowman was obliterated, on the ground, nothing more than an untidy pile of snow.

When he went inside again Holly refused to give up. She sat on the porch step, but she didn't knock again. Instead, she stayed there thinking about everything that had happened between that day at the end of November when she'd stumbled upon this cabin and now. She'd let Mitch calm down, then knock again, certain she could make him see sense.

But the time ticked on by. It was dark by now and getting colder. She contemplated making another snowman, if only to rile him so he'd come out, but she was shivering even through all her layers. She blew onto her gloved hands and willed the snow falling from above not to get too heavy and make it impossible to get up the track. It'd be challenging enough in the dark and she only had the torch app on her cell phone for guidance.

A couple of times she thought she saw Mitch in her peripheral vision come to the window but every time she turned there was nobody, and after a couple of hours she called time on the craziness. Mitch wasn't going to open the door to her, she needed to leave and hope he eventually calmed down. She climbed the hill, cursing under her breath every time she slipped on a patch of snow or a hidden icy part.

In the car earlier, when she'd realised Pierre was up to something, he'd refused to share the details. He said it was business, nothing personal, and then when she pried some more he accused her of having feelings for Mitch, which of course she couldn't deny. He got angry and they rowed – him accusing her of pitying a man and changing since she left her real job. She yelled at him for being so shallow and for never taking her change of career seriously. In the end she'd said she thought their relationship was over, got out of the car and stomped up Main Street towards the Little Knitting Box, leaving Pierre to speed off in anger. But she hadn't gone far when she realised she needed to warn Mitch that Pierre was about to play dirty. And so she turned back and headed towards the top of the track. What she hadn't expected was to see Pierre's car still parked on the street with no sign of the man himself. Her stomach had churned when she realised he'd gone to confront Mitch and she'd gone down the track as fast as the icy surface would allow, in time to see Mitch tackle Pierre to the ground and then Pierre threaten Mitch with adding details of their brawl to some sort of press release.

She took the fork in the path as she made her way up the track now. It was time to confront Pierre and get some answers. But before she got much further, a kid came running towards her.

She was less scared when he hurtled past and she realised it had to be Jude. 'I wouldn't go down there if I were you,' she advised.

'I can handle him,' the boy called back.

'Wait!' Holly set after him and he stopped at her voice. 'You're Jude, right?'

'And you're Holly.'

She smiled, wondering whether Mitch had mentioned her before or whether the boy had picked up her name on the grapevine. 'I sure am. Look, I know you're a good friend of his, but he's had a run-in with someone and I don't know why he's so mad, but I'm going to try to find out.'

The kid took a cell phone from his pocket. 'I think I know what happened. Follow me. No reception down here unless you're right at the cabin.'

Holly followed obediently and they ran all the way up to Main Street, where Jude got enough of a signal. Pierre's car was long gone by now – he'd be back at the hotel, and Holly knew she'd have to go there for answers.

Jude scrolled through his cell phone looking for something. 'My friend Cal's mom used the spa at the hotel, she signed up to the hotel blog for offers and got a good deal for New Year's.'

'Okay...'

He tipped his head side to side as though to hurry up his thoughts and explanation. 'She got the most recent blogpost about twenty minutes ago. She was in the café, Cal showed me, and I came straight here.' He found what he needed and handed her the cell phone.

Holly looked at the screen displaying the Hatherleigh Group logo at the top and then the name of the hotel and, scrolling down, she saw a blogpost with a timestamp that showed it must've been published while she'd been trying to get Mitch to open the door. If Pierre was responsible for this, he must've given the go-ahead after he stormed away and the second he'd got a cell-phone signal. The post was titled 'Thousands of new jobs and a significant boost to local economy'. At first it seemed harmless. The opening paragraph talked about the hotel group and what it had already brought to the area, it detailed the golf course everyone knew about and next up was the proposed building of fifty log cabins on the land adjacent to Main Street. They wouldn't spoil the look of Main Street, they'd be hidden down in the woods, nature wouldn't suffer.

But Mitch would. This was his land they were talking about and he hadn't agreed to the full sale, had he?

'Keep reading,' Jude urged.

She scrolled through some quotes from local residents – Noah from the bakery had said 'an escape to a log cabin in the woods would be perfect', Nessa from the library said 'my husband and I can't wait to take golf lessons', Enid from the café was looking forward to 'a thriving business with more visitors coming to Inglenook Falls'. Holly really didn't see the problem with the article. If Mitch didn't sell the land then this would be nothing more than wasted publicity, but if he did, well, then that was his call. But when she reached the final paragraph, things began to fall into place. She read on: 'The Hatherleigh Group are currently in talks with local landowner Mitch Baldwin and would like to support him in rebuilding his life after hardship came his way four years ago. Mitch lives alone and rarely sees or speaks with anyone in the community since his wife and child disappeared, and following his release from a Connecticut mental-health facility.'

'No wonder he hates me,' she muttered. The article revealed the secret Mitch hadn't told anyone about, it painted him as a sad and lonely man who'd lost everything. Which was true in many ways but putting it out there along with photos showing his worst side was a hundred steps too far. Holly was surprised Mitch hadn't strangled Pierre down there in the woods earlier. And those photos? They were her photographs she'd taken when Mitch had helped her that day. Pierre had stolen them to crucify this man and her heart nearly broke in two.

'I'll go talk to him,' Jude offered. 'I'll make him see reason.'

'Do you think he will?'

He shrugged. 'No idea. Can I ask, was it you who told your boyfriend about Mitch spending time in a mental-health facility?'

'No! I didn't say a word, honest to God.' He was thinking about it, she could tell. 'Wait, did you know before this blogpost, article, whatever it's called?' Trash, slanderous accusations, she could think of a few ways to describe it. And she was sure Mitch could drag Pierre through the courts for this if he wanted to.

'I've known for a long time. A few people in town know but never mention it. Despite what Mitch thinks, people care and don't want him to come to any harm. I wish he'd see that. I need to make him understand.' With renewed energy he took off down the track.

Holly didn't see how the boy was going to get through to a strapping man who'd made his mind up already and who was renowned for his stubbornness. But then she had an idea. 'Jude! Wait up!' She ran after him.

'Watch it.' He put an arm out to steady her when she slipped on ice under foot. 'You okay?'

She took a deep breath, reminding herself to be careful. 'I have an idea. Will you help me?'

'What kind of an idea?'

'We need damage control. Are you any good with a camera?'

He pulled out his cell phone and clicked the photos app to show her a handful of shots. 'I can point and shoot.'

'Actually, these aren't bad. I'll have to let you have a go with a real camera sometime.'

'Yeah?'

'Yeah.' She liked the boy. And they were on the same side, which counted for a lot right now. 'But first, my plan.'

* * *

After talking with Jude, Holly wasted no time in going to the hotel, where she found Pierre working on his laptop in the restaurant.

'Holly?' When he looked up his smile didn't last long because her face said it all. 'Should we go somewhere private?' He picked up his things.

She leaned forwards so nobody else would hear. 'You get that blogpost deleted right now, and then we'll talk.'

He opened his mouth to say something but changed his mind. He took out his cell and called whoever was presumably responsible. He offered no explanation but told them it was a matter of urgency and it should be done immediately. His actions told Holly he knew he was badly in the wrong, but she hadn't even begun to get going with what she'd come here to say.

'Call me when it's done,' he instructed whoever was on the end of the phone.

He picked up his laptop and motioned for her to follow him. They went out of the restaurant, upstairs to his suite, and Holly waited for him to shut the door before she launched into the tirade that had been brewing ever since she'd found out what he'd done.

'How could you?' she yelled. 'Of all the nasty, underhand things to do!'

'It's business, Holly. You should know that.'

She wagged a finger at him. 'Don't you dare compare anything I do to what you've done. It's not business, it's desperation. Wanting to get your own way, impress the company. Whatever! And how did you even find out all that information about Mitch?'

'I did a bit of digging. He thinks nobody knows a thing, thinks it's a big secret, but you charm people enough and they start talking.'

'He could take you to court for slander!' She had no idea of the intricacies of doing so but her fury wasn't vetting what came out of her mouth.

'Why do you feel the need to stick up for him?'

'Because I'm a decent human being!'

'Stop yelling.' He led her away from the door. 'There are other guests to consider and *that* really is business.'

She sat on the edge of the bed, its luxury meaningless. 'He thinks I fed you the information about his time at the Bampton Lake Lodge.'

'Ah, so that's what this is about.' He'd undone his shirt cuffs and rolled up his sleeves.

'What's that supposed to mean?'

'It's about him, that man. I saw the way you looked at him when we were outside the log cabin.' He shook his head. 'So you've found someone you like better. Wow... I really didn't see that coming.'

'Pierre...' Her voice softened because the attraction to Mitch had come out of nowhere, but the doubts about this relationship with Pierre had been simmering away for some time.

'Part of me hoped you just felt sorry for him. But I don't think that's true, is it? I mean, how do you even know him?' But he held up a hand. 'You know what, I don't need to know. The fact you didn't come after me today but stayed there for him tells me everything I need to know.'

'I didn't plan it, I swear.'

'But you're attracted to him? I don't see why. I mean the guy had a haircut and a shave but he's a sad, lonely recluse.'

It angered her the way he spoke about a man he didn't understand. 'I'm attracted to his kindness, his ability to put other people first, his vulnerability and everything he's been through yet he's still standing.' A man so different to you, Pierre.

'You make him out to be some kind of hero.' He slumped down onto the bed at a right angle to where she was sitting.

'Actually, he is. Remember the bruise on my head?' He didn't speak. 'Well, it didn't happen quite like I said. I fell on the track leading towards the cabin when I was trying to get away from someone I thought dangerous.' She couldn't help a small smile move across her mouth. 'I was concussed, he looked after me without question. And here you are painting him a monster.' With a shake of her head she said, 'I really don't understand you, Pierre. You're a good man most of the time, but that blogpost, it was a terrible thing to do. And you stole my photographs from my laptop.'

It took Pierre quite a while to speak. 'I apologise. I shouldn't have done that.'

'Damn right you shouldn't.'

'I was angry. He was standing in the way of the development that would've most likely seen me get promoted. It was an empty threat, I didn't want to ridicule someone who'd had a hard time, but when I saw the way you looked at him today and you stayed with him rather than come after me, I was so pissed I made the call to publish the blogpost.'

'So jealousy and money drove you to do it.' She couldn't look at him.

'We're good together, Holly.'

'We were at first when it was all new, but I changed quickly when I left the magazine and you haven't seemed to be behind me in my decision.'

'I want the best for you.'

'I know.' As unsupportive as he'd been, she'd never once doubted he wanted her to succeed. But it was succeeding on his terms that she couldn't quite get to grips with.

'When we first got together we seemed to want the same things, which is why I was trying to get you to come back to the corporate world, work for the business.' His cell phone rang and he answered it, the conversation short, and when he hung up told Holly, 'It's done. The blogpost is gone.' He clicked on his laptop and the website to prove the blog section had no trace of what had been there earlier.

'But the damage isn't.'

As if she hadn't spoken he carried on. 'I saw us travelling the country together, working on huge projects like this hotel.'

He would never see the real Holly. He wanted Holly the editor, the Holly who wore suits every day and walked into an office with a presence, the woman he'd started dating. Some couples stayed together through change, but other times they went their separate ways. And it seemed they were the latter type.

'I'm sorry, Holly.' He rubbed his hands across his face. 'The company could come down on me hard for this if they get wind of the blogpost, if Mitch starts any trouble.'

Could he get fired for something so underhand? 'Why don't you go to them first, come clean, explain it's been deleted?'

'Explain I don't have the extra land for the plans I got them all excited about.' He seemed resigned.

With Jude working on what she'd asked him to do, it was time for Holly to step up. She had to do this for Mitch – he didn't deserve what had happened and it was she who'd been a part of Pierre's thinking behind it all, so some of the responsibility lay at her door. 'I have a proposition for you,' she told him.

'I leave for Munich in a few days.'

'Then we'd better get started.' And Holly crossed everything from her toes to her fingers that it would work. That Mitch would get his life back.

22

MITCH

Since the fight with Pierre some twelve days ago, and Holly begging for him to hear her out, Mitch had only left his cabin when entirely necessary. He'd felled trees and driven them out to various locations but refused to talk to Jude about anything other than business. A couple of times he'd had people knock on the door but he'd ignored it, knowing it would be Jude, Holly, or people in town telling him to get the hell out of here. They didn't want some mental case roaming the streets and with that press release going out as a blogpost, everyone would know the truth by now. He wasn't a whizz on social media but he knew enough to know that news covered the globe very quickly these days.

He looked in the bathroom mirror. It was early and still dark, the morning before Christmas Eve, supposedly the most magical time of the year, but he couldn't feel any of the seasonal spirit. His beard had begun to grow back, the cabin was a biohazard it was so messy, and since the altercation with Pierre, Mitch had felt defeated and found himself considering whether he should get it over with, sell up, and start over.

He went back through to the bedroom, lost himself in the tangle of sheets, and fell asleep wishing he could obliterate everything around him.

When he woke up again the sun was streaming through the window and he squinted before turning over. He shut his eyes again but instead of lulling himself to a slumber, his eyes opened at the ringing of his cell phone. He was tempted not to answer but when he saw Jude's name on the display his conscience got the better of him and he picked it up. The boy could be in trouble and Mitch would never let anything happen to him.

But Jude was fine. All he'd wanted to do was ask Mitch whether his help was needed today, but Mitch assured him it was time he spent the festive season with his gran. They'd sold plenty of trees up until now and Mitch couldn't face trying to sell any more. But what Jude's call did do was spark him into action. He looked at the clock, still early enough that if he left now with his camping gear he could hike all afternoon and into the evening, hike all day tomorrow and the next day and wipe out any thoughts of Christmas until it was over. Maybe he'd hike for a couple of weeks, get Jude to do what was needed at the Christmas tree farm, then he'd come back and see where he went from there.

He dragged his hiking boots out from the cupboard but when he took them downstairs he was ashamed at the mess. He shivered. He'd let the log burner go out early last night, come to bed with a beer, the bottle lying there taunting him from his nightstand when he woke up before, reminding him what a mess he was. And when he looked at the document carrying case Holly had brought her photo in, ready to be framed, he wondered about the woman he'd begun to trust, care about, and probably love a little bit. What sort of a person could betray you in that way? She'd told that snivelling businessman his secrets, the things he'd entrusted to her when he had no place else to turn. She'd given him photographs. He'd known they were her work because she must've taken them that day she'd fallen down and he'd taken her up to his bed. She'd trusted him so little then that she was probably gathering evidence in case he should do anything terrible. But he hadn't. She had.

But rather than thoughts of Holly making him sink into a pit of misery again, thinking about her reminded him he'd almost pulled himself out of the mess he'd been in, and he never wanted to go back to those depths of despair again. Before he knew what he was doing he'd picked up the razor Holly and Cleo had left for him and hoped it was sharp enough. The straggly beard was on its way back and he'd hidden behind it once, but never again. He'd clean himself up, go hiking over Christmas and get some perspective, and then he'd think about claiming his life back, and that included Albie.

After he'd sorted himself out and showered, he tidied the upstairs while the cabin was still cold, as though he needed the air to circulate and bring him to once more. He went into the kitchen, by far the worst room in the house. He threw away food detritus from plates, scraping with a knife to remove what had dried hard on the surface. He threw out beer bottles, ran upstairs to retrieve the one from by his bed, he scrubbed at a sticky patch on the countertop, he wiped the cooker that had been splashed with soup that puddled near the burner, he swept the floor, wiped the fridge door where his grubby fingers had ripped it open to get another drink.

It was done. The place was clean, he was presentable again, and he wasn't going to let this setback beat him. Pierre could go to hell. And Holly... well, he wasn't sure what he wanted for her. He picked up the basket from beside the log burner. He'd stock up so that when he came back to the cabin in a few days or weeks, depending how long he needed, he'd be able to warm the place up. He'd bring in kindling too, so it was all ready to go.

Bundled up against the cold, he ventured out onto the front porch. He immediately saw what was missing. The snowman. No longer there after he'd kicked it down, taking his temper out on

anything he could find. Pierre had got away lightly, but the
snowman hadn't. He left the basket on the porch by the door and
went over to the shed, from where he took out the axe. He pulled
out some bigger logs from the end section of the tarp and dragged
one to the upturned log where he'd split it into pieces small enough
for the log burner.

It was nearly Christmas. Almost time to mark the end of
another calendar year without Albie. But next year would be different, he'd make sure of it. And he'd do it without Holly's help. For a
moment there he'd imagined them together, both pulling in the
same direction, but it seemed all along she'd had her own agenda
and he felt like a prize idiot. But on the positive side – the side he
was really trying to see these days – he'd made money from his
paintings, Nikita wanted more, his picture frames were popular and
selling well and the Christmas tree farm could open to an eager
public if he could ever get the nerve to do it. And he had Jude, and
Jude had him, and that was partly the reason he couldn't fall apart
as spectacularly as he'd done before. Jude's parents had never done
right by their boy and Mitch wanted to prove to him that not all
adults were assholes.

He shook his head. Time to get sorted, chop this wood, and get
out of here. Stick one finger up at the town's decorations as he drove
away, avoiding Christmas at least for one year. And then he'd take
any flack they wanted to hand out in the New Year. He split a few
pieces of log, then split them again and again, and dropped them
into the basket on the porch, adding scrap pieces for kindling. And
then he dragged more big pieces around to the upturned log and
carried on. Once the basket was half full he decided he'd do one
more for good measure. He picked up his axe once the wood was
waiting on the upturned log and in the corner of his eye saw Jude,
who as usual had ignored his insistence that he didn't need help
today. 'Come help chop now you're here,' he called matter-of-factly,

turning back to his task. 'You always boast how strong you are. Make yourself useful and drag over another log.' He'd get the boy to help then he'd surprise him by taking him for a hot chocolate at the café. He'd ignore anyone else in this town but make this about Jude. Jude would think he'd lost the plot!

But then another figure appeared in his peripheral vision. This time, a woman. Mitch set the axe down and took a couple of steps forwards.

The axe fell to the ground, Mitch put one hand on its handle to hold it upright or was it to steady himself?

The boy stepped towards him some more and Mitch realised it wasn't Jude at all. The woman hovered behind, unsure whether to get any closer.

Mitch was rooted to the spot. Because he was looking right at his son. The son who'd been barely hip height against him the last time he'd hugged his boy but who now looked as though he'd easily reach his chest.

Mitch didn't believe in Christmas miracles. He believed in reality and what he could see. But it appeared they were one in the same thing right now.

He stepped forwards. 'Albie.' His voice wobbled and he opened his arms ever so slightly, daring to hope.

Albie hesitated, but Shannon edged closer to their son and squeezed his shoulder gently in affirmation. And then there was no stopping the boy. He ran towards Mitch, through the snow on the ground, the resistance no match for his determination as he raced into his dad's arms.

Mitch cried, he laughed, he held his boy close. 'It's really you? Oh, it's really you.' He kissed Albie's head beneath the chocolate-brown, woolly hat. He took off his gloves so he could feel the skin on Albie's cheeks beneath his fingers. He hugged him again and again until Albie's tears gave way to endless laughter.

Shannon braved stepping closer herself. 'You look well, Mitch.' It was all she said before she burst into tears.

He couldn't be her comfort, not after everything that had happened. 'Would you like to come in?' he asked when she eventually calmed herself down.

She nodded. 'I would, very much.'

Mitch led them all into the log cabin, unable to take his eyes away from Albie. It was enough of a wrench to let the boy pull free of him to take his shoes off and hang his coat. He didn't want to let him out of his sight. He had no idea why they'd come, why now – all that mattered was that they were here. He leaned out of the front door again and put one hand on the basket of logs.

'Would you like to help?' he asked Albie.

'Sure.'

Between them they lifted the basket to beside the log burner, opened up the front, and Mitch guided his son in how best to place a few of the logs. Albie got into the task and, when they lit the kindling, sat mesmerised, his bottom on his heels as he watched the fire take hold.

Mitch offered coffee but Shannon declined so he made one for himself anyway. He needed to occupy his hands, stop himself from strangling the woman who'd caused him so much pain – although she looked as though she were in a world of hurt of her own and it kept him level-headed somehow. He knew that if she'd shown up a couple of weeks ago he might not have been so rational, and Holly had played a big part in his transformation. For that, he would always be grateful.

He didn't get long in the kitchen to gather his thoughts because Albie was at his side in seconds, firing question after question his way. Was the log burner the only source of heat in here? Did he have hot water? Were there bears in the area? How many Christmas trees did he have? Why hadn't he decorated the cabin for the holidays? Did he kill and cook his own food? It reminded Mitch of Jacob that day in the Little Knitting Box, his imagination running wild.

'He's into asking a lot of questions,' Shannon explained when she joined them after Mitch had patiently answered every single one. Her light brown hair was shorter than it had been, but it suited her. Her make-up was still the same, a little bit on her eyes, lips always painted. She'd always liked to maintain her appearance. When he'd gone the opposite way it must've been a huge shock as well as trying to fathom his emotional state.

'It'll help you learn at school, and it shows you're listening,' Mitch told his son instead of voicing his real thoughts, which were that he and Albie had a few years to catch up on and so of course the boy had questions. He reached out to touch Albie's hair, the same dark blond as it had always been, cut short and neat with a fringe on the cusp of needing a tidy. 'Would you like a drink, Albie?'

'Do you have hot chocolate?'

'I think I may have used the last of it for a friend of mine. Jude, you'd like him.'

'Is he your age?'

Mitch laughed. 'No, he's fifteen, much closer to your age than mine.'

Albie had a few sips of water and asked whether it would be okay for him to go off and explore the cabin and Mitch said that of course it was. The boy had been raised with manners and had turned out well even with the obstacles that had been thrown in his way.

'I will take that coffee,' said Shannon when they were left alone. 'If I may.'

He nodded, plucked another mug from the hook beneath the cabinet and poured out the coffee from the pot.

The air in here was polite, stilted, not yet giving way to everything that needed to be said. And when he heard the front door open he said, 'I better see what Albie's up to.'

'Good idea.' She managed a smile and followed on, coffee mug clutched in her hand.

When Mitch reached the door he saw Jude standing on the porch, dumbstruck at the sight of Mitch doing what you might call entertaining. 'Hey.'

'I saw him coming towards the cabin,' Albie explained, 'from the upstairs window.'

'Albie.' Mitch put a hand on his son's shoulder. 'This is Jude, the boy I was telling you about. He's a very good friend of mine.'

'Good to meet you, Albie.' A smile spread across Jude's face. 'I came to have a word with your dad, it's kind of important.'

'It'll have to wait,' Mitch told him. Right now, he had enough to worry about. And then he had a thought. 'Could you do me an enormous favour?' He sensed Shannon's presence behind him, checking what was going on.

'Anything, you know that.'

Actually, he did. 'Would you be able to go to the store and get some hot chocolate for this one? He doesn't do coffee.'

Jude grinned. 'Tell you what, better still, I'll take him to the café, let you have some time.' Shannon appeared then. 'If it's okay with you, Mrs... er...'

'It's entirely up to Mitch,' Shannon added after she'd introduced herself to Jude.

Mitch found his wallet, gave them twenty bucks and told them to watch out for each other. And he and Shannon stood at the door after he helped Albie on with his coat and hat and watched them traipse across the snow-covered ground to meet the track. Already they were talking about Christmas, about the best snowball fights they'd ever had, and they were laughing. It was the best sound Mitch had heard in years.

Mitch shut the door to the cabin, and then it was just the two of them. 'Thank you for trusting my judgement.'

'I owe you that.'

He said nothing as he went through to the kitchen and picked up his coffee. As much as he didn't want to let his son out of his sight ever again, he needed to be with Shannon alone, for Albie to leave them to it, and Jude had come to the rescue yet again.

'You took my son,' he said, with no preamble.

She set her mug on the table and her face crumpled as she sat down. 'I ran. I got scared.'

'When the going got tough, you didn't stand by me.' He stayed leaning against the countertop.

'I know.'

They sat in silence for a while, the clock his dad had made ticking away as time passed slowly. 'You didn't even let me know where you were,' he said eventually.

'I didn't want you coming after us, not at first.'

'What do you mean, not at first?' He abandoned his coffee, he couldn't stomach it.

'You were in a bad way, Mitch. I tried to support you at the start, but our home had gone, you were in a place I couldn't seem to reach.'

He hadn't pushed Albie away but he knew he'd kept his wife at arm's length. He'd watched her run the household, work her own job, take care of their son, but he'd felt such a failure he hadn't been able to let her in.

'I was frightened, Mitch.'

'Of me?'

'Partly. Not that you'd hurt either of us physically, but that you'd damage Albie somehow as he watched you get worse. I had to do what I thought was right.'

'Where did you even go?'

'Durango, to Mom and Dad's at first, but you know my parents.'

'I can imagine they harped on about how much of a mess you'd made, marrying me.'

She smiled. 'Actually, they told me how much of a mess I'd made leaving you and walking away.'

Now that, he hadn't expected. 'But they never really liked me, I could tell.'

'Dad would never have liked any of my boyfriends. Mom longed for me to meet a country boy and move back to Durango to be near them, look after them in their old age. The irony is, looking at you now and the way you prefer to live, she'd probably prefer this Mitch. I think you're more the sort of man they saw me settling down with.'

'I've changed a lot.' He walked through to the lounge, added another log to the burner.

Shannon joined him and sat at the opposite end of the sofa. 'After Durango we went to Chicago to stay with a friend, then moved to Boston to stay with someone else, but I couldn't keep dragging Albie around. I needed a job for a start, and so we came back this way and settled in Brooklyn.'

Their eyes met. 'You've been that close, all this time.'

'I found a great school, he made friends, but he never stopped asking about you. He told me he hated me for taking him away.'

Good! Mitch felt an odd sense of satisfaction. 'You never thought to come see me, give me another chance?'

'I found a job quickly and then I put it off. First it was the hours I was doing that gave me an excuse, then it was Albie settling in and I didn't want to disrupt that, then my parents said you'd sent them letters begging to know where I was and I got scared. They said they'd heard from people in town that you were a mess.' Her face fell. 'It frightened me when Mom said how angry you were in your letters.'

'Are you surprised?' He didn't mean to raise his voice quite so much but the words were out before he had a chance to let what she was saying sink in. Because she was right – not that he would've hurt her, but that he was unpredictable, a mess. He'd spent day after day sitting in a chair feeling sorry for himself, barely speaking a word to anyone, biting their heads off when he did, letting his appearance go downhill because he couldn't muster the energy to care.

'Your eyes scared me the most.' She looked down at her hands and it was now he noticed they were playing with a tissue, tearing it into sections, the thing still soggy with her tears from earlier. 'Where once I'd seen enthusiasm and love, I saw your devastation. I wanted to help you, I tried, but then every time I came near you, you'd bark at me to leave you alone. It was like the Mitch I'd married had gone and I didn't know how to get him back.'

He stood, went to the window, calmed by the sight of tiny innocent flakes fluttering to the ground. 'Neither did I.' His shoulders slumped, the weight of the last four years overcoming him with emotion. 'But I'm getting there now.'

She'd appeared at his side without him realising she'd left the sofa. 'I know you are.' They watched the flakes silently. 'This place looks really good, you know.'

'Dad had it pretty organised, I haven't had to do much.'

'But it's in order.' She cleared her throat in the way he remembered she did when she got nervous. 'I didn't know what to expect, coming here, but I'm glad I found a man who's risen up from the crap life doled out to him.'

'I know I brought some of it on myself.' Perhaps they'd still be together if he hadn't lost his job and then their home. Or perhaps they wouldn't if she'd run at the first sign of trouble.

'I met someone,' she said, and he realised he wasn't sorry to hear it.

'Well, I don't need to worry about you taking my son away, because you already did.'

She looked up at him, accepting his unkind words, her silence an admission of the wrongs she'd done. 'I deserved that,' she said after a while.

'I've had a lot of time to be angry at you, Shannon, a lot of time, and you probably were right to keep Albie from me when I was in that state, but to take him from me for so long? The not knowing nearly did me in. And part of me will never forgive you for that.' She said nothing. 'But you're a good mom, you were protecting him.'

'I was.'

He took a few deep breaths before he spoke again. 'Tell me about this new man in your life.' He was a father, he needed to know details if his son was spending time with another man.

She briefly told him about Luke, the geologist she'd met in her new neighbourhood. 'Albie gets on with him well, I wouldn't be with him if he didn't. But keeping Albie away from you and meeting someone else, well, no one would ever have taken your place. Albie never stopped pushing me for answers, you know. Can't imagine where he got his persistent streak from.' She gave a wry smile. 'Luke and I have talked about getting married.'

'So you want a divorce. Is that why you came?'

She tilted her head in that way that said he was talking nonsense. 'I wasn't even going to mention it today, or Luke.'

'Right... well, I guess a divorce would be easy if we both agree.'

'I guess so.' They stared out the window some more, the perfect position to have this talk. Staring directly at one another would have made everything so much harder, but the snow outside, the peace, it had a calming effect.

'The Christmas tree business seems to be going well.' Shannon always had been one to change the topic if it got uncomfortable, but also one to move things on in times of difficulty, which was what she was doing now and it was welcome. 'I understand the tree at the library came from here.'

'You've been to see Nessa?'

'Couldn't avoid it. I'd just parked up at the top of Main Street ready to sneak on down to the cabin when she spotted me. No doubt I'm the talk of the town.'

He laughed. 'At least it'll give me a bit of a break then.'

'They're good people around here, I kind of miss that.'

'You think you'll come back?'

'I doubt it. Luke's job is in the city, so is mine, and Albie's happy at school.'

'Right.' His hopes faded, but he had a right to demand to see his son, a right to claim time with him. Yet he was anxious to tread carefully. After what Jude had told him about his parents and how they'd used him in their games, he never wanted Albie to feel in the middle of anything. He and Shannon were never getting back together, she and Albie had Luke in their lives now. All Mitch needed to know was how much room there was for him.

'Can I see Albie again after today?' he asked.

'He's your son, I was wrong to take him out of your life.' She put a hand to his face, the smoothness of his jaw she wouldn't have seen or touched for a long time. 'You can see Albie as much as you like. I'd rather keep him in school where he is, but you can come to Brooklyn, he can come stay at the cabin.'

Mitch let her words settle as they sat quietly for a while. He listened to the ticking sound of the clock in the kitchen, its steady rhythm grounding him as he accepted this moment for what it was.

'I made him a gift every year, you know,' he said eventually. By now the boys were back and were outside, laughing, packing together snowballs and pummelling each other. 'Every birthday.

Every Christmas. I figured if I ever saw him again, he'd need to know I'd never once forgotten him.'

Her tears got the better of her and this time he went to fetch a box of tissues from the kitchen. 'Here.'

'Thank you.' After a moment she said, 'I underestimated you and I'm sorry.'

She wouldn't be the first to do so. 'Do you think I could spend next Christmas with him? It's been so long.' His eyes stung with tears of pain he'd held in since seeing them both and he pinched the top of his nose to stop them flowing.

'Listen, why don't you come to Brooklyn this year and have Christmas with Albie, Luke, and me?' He shook his head. 'Do you already have plans?'

'I'll go hiking. Jude invited me to his place but I'd rather get away, you know.'

She watched the boys. 'Jude seems like a good kid.'

'He is and he's had it tough.' He briefly recapped the tale of the boy's parents.

'Sounds as though he's done well to find you. I bet you've kept him on the straight and narrow, shown him the way.'

'I think he's shown me the way too.' He gulped, realising the honest truth in his statement. 'I enjoy his company and he helped me find myself again, he gave me a purpose.'

The boys came flying towards the door, laughing and joking, as Mitch stopped them before they brought the outside in with them. 'Come on, Dad!' Albie yelped. 'Snowball fight! Mom?'

'I'll pass, thank you.' But she smiled. 'You go on,' she urged Mitch.

He didn't need any convincing. The way his son had called him Dad had almost floored him but for the next half an hour the three males of the party dipped and dived away from snowballs, Shannon gasped and stood back when Albie accidentally threw one at the window and then froze to see if he'd get told off. He was a normal kid, Mitch felt like a regular parent, and he was loving every second.

When they finally finished, with Mitch spent and buzzing with a euphoria he hadn't felt in a long while, the boys made snow angels on the ground and Shannon stepped out to join him on the porch. She had her coat, scarf, and gloves, and her bag. His heart plummeted. 'Time for you to go, I guess.'

'I'm afraid so.' She took a step past him but turned. 'Look after him, won't you?'

'What do you mean?'

'Albie. How about you have him for Christmas, I'll pick him up Boxing Day?'

'Are you serious?'

'On one condition.'

'What's that?' He'd do anything!

'Put up some holiday decorations, Mitch. This place looks miserable without them. And it's Christmas Eve tomorrow.' She went over to talk to Albie, who seemed pretty taken with the idea.

'What about all my presents under the tree at home?' Albie wanted to know. 'And how will Santa know where to come?'

So Albie still believed. Mitch couldn't deny he was pretty happy about that.

Shannon hugged her son so tight Mitch knew this wasn't easy for her and he appreciated the effort despite how much he'd resented her over the years for doing what she did. 'Santa will leave presents at our house, he'll know you're doing something really important right now. And then how about I pick you up Boxing Day and take you home so you can see what he brought you?'

Albie threw his arms around his mum. 'I guess that would be okay.'

Mitch nodded a thanks to the mother of his child. Not getting presents on Christmas would be hard for a kid to understand when

Santa managed to go everywhere, but Albie's response told Mitch how much his son had missed him and how desperate he was to be with him now.

'Don't worry about clothes,' said Jude. 'I've got some stuff I've grown out of that I can lend Albie. How about I leave you to it and come back tomorrow with some things?'

'Thank you, Jude,' Mitch smiled.

Jude did some kind of weird boy-like handshake with Albie and off he went up the track with Shannon as she headed back to her car. Mitch meant to ask Jude what he'd wanted to talk to him about but he guessed it could wait.

'Dad?' Albie asked when his mum and Jude were out of sight.

'Yes, son?' Would he ever get tired of calling him that?

'I wish you had a Christmas tree in your cabin.'

Mitch's laughter came out in little puffs of white air against the cold. 'You know, I think I might know a place where we can get one.' He put his arm across Albie's shoulders. 'And you'll have the pick of the bunch.'

* * *

Mitch and Albie spent the rest of the day bonding over more snowball fights than Mitch thought he'd ever had in his entire life. He showed Albie around the fields, they chose a fine specimen of a tree, and between them carried it back to the little log cabin, where they left it while they drove out to a Christmas store on the outskirts of the next town. They returned with garlands they wound around the bannisters of the staircase Mitch's father had lovingly crafted, they used enough Christmas lights on the branches of the tree to cover Connecticut, before adding sparkly threaded angels, little toy drummer boys, silver bells, baubles, and a set of glass reindeers. And when Mitch presented Albie with everything he'd made over the years, Albie in return produced items from his backpack.

Mitch's eyes filled with tears. 'What do we have here?' He looked at three baubles as Albie unwrapped them from their protective packaging.

'I made one for you every year and hung it on the tree so it would remind me of you.'

Mitch hugged him hard. 'I always thought of you too. Not only at Christmas, but all year round.'

'Do you like them?' Albie could barely talk he was being held so tight.

When Mitch pulled away he waited for Albie to explain each decoration to him. First up was the simplest one, a silver bauble with Daddy written in glittery letters. 'That was the first year, my favourite colour was green.'

Mitch grinned. There was so much to learn about his boy. 'And this one?' He picked up the second, a deep red with green leaves and white berries. 'What made you paint mistletoe?'

'Everyone at school paints Santa, or a snowman, or a Christmas tree, but I wanted to be different and I remembered seeing it at a flower store near where we lived and made Mom buy some that year so I could draw it. I thought it might bring her someone to love too, because she was always so sad.'

Mitch hadn't expected the frank exchange between them but it was good to be reminded that as angry as he'd been at Shannon, none of this had been easy on her. She'd made a mistake and no doubt paid for it with guilt and by being too frightened to put it right.

'Now this,' said Mitch, taking out the third bauble, 'is wonderful.'

Albie's chest flared with pride. 'I painted it last Christmas. It reminded me of this cabin with all the trees and snow.'

'You're very talented.' The design was against a midnight-blue bauble, white snow covering the roof of a log cabin, trees in the background and surrounding it.

'Mom says I get my talent from you.'

'Does she now?' When he'd first met Shannon he'd painted but had soon found his job kept him way too busy for a hobby. It was only when he reached rock-bottom that he realised his true passion could perhaps lever him out of the place he was in.

'I wish I could make things out of wood too.'

'I'll teach you.'

'Really?' Albie's eyes sparkled. 'And one day I'm going to make another sledge like the one Grandad Albert made me.'

Mitch's heart thumped. 'You still have it?'

'It's a bit battered now, but still goes fast. I'd like another one so we can race.'

Mitch lifted a hand to high-five his son. 'You're on. One day. And are you sure you don't mind there not being any gifts beneath the tree? I kind of wasn't expecting anyone. And Santa will have planned to go to your house in Brooklyn,' he added hastily so he didn't shatter the illusion.

Albie shrugged. 'I have all the things you made me.'

And Mitch certainly didn't need anything himself. He had everything he'd ever wanted, right here in this room.

That night, after Albie told him he still had the toy car collection and had added to it a lot over the years, and that Mitch should come see it sometime, he put Albie to bed in the second bedroom, which was empty apart from the inflatable mattress that usually stayed in its box. He'd found enough spare sheets and blankets to cover it over, Albie had positioned his wooden pieces on the window sill, and after each of them making up a story to tell the other – monsters were very much included in the tales – Mitch stood and watched his son sleep, stolen moments irreplaceable but a certain sense of peace washing over him at being able to experience this now.

When fatigue caught up with him too, Mitch wished he could tell Holly about Albie, his miracle at the little log cabin. But they were done. And as he turned in he realised that in the time Albie had been here, he hadn't thought once about that blogpost. Perhaps it was as they said... today's news soon became tomorrow's trash can liner, or whatever the online equivalent was these days.

* * *

The next morning Mitch and Albie went to town after a father and son breakfast of blueberry pancakes. Mitch had told Albie to call his mum and Albie admitted he'd already sneaked off to do it. He hadn't wanted to upset Mitch but he hadn't wanted his mum to worry either.

'Don't ever be afraid to tell me things like that,' he told Albie as they sat in the café. 'Your mom and I aren't together but we do share you.'

It was Christmas Eve and Enid was doing her best not to look over but her eyes had danced as she'd taken their order for hot chocolates with marshmallows and whipped cream. Mitch would come back another day to talk to her properly, he owed her that much. He'd known her for years and she'd never had an unkind word for him even when he was so down on his luck he couldn't see any way out.

After the café they stopped at the bandstand and admired some of the snowmen nearby. Albie went to have a chat with Santa himself and when they left they saw Dylan with his kids waiting in line. And if Dylan was shocked to see his transformation and the presence of his kid, he didn't show it. Dylan reiterated his offer to help with Mitch's website and this time Mitch agreed a day and time, already looking forward to it. And Jacob gave him a conspiratorial wink as though Albie's appearance had something to do with Christmas and the presence of a Santa Claus.

Albie spotted the Christmas markets on the fields across the way but Mitch couldn't face a big local event and he suggested they go next year instead. They had a few years to catch up on, after all. Albie hadn't seemed too displeased either. Much like Mitch, he seemed to want to get to know the part of his life that had been missing for too long.

Next it was on to the Little Knitting Box, somewhere he thought he could cope with. 'I think we could both do with a new pair of gloves,' he told Albie. 'I have plans for yours later.'

The store was crazy busy on Christmas Eve, with a colourfully dressed girl carrying a box of yarn through the store to take over to their market stall, he heard her say to Cleo. Cleo was straight over to help Mitch and Albie but not before she'd offered them a cinnamon-and-sugar-topped cookie. She set the plate down, found what they needed, and acted as though he were any other customer. Any other normal part of this town. Which he supposed he still was.

They left the Little Knitting Box before Albie could get crumbs on all that lovely yarn. He was munching another cookie and Mitch wouldn't mind betting the boy had built up an incredible appetite after the antics of the last day or so. And before they turned down the track Mitch managed a wave across to Nessa, who was in the window of the library arranging a display of Christmas-themed books. Her smile said it all. He'd talk to her soon too, make peace, he owed it to a few people.

They headed down the track making plans for the most important task of all on Christmas Eve, even more important than decorating the cabin, Albie had said. And they got to it straight away. Snowmen. They wanted to build two, father and son, and with a fresh blanket of snow having fallen overnight, they balled up the sparkling white powder and went back and forth so the ball increased in size to make every part they needed. When they were done they even dolled up the characters, adding twig arms Mitch had foraged for out in the nearest field. They added a couple of old hats, Mitch's threadbare gloves and Albie's that he'd already exchanged for the new burgundy pair, plus big lumps of coal for the buttons, three on each snowman.

They were sitting on the porch admiring their handiwork with the snowmen when Jude came down to the cabin, out of breath from rushing.

'What's the hurry?' Mitch got to his feet. 'Is your gran okay?'

'She's fine.' He handed Mitch a bag first. 'Here's the few clothes I said I'd bring for Albie.'

'Thanks, appreciate it.'

He recovered a little more and handed Mitch the envelope he'd been clutching. 'I've been looking everywhere for you, you weren't here earlier so I went up to Main Street when I saw your truck, but just missed you at the café, then at the Little Knitting Box, then Nessa told me she saw you coming back here.'

'What's this?' He hoped it wasn't another bundle of anything that could take away his good mood.

'No idea. It was passed to me yesterday but I could see you were busy with Albie here.' He smiled at Mitch's son. 'Sorry, it's a bit crumpled, I shoved it in my jacket most of the day.'

'Who's it from?'

'Open it.' He rolled his eyes with all the impatience of a teenager in the company of a generation he didn't quite get.

Mitch opened the envelope to reveal a formal-looking document and then spotted the logo on top. The Hatherleigh Group. He might have known. He read on, his eyes scanning the sentences, absorbing the words in the paragraphs.

'What is it?' Jude asked.

'Yeah, Dad, what is it?' It still floored him when Albie used the D word. The boy probably had no idea what music it was to his lonely ears.

'It's a contract.' His son didn't know everything that had gone on so it would be pointless to try to explain. But inside the envelope was a letter from Pierre's company making an official offer for part of his land. Not all, only the fifty acres Mitch had proposed, but the amount offered was three million dollars. Mitch sat down on the porch. The Hatherleigh Group were proposing a twelve-month delay to any work to give Mitch a chance to organise the land he'd have left, move trees, alter irrigation systems, erect fencing. And there was no proposal for additional vacation dwellings, only the golf course. There was no mention of the blogpost either, the defamation Mitch was sure he could've had a field day with if he'd liked, but the subtext of that mighty financial offer had to be that he wouldn't breathe a word of it. And he wouldn't. He'd already let it go. He had to. Holding a grudge, holding onto anger, had never helped him in the past.

'Dad, what is it?' Albie persisted.

Jude shrugged when the boy looked at him. 'Hey, I don't know either. I do know who gave it to me to pass to you though.'

'Pierre, surely.' Mitch looked up, squinting in the winter sun that came for him through the trees towering high against the blue skies of the day. Pierre was probably too scared to come down here again himself.

'It was Holly.'

'She's done enough.' Mitch slid the document back into its envelope and stood to go inside, but Jude was quicker and blocked the door.

'Now listen up,' said Jude, 'you got this because of what she did for you.'

Holly pushed for this? She'd made it happen? 'Well that'll be her guilt talking.'

'She didn't do anything, Mitch. It wasn't her who told that jackass... man, about your past.' Mitch had reprimanded him once about foul language and Jude was usually on his best behaviour. 'People have known a long time.'

'What?'

'I've known for a long time.'

'You knew I was in a... in an institution?'

'You were hardly in a straitjacket.' Jude rolled his eyes heavenward, his candid tone the usual one he used with Mitch. 'But I always said you underestimated the people of this town. When you were stomping around demanding answers they were scared but believe it or not they did want to give you a chance to prove yourself, you just never took it. Yes, that's right, I've been talking about you with people for a while, but only because we all care.'

Mitch hardly knew what to say.

'Now what's in the letter?' Jude asked. Albie was following the conversation, looking first at Jude, then at Mitch.

'An offer for part of my land, not all.'

'You gonna take it?'

'Don't know.' He looked around him, at his cabin, his home, the land he'd never leave. 'Thank Holly for this.' And he tried to go inside again.

'You're an idiot!' Jude followed him to the doorway and waited to get a signal on his cell phone, then brought up something on the screen.

'What is it?' Mitch asked when Jude thrust the cell phone at him.

'A blogpost.'

'I already know what's in it.'

'Not that blogpost. That one has gone. Dead and buried.' He waved the cell phone at Mitch again.

Mitch took it this time and staring back at him was another blogpost, except this time it was completely different. Every photograph of him was a flattering one, clean-shaven, together, his successes in art, framing, and the Christmas tree farm were celebrated, and at the end of the piece was a brief paragraph about Mitch, how he'd always wanted to hand the business over to his own son one day but that Albie wasn't in his life right now. It said he hoped perhaps this year he would get the only gift he'd ever wanted, to be reunited with his son.

Albie came closer to see what was going on. 'That's the article,' he said, tugging Mitch's sleeve so he could see it for himself. 'I saw it at my friend Beau's house. His mom is a food blogger and left her laptop open on the kitchen table. I was waiting for Beau to get ready and I saw it said Inglenook Falls.' He looked at the ground beneath them, scuffing his shoe against the snow. 'I read the article. Beau wasn't happy with me, said his mom goes mental if anyone touches her laptop. But I wrote down the website and when I got home I showed Luke. He showed it to Mom. That's why we turned up.'

Mitch couldn't believe it. 'But who...' He didn't really need to ask.

'Holly didn't tell Pierre anything,' Jude added. 'He asked around, charmed people, most likely women, willing to drop their —' Albie giggled. 'Women willing to talk to him, a good-looking, rich and successful man. He wrote the whole thing, emailed the photographs to himself from Holly's laptop. She went crazy at him. Demanded he delete the blogpost. In the meantime I took photographs of the land, gave her some pictures of our trees selling in Bampton, photographed the tree at the library and the one on the bandstand, and she put together her own write-up.'

'How the hell did people see it?'

Jude shrugged. 'Said she had contacts all over America, editors, magazine people, lots of social-media presence. You know, you should get in with that, drum up business,' he added. 'You gotta get with the times.'

'Thanks, I'll try to remember that.' He was still trying to come to terms with the fact Holly had been responsible for Albie coming back to him, that she hadn't been the one to tell Pierre, that she'd been on his side all along.

Had he chased away the one person who had been there for him?

'What are you thinking?' Jude asked.

'Yeah, Dad.' Albie mimicked the jaunty stance of Jude, already in awe of this role-model in his life. 'What are you thinking?'

'I'm wondering if you'd like to help me out with something.' He addressed Jude.

'I don't know, I helped Holly out, I'm not sure I want to be seen with the enemy.'

Mitch grinned. 'Maybe I'm not really the enemy.'

'Keep talking.'

And as all three of them went inside the log cabin, Mitch told them his plan.

The first miracle had been Albie showing up, the second was feeling a part of Inglenook Falls again. Was it too much to hope for a third?

23

HOLLY

New York City was thriving and ready for Christmas. It was hard to believe that this time last year was Holly's first Christmas in this amazing city. It had been a year filled with surprises, some sad, some amazing, but she felt at home here now. This morning she'd submitted a fiction piece to a San Francisco magazine, plus another few photographs taken around the city to an images library. And now she planned some time off over Christmas, although it felt indulgent when she worked for herself, as though she was playing hooky.

Bundled up, she made her way over to the Inglenook Inn for the annual Christmas Eve party. Warmth from cafés and bars spilled out onto the sidewalk, street carts filled the air with the scent of mulled cider, the aroma of roasted chestnuts, people rushed to and fro on the last day to enjoy the holiday markets, crowds of people hurried home to loved ones or out on the town for winter cocktails.

She reached the stoop of the familiar brownstone, climbed the steps, and paused at the top, standing in the same place Myles had proposed to Darcy last year and they'd begun their happy ever after.

She couldn't think of two people more perfect for one another, apart from Cleo and Dylan of course, who were to be married next year. A couple of weeks ago she'd thought perhaps she and Mitch could've started something, but not now. Since she'd had Pierre take the blogpost down and she'd had him draw up a new proposal for Mitch that she thought he'd be very happy with, she hadn't heard from Mitch even though Jude must have passed him the details by now. And she knew from Cleo that his son had come back. She'd got the text from her friend this morning and she'd cried with joy knowing Mitch finally had the part of him that had been missing. She'd worked her ass off to get the word out about him and his situation, using Jude's photographs and her own as well as her contacts in the business. She'd got in touch with bloggers, editors, friends, ex-colleagues. She'd reached out to Daisy, who as predicted was doing Holly's old job, and Daisy had got dozens of bloggers straight on the case. Even Jason from the magazine had come through with his connections and within three hours they'd trended on Twitter, her photographs on Instagram had generated lots of interest, and now all she could do was hope that in the new year Mitch would put all the pieces of his life back together.

She breathed in the smell of winter, the cold, the feel of Christmas. She guessed the new proposal and the blogpost hadn't been quite enough to convince Mitch to change his mind about her, but at least now, he knew the whole truth.

The door opened behind her. 'Holly!' Darcy wrapped her arms around her friend and then ushered her inside.

Holly had texted Darcy earlier to say she wasn't sure she was feeling up to a party, she felt so down about Mitch and everything that had happened, but Sarah's voice had been there in her head again urging her to live this life the best she could.

'Grab a champagne,' Darcy insisted, and led her over to the bar in the communal lounge where glasses were lined up and waiting. 'It's your favourite, I remembered from last year.'

'Don't mind if I do.' The bubbles rose welcomingly in the vessel as she lifted it to her lips.

'What have you been up to? I haven't seen you in ages.' Darcy was a bit preoccupied, watching guests, making sure they were all looked after.

'I've been swamped, but now it's Christmas.'

Darcy smiled but she seemed distracted. 'You deserve a rest.'

Music played softly in the background, the next track, 'Let It Snow!', one of Holly's favourite Christmas tunes. 'Something smells wonderful.' She smiled. Here with friends, maybe it was exactly what she needed tonight.

'Our chef Rupert is the master of canapes.' Darcy looked this way and that, through the crowd of partygoers, presumably to locate a tray circulating and prove her claims. 'We've got crab brioche bites, bruschetta, turkey and cranberry blinis, and you definitely should try the fig and goat's cheese puffs. And that's before he serves the white-chocolate cherry bites.'

'You'll never eat Christmas lunch tomorrow with all that lot.'

'Oh, we'll be fine by then,' Darcy grinned. 'Another champagne?' She didn't wait for an answer before she topped up Holly's glass.

'Thank you.' She wasn't sure she could keep up if this was the pace Darcy was going to make her go at this evening.

This time a much younger waiter brought over a tray of canapes and she grinned, betting he was a relative of Rupert's or Darcy's, here to earn some extra pocket money over Christmas. 'Madam, may I offer you a Santa-strawberry?'

'Now these look interesting.' She picked up a strawberry, its top section sliced and filled with cream to make a face and beard that had chocolate pieces for eyes and a nose. Another dollop of cream made the top of Santa's hat. Holly popped it in her mouth in one go. 'Very good,' she said when she'd finished. 'You'll have to say thank you to Rupert, these are wonderful.'

'Rupert didn't make them,' the boy told her. And then he set the tray down and held out a hand for her to shake. 'It's nice to meet you, Holly. I'm Albie.'

She shook his tiny hand and realised where she'd heard of Santa-strawberries before. Mitch.

'I saw your article, so did Mom.' Albie stood back and gestured with his hand out towards the direction of the dining room. 'Ma'am, if you'll come this way, Da... I mean, Mitch is waiting for you.'

'He's here?' Suddenly her legs lost all feeling. Her hands shook. She felt self-conscious. Had she chosen the right outfit today – the high boots with jeans, the cream silk shirt that nipped at the waist, the silver heart pendant? She caught sight of Darcy, hands together in prayer position as she watched on, clearly very much a part of all this. And in a trance-like state she followed Albie out to the dining room.

Mitch had his back to them, facing the Christmas tree, this year a second freshly cut tree for the inn, filling the room with its authentic scent. He turned at the sound of them both and when Holly looked for Albie the boy had already gone, shutting the dining-room doors behind them.

Mitch picked something up from the floor, gift-wrapped with a big red bow. 'Merry Christmas, Holly.'

Her picture. 'Can I open it?'

'Of course.'

She tugged the bow and delicately unwrapped the gift. 'It's beautiful.' She set it down on the nearest table so she could run her fingers along the smooth wood of the frame, damaged in parts from other events in life, things that had come its way, but smoothed over with varnish that held those flaws in place so they became a thing of beauty. 'I love it. And I know Sarah would love it too.'

'I like to think she would.'

'How much do I owe you?'

He shook his head. 'It's a gift.'

She took a deep breath. 'I didn't get you anything.'

He stepped forward, held the top of her arms with his hands. 'Are you kidding me?'

She smiled. 'Albie seems a great kid, and those Santa-strawberries are pretty good too.'

'He made them all himself, wouldn't let Darcy help at all.'

'He sounds determined, like his dad.' She looked down but then met his gaze again. 'I never thought it would work, you know, but I had to try.'

'Thank God you did.'

'Yeah.'

'Holly, I'm sorry I doubted you even for a second.'

'You weren't to know. If I was you I would've thought the same.'

'And was it you who persuaded Pierre to make the offer on the land?'

'I thought it was the least he could do under the circumstances.'

He smiled down at her, stepping that little bit closer. 'Is it over with Pierre?' he asked, his lips dangerously near to hers.

She could smell a scent that was familiar and reminded her of the night at the art gallery when she'd really begun to get to know him. 'It's over. It was over the day I met you.'

'Really?' She felt his breath in her hair, then again on her face.

'Well maybe not on the *actual* day,' she grinned.

'You don't want me to grow the hair and beard again?'

'Dear Lord, no.' She began to laugh. 'But there was always something about you. At first I thought it was my journalist mind, the inquisitiveness. Then it became about helping someone out who was stuck in a rut, who had goodness in his heart but had been beaten down. It all changed that night at the Winter Village in Bryant Park.'

'Really?'

'I wasn't scared of you that night. But you got to me, you frustrated me, you were so stubborn.'

'Always have been.' He moved even closer until she could feel the tingle of his skin almost touching hers. 'I've wanted you since the day I scooped you up outside the cabin. But it'd been so long since I'd been fit for friendship let alone a relationship that it was easier to dislike you and bite your head off than give you any part of me.'

This time his lips collided with hers, gently at first, then with an urgency that threatened to undo her.

She kept her eyes closed when they pulled away and touched a finger to her lips as if to make sure it had been real. And when she opened them he was down on one knee.

'Holly...'

She couldn't speak.

'Would you do me the honour of spending Christmas day with me?'

A giggle of relief escaped that it was a proposal of sorts yet taking one step at a time. 'You mean swap all the glitz and glamour of New York City for a little log cabin?'

'Yeah.' He bit down on his lip, anxious to hear her answer. 'What do you say?'

'Only if you have a turkey.'

'Ah...' He stood up, a look of conviction on his face. 'We'd better go get one and hope there's something still open at this time on Christmas Eve.'

Before they left the room she said, 'You know, you'd better have a Christmas tree sorted, the cabin looks as though the biggest Grinch of all lives there.'

'He did once upon a time.' Mitch took her hand as they went out into the hallway and he beckoned for Albie to join them. 'He doesn't any more.'

Mitch helped Albie on with his coat while Darcy rushed forward with a smile on her face. She hugged Holly. 'Merry Christmas.'

'Merry Christmas, Darcy.' She asked her friend to store her framed picture for now and off they set, out onto the stoop and into the snow falling in and around Manhattan. Albie was already twirling around on the spot on the pavement, tipping his face up, eyes closed, feeling the magic of snowfall on his face.

'Do you believe in Christmas miracles?' Mitch asked as they pulled on their gloves, left the Inglenook Inn behind and prepared to find what they could for a Christmas feast.

'I'm starting to.'

Holly could never have predicted what would happen tonight, how things could change so quickly. But they had. And tonight, when she went to sleep on Christmas Eve, she'd know that she didn't need any gifts wrapped beneath the tree. Because everything she wanted would be right there with her.

24

HOLLY

Mitch, Holly, and Albie had found a turkey and everything else they needed at a store near Union Square. They'd gone on to Holly's apartment after that, so she could pack an overnight bag. 'Make it enough for two or three nights,' Mitch had whispered in her ear. Albie had been preoccupied running a hand along the iron railings out front so his gloves gathered up the snow at the end. 'Albie's going to his mom's the day after tomorrow.'

She'd grinned then and suggested they meet her at Penn Station while she finished packing and grabbed Albie some last-minute gifts. She couldn't stand the thought of there being nothing under the tree for him. And Mitch had leant in and kissed her like they were a part of a team. 'I don't deserve you,' he'd said, and she'd replied with, 'Don't worry, you can spend a few days making it up to me.'

Now, at the little log cabin in the woods on Christmas Day, picture-perfect with its tree bedecked in a whole host of ornaments including a few homemade pieces Albie had decorated during the time he was separated from his dad, wrapping paper was strewn across the floor as Albie played with the few gifts Holly had snuck off to buy yesterday. She'd found a heavy cargo transport Lego set, which was above his age range but she figured it was something he and Mitch could work on together at the cabin. She'd also found a chemistry set so Albie could experiment with crystallisation and separation, acids and bases, chromatography. She bought a few smaller things to fill a stocking too – chocolate, marbles, a pack of playing cards, some funny rainbow slime that was apparently very popular according to the assistant restocking the shelves.

With music filling the cabin, the three of them sat down for lunch around the small kitchen table, the scent of roast meat filling the air, golden crispy potatoes shared between them, vegetables and gravy passed from one person to the next. And when they were done Mitch kept his role of being the dad and insisted Albie help with the dishes so Holly, who'd done most of the cooking as the boys scattered Lego pieces everywhere and made a start with construction, could put her feet up. She'd almost offered to help but they'd looked like they were in their own special bubble. Father and son, both with aprons on, one whose apron trailed on the floor as they bopped to Christmas music about rocking around a Christmas tree. Albie had added some interesting moves with a wooden spoon waving through the air until Mitch had pointed out bits of gravy were flying off it so they'd better stop.

Holly went out to the porch instead of retreating to the sofa. She took a big tartan blanket with her from the blanket box upstairs and sat on the rocker looking out at the trees, the stars lurking above. The snow came down lightly for now, forecast to be heavy as of tomorrow afternoon. But Holly didn't care if she was snowed in at the little log cabin for a long time. She'd phoned her parents this morning and tried to recount the entire story and all they'd wanted to know was whether she was truly happy. And she'd admitted that, for the first time, she really was.

She'd only just wrapped herself in the blanket when a text

pinged on her cell phone. She'd meant to turn it off and intended to do so but saw it was Pierre. She opened the message, which was brief and to the point. He said Merry Christmas, wished her well, and told her someone else would be overseeing any further changes to the hotel from now on. He'd moved on to something else now Mitch had agreed to a partial land sale.

She didn't write back; she didn't need to.

'Hey, Holly.' It was Jude, emerging from the trees as he came down the track with a gift tucked beneath one arm.

'I didn't expect to see you today. I thought you were spending Christmas with your gran.'

'We've eaten and she's sleeping it off, I got a bit bored.' Holly suspected he also missed Mitch a little, the man who'd stepped in as a father when the boy didn't have many people on his side. 'Our neighbour is coming for a game of cards later so I think Gran's glad to get rid of me for a while.'

Mitch came out onto the porch. 'I thought I heard voices. Merry Christmas, Jude.' He ignored Jude's outstretched hand and surprised him with a hug instead.

'Dad!' Albie hollered from inside, but he soon changed that to 'Jude!' when he came out and saw who else was there.

'Hey, Albie. How's it going?' He handed Albie the gift he was holding. 'I got you something. It's not new I'm afraid, it's been mine for years, but I thought you might like it.'

Albie took the present and wasted no time in ripping it open. 'A dartboard! Great!'

'It's very kind of you,' said Mitch. 'Thank you, Jude.' He went inside and came out with a couple of parcels himself and handed over the first. 'I was going to give this to you when I next saw you. Now, you can exchange it if you don't like it.'

Jude looked a lot younger than fifteen when his eyes lit up and he tore off the paper almost as quickly as Albie had done with his.

He pulled out a sweater and didn't hesitate to give Mitch another hug, something you didn't normally see a boy of his age do, but then their relationship was unique, special in a way not many would understand.

Mitch handed him something else, an envelope wrapped in festive paper. 'What's this?'

'Another something for you.'

Bewildered, Jude opened the gift and took out what looked like a cheque. 'I can't take this.'

'You can and you will. It's to help you, your gran, and the only condition is that you don't take the money and run. I want you in my life, buddy. And I think Albie might too.' He looked at both boys. 'Between you and me, I'm useless at darts, he's going to need someone to teach him properly.'

'In that case...' Jude grinned. 'Where are we going to put it up?'

'The landing?' said Albie. 'You could move some of the photos up there.'

'But they're of you, I like them there,' Mitch chipped in.

Holly grinned at the look on Albie's face when he said, 'It's kind of weird, like a shrine. We learned about them at school.'

'Yeah, it's kind of a bit freaky up there,' Jude agreed.

'I'll see what I can do,' said Mitch. 'Why don't you show Jude the Lego for now,' he suggested.

They escaped inside and left Mitch and Holly on the porch.

'You know,' Mitch began, 'I think you're my third Christmas miracle.'

She smiled in recognition, as happy as he was. 'I think you might be right.'

'Stand up,' Mitch prompted.

'I'm not sure I can after that lunch.' But she did as she was told and he took the rocker himself before pulling her down on his lap, wrapping the blanket over the both of them. 'I might squash you after all that food,' she laughed.

'I'll live.'

'Well, I know what to get you next Christmas now.'

'And what's that?'

'A porch swing, for two.'

'I could make us one.'

'Even better.' The snow had left a gentle layer on the ground on top of what was already there, but in a day or so this place would be covered, isolated, and it would be just the two of them as they got to know one another properly for the first time. Last night they'd hugged each other close, the desperation to explore one another's bodies almost too much, but had agreed to wait until after Albie went to his mum's tomorrow.

Mitch kissed her neck, pulled her even closer beneath the blanket. 'I'm not sure I can hold out another night.'

'I'm worth the wait, you know.'

And as they rocked away on the porch at the little log cabin, he told her, 'Of that I've no doubt.'

MORE FROM HELEN ROLFE

We hope you enjoyed reading *Christmas Miracles at the Little Log Cabin*. If you did, please leave a review.

If you'd like to gift a copy, this book is also available as an ebook, digital audio download and audiobook CD.

Sign up to Helen Rolfe's mailing list for news, competitions and updates on future books.

https://bit.ly/HelenRolfeNews

You can now order the next book in the New York Ever After series, *Christmas Promises at the Garland Street Markets*.

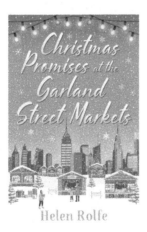

ABOUT THE AUTHOR

Helen Rolfe is the author of many bestselling contemporary women's fiction titles, set in different locations from the Cotswolds to New York. Most recently published by Orion, she is bringing sixteen titles to Boldwood - a mixture of new series and well- established backlist. She lives in Hertfordshire with her husband and children.

Follow Helen on social media:

 twitter.com/hjrolfe

 facebook.com/helenjrolfewriter

 instagram.com/helen_j_rolfe

Boldw∞d

Boldwood Books is an award-winning fiction publishing company seeking out the best stories from around the world.

Find out more at www.boldwoodbooks.com

Join our reader community for brilliant books, competitions and offers!

Follow us
@BoldwoodBooks
@BookandTonic

Sign up to our weekly deals newsletter

https://bit.ly/BoldwoodBNewsletter

Lightning Source UK Ltd.
Milton Keynes UK
UKHW040256010722
405215UK00002B/273